T0129104

EVERYBODY GOT ISSUES

EVERYBODY GOT ISSUES

V. ANTHONY RIVERS

A
SBI
PUBLICATION

A STREBOR BOOKS INTERNATIONAL LLC PUBLICATION
DISTRIBUTED BY SIMON & SCHUSTER, INC.

Published by

Strebor Books International LLC
P.O. Box 1370
Bowie, MD 20718
http://www.streborbooks.com

ISBN 978-1-59309-003-6
LCCN 2003100152

Distributed by Simon & Schuster, Inc.
1230 Avenue of the Americas
New York, NY 10020
1-800-223-2336

Cover Photography: Keith Plummer

First Printing July 2003
Manufactured and Printed in the United States

10   9   8   7   6   5   4   3   2   1

I REMEMBER ONE DAY WHEN THE SKY OPENED UP and shined a ray of light upon the beautiful green pasture below. Someone special at my side witnessed this moment as well. We were not too far from St. Augustine's Church and very close to the Cane River. It was such a peaceful day in this part of Louisiana. We pulled over and held each other tight. Then we argued about taking a picture of the sky and whether or not we were close enough to get a good shot. For a split second we had "issues" but we got over it. We later made a pact that there was nothing we couldn't get past or endure, together. I dedicate this novel to the woman who once told me "I love that you know how to live."

Thank you,
V. Anthony Rivers

ACKNOWLEDGMENTS

Wow, my second book and it's been a blessing to be able to continue to meet and discover new characters inside my creative soul. I thank God for that and for allowing me to continue this dream in the making. Special thanks to Zane for her continuing guidance and support. I'm so inspired by you like you wouldn't believe!

Thanks so much to JDaniels for the inspiration, the wisdom, the guidance, the friendship and endless help. You are the bomb in so many ways. Thanks to Shonie Bacon for all the emails, the laughter and lessons about life and writing...You are awesome and a real friend besides being an inspiration! Thank you Darrien Lee for everything and then some... Friendships and support teams can't get any sweeter.

I'd also like to thank the incredible Martina Royal and Tanya Lewis, never forgetting to say hello and keeping me pointed in the right direction. Y'all mean a lot...

Very special thanks to Jamise L. Dames. Your friendship and kindness has blessed me in so many ways. You are an inspiration that tells me that success can go hand in hand with humility and looking out for others.

Thank you to Gayle Jackson Sloan for being my big sis in and out of this writing arena. You are beyond wonderful and so funny too!

Shoutouts also go to Shennice Pruitt-Gober, Karen Lemmons, Laurie

Hunter-Gilbert, Cheryl Floyd-Miller, William Fredrick Cooper, Earl Sewell, Miguel Wilder, Tonya Howard, Deayah, Valerie "Brownwoman" Williams, Charaine, Kim Roseberry and also the Nubian Chronicles family.

Now I'd like to give special thanks to some dear family members. They are the foundation for so much in my life and definitely the inspiration for perhaps some stories down the line.

I grew up with my uncle, Richard and cousin, Vaughn. As an only child, I never felt like I needed siblings with them around. Thanks to my beautiful aunt who deserves her name in lights, Tamer Moorings. Always warm hugs for my Mother and Grandmother, Gloria and Alzata.

Special shoutouts to above as I have to believe that my Father, Grandfather and Grandmother, Virgil "Sonny" Rivers, Virgil Sr. and Senora Rivers respectfully, are watching down on me with pride and big smiles. The anchor of their love is planted so firmly in my heart and in that wonderful little town called Mt. Pleasant, Texas.

Never the last and never the least, I could never thank my cousin George of Daingerfield, Texas enough for introducing me to my family history and the wonderful church originally built after slavery that bears the name of my great-great-grandmother Moriah, otherwise known as, Mt. Moriah Missionary Baptist Church. Big ups to everyone there!

One day when I came walking out of the Rivers Cemetery, there stood Cousin George with open arms, a warm smile and plenty to talk about. He passed down a legacy and I'll forever be grateful. A strong part of that legacy has been "Love" and with that love I'd like to give a special mention to cousin, Maggie Johnson and also to Big Mama for blessing me with some of that special BBQ sauce on my chicken after church service one Sunday morning. (Smile)

Thank you to "Babycakes" for bringing it all together and creating dreams that look like yesterday. Thanks for coming out to Starbucks! January 19th set it off for us and it's been a magical, often spiritual ride ever since.

Also want to send some warm love to the always clowning, Lois Casey!

Once again, I'm so grateful for this opportunity to share another story with new characters that feel like a part of my family now. Thanks so much to those that wrote to me and told me how much my first novel *Daughter By Spirit* touched their hearts.

Deayah, thanks for keeping my message board hot with visitors. Special thanks to all the African American bookstores that have shown wonderful support. Thank you to EsoWon, Zahras and Maliks books for providing great reads to the local AA community. Special nods and winks go out to RAW Sistaz, Sisterdivas, APOOO, Black Writers Alliance, Imani Bookclub, Ladygodiva, ASAP-Online, Prolificwriters, and Black Images in Dallas. It's a great feeling to be able to walk in a store and see your work on display. It's an even greater feeling to witness someone on a mental journey, walking inside the shoes of a character you've created. Thanks and more thanks for those feeling what flows through me, truly...I'm forever grateful...

Warm Blessings to all...

Introduction to Avonté

A brother in the '90s has plenty of options for advancement. I've learned that recently and especially because I'm due to graduate in about two weeks. I'll finally earn my master's degree in advertising, and it's about damn time.

I have to admit that my motivation for going to school in the past was a little suspect but I forced myself to finish this year. I used to be about the ladies and the opportunities in between classes, but I guess I woke up, just a little bit. Now in the year 1999, Avonté Douglas is about to make his mark in the world. I have plenty of interviews lined up. And, I bought a couple of suits from the Men's Wearhouse so you can definitely say I'm ready. I'm gonna be pissed off if the only thing I find is a job in the mailroom, but I've got to remain confident.

Friends of mine tell me to just think positive and my grandmother told me to go to church and pray. I've been doing my best to be optimistic. At times I'm probably overconfident. Maybe a little egotistical. I've been sending out resumes like crazy. When I put together my first draft, I described myself as a "Tall handsome man of color." After I finished, I had the best looking profile for a dating service that I'd ever seen in my life. I put that in my desk drawer for later and made a second attempt at writing a "real" resume. The women are just gonna have to wait until after I start making some dollars.

The last two years have been a little bit hard on me because I believe I should be a lot farther along in my life. I'm living with my mother so I can save some money. That's been an okay situation but it cuts down on the amount of nights that I'm able to spend with the opposite sex. Whenever I want to spend the night with somebody, I have to get a hotel room. My budget has been tight, so needless to say, I haven't been getting any—lately.

Avonté can catch the ladies, but developing a situation beyond the initial attraction is something that doesn't happen too often. That dreaded word "relationship" is something that I only know how to spell right now. But then again, since I'm not where I want to be, why try to have somebody all up in my grill trying to pass themselves off as my significant other? I'm too young to be worrying about that right now any-damn-way; especially since I just chase the ladies for sex—and relationships? I haven't had a girlfriend since the '80s, back when I was sporting a high-top fade.

I took on a new journey when I got into college. I discovered the pleasures of being immune to a deep commitment. Bells ring in my head when a lady just tells me she wants to have fun. I start smiling like the Grinch just about to steal Christmas. Of course, I'm stealing more than just holiday time. But as I said earlier, that's no longer my focus. I'm about to graduate and as soon as I get a job, then maybe I'll enter new arenas where the ladies are concerned. I can visualize myself already going to sports bars during the week and nightclubs on Saturdays and Sundays. I'm gonna live the lifestyle of a young "Buppy" to the hilt. I know I'm looking ahead but my friends said to think positive. I'm thinking positive and then some. Spending my money before I even cash the check, one might say.

Celebrating too soon is always a habit of mine and today is no exception. I'm on my way to an interview and because I want this particular job so much, I know it's gonna be mine. I threw on my best suit and a funky fresh tie to go with it. I also brought a more conservative tie with me; just in case I change my mind. I'll probably change it. This position

I'm going for is entry level, but they assured me that there's rapid growth potential. I had to catch myself when I talked to them over the phone.

"How rapid?" I wanted to ask.

I'm glad I didn't say half the stuff that was on my mind. I played it cool and professional. I acted like a straight-A student with a respect for authority rather than the B+ egomaniac that I really am. Nobody needs to see my true colors until I've passed the probationary period. After that, I'm taking over!

Thinking is always one of my favorite pastimes. I can sometimes see my entire life before me. I visualize nothing but good times and opportunities. I guess that's why I get accused of having a devilish smile. That's my trademark and I haven't met a woman yet who wasn't attracted by it.

"You here for an interview?" a female voice asked.

"Excuse me?"

"I noticed there's only two other people here. I was expecting a lot more to show up for this job," the lady spoke softly.

"Probably so, but I just try to stay focused on me. Know what I'm saying?"

"So, you and I are gonna be competing for it then, huh?"

"Competing?" I asked.

I looked at homegirl like she was no competition at all.

"My name is Vanessa Jenkins."

"Sup, I'm Avonté."

"Nice to meet you, Avonté."

The girl had very lovely hands, a brown-skin complexion, and was beginning to take me out of my focus. That wasn't too cool, at all.

"My pleasure, Vanessa."

I glanced at the rest of Ms. Jenkins when she turned her attention toward someone walking into the office. She was wearing a champagne-colored, polyester-crepe business suit with a long skirt. Even her nails and lipstick had that same champagne color and she wore it well. Her suit looked like it came straight from the same JCPenney catalog that I ordered my size 13 rugged leather boots from. I almost felt compelled to turn on the charm a little and see if I'd get a smile out of her. Maybe make her cross her legs in my direction.

"So, what's this I hear about me having competition? Who, pray tell, would give a brotha like me some competition?"

"This sista right next to you," she responded.

I liked the way she sat up, crossed her arms and gave me a cocky smile of her own. I was enjoying this. It's a shame that I may not see too much of Vanessa since I'm the one they're gonna hire for the job.

"Hey, Vanessa," I said softly.

"Yes?"

She still had her arms folded. Seemed like she was anticipating in a cute way what I might say next. She was shaking her head, gesturing for me to continue, but she still had that smile.

"Vanessa, since I'm all up in your area here..."

"Huh?" she interrupted.

"Let me finish. Since we seem cool with each other already, how about we share a cappuccino or something and let bygones be bygones, so to speak."

"I hope you're not going talk like that in your interview."

"Nah, I'm gonna be professional."

"I hope so."

"What about my offer?" I asked her.

"Coffee sounds nice but I'm not sure what you mean by letting bygones be bygones?"

"Yeah, well, uh, I don't want you coming after me when they hire me instead of you," I told her.

"Oh, is that right?"

"Yep. I wouldn't have bought this new suit if I thought I wouldn't get the job."

"I hope you saved your receipt and didn't remove the tag."

Homegirl was flashing all her attitude, even though she tried to keep our conversation on the down-low. I was having fun talking to Vanessa. This kind of fun was making my focus so cloudy, too. I felt it was time to relax my efforts for the moment.

"Let me stop talking to you. We're still on for coffee, right?" I asked.

"Uh, huh."

Vanessa went back to thumbing through magazines and I returned to my usual active imagination. I was doing a mental balancing act. I was visualizing Vanessa in her panties on one side and celebrating 'cause I got the job on the other. Life feels good when you can imagine more than one way to have fun.

"Vanessa Jenkins?"

Someone stepped out from inside the office and called the next interview. I thought I was the next person but that's cool. Vanessa looked good walking inside. Maybe she was my competition because she walked in there like she already had the job. She was trying to play the role by asking if that person had a good weekend. Now if I go in and ask the same thing then I'll sound all fake and shit. I wish I could hear what else she's saying in there. I feel like I'm back in school because I'm letting a female mess with my head—again.

An hour went by before the door slowly opened. I was beginning to doze off from waiting so long. Plus, they had it cold up in there like they thought it was 100 degrees outside. I should've gotten up and checked my eyes to see if I look tired but I didn't want to leave and miss my name being called. I could see Vanessa slowly coming out of the door. Seems like whomever she was talking to didn't want the conversation to end. I didn't like what I was feeling. Going in there could've been a waste of my time and another opportunity to be embarrassed. Finally Vanessa made it all the way through the door. She flashed a sweet smile and stood in front of me.

"I don't think I'll be able to have that coffee with you, Avonté, but give me a call, okay? Here's my number," she said, handing me a small piece of paper.

I looked up at Vanessa with my sleepy eyes, not knowing what was going on. I couldn't match her enthusiasm, but it was cool to get her phone number.

"Okay, I'll give you a call."

"Talk to you soon?"

"Okay, Vanessa."

She walked out the door and as soon as I turned around, the office door opened.

"I think you're next. Avonté Douglas, right?"

By the way this lady was looking at me, I could tell this would just be a formality with her. I could play this interview in my mind already. I knew the conclusion wouldn't be in my favor. I'm just sleepwalking through this entire experience.

"How are you today?" the lady asked.

"Good."

"That's excellent. Listen, I guess we should cut to the chase. We've found someone to fill the position, but I'd like to hold on to your resume for a possible opening that may happen soon. Would that be okay with you?"

"Yes, Ma'am, that would be fine."

Here I was, sitting like a young boy who'd just gotten his heart broken. Still, I tried to be professionally humble. It appeared that Vanessa did her thing and got the job.

My mind was going blank as I sat across from the interviewer. She was talking about the company, and all I could see was her mouth moving in slow motion.

"I'm sure you're a little disappointed but we here at Montaqua Publications are always interested in young creative minds. Please don't be discouraged."

"Oh, thanks, I won't be. I guess it's a learning experience as they say, huh?"

"Exactly. Plus, you never know because we could be calling you back very soon. You seem to be someone that would fit well inside of a creative environment such as this one."

"It would be a dream come true, Ma'am."

"Well, don't give up on that dream. Not enough people have the patience to start somewhere and work their way up."

"Thank you," I responded, not liking the hint she was giving me.

As I walked out the office, I took a look at the piece of paper with the phone number that Vanessa had given me. I started to crumble the page and toss it in the trash, but I didn't. I almost said a few curse words about my competition, but I passed on disrespecting her that way. I remembered how cool she seemed. Maybe she had more going for herself on paper than I did. My jealousy kicked in for a second and I returned to my thoughts of tossing the phone number. I didn't. Instead, I found a pay phone in the lobby and tried calling Vanessa. I had a feeling it was her beeper number. Even though I've been blessed to receive phone numbers without really trying hard, I figured a woman like this probably wouldn't give hers out so easily. I waited for the message after I heard the dial tone for the fourth time.

"Hello?"

The sound of her voice was like drinking down one of those smoothies on a hot day. She sounded so sweet.

"Hello. Is someone there?" she answered a second time.

"Vanessa?"

"Yes, who's this?"

"Oh, wow!"

I guess she proved me wrong again. I was batting a thousand with my assumptions today.

"Do I know you?" she asked.

"Hey, Vanessa, this is Avonté."

"Hey you, how did it go?"

"What you mean, how did it go? You got the job!"

"I thought maybe you could still talk your way into getting something. You had me smiling, even though I tried to hide it."

"Is that right?"

"Yes, you did and I was thinking about you, too."

"You were?"

"Yes."

"Damn, you got me in this lobby perspiring..."

"Doing what?"

"Sweatin', Gurl!"

"Oh, you are funny, Avonté."

Vanessa had me forgetting all about the fact that she stole my job. Talking to her on the phone was just as cool as it was in person. I felt like I was still sitting next to her, glancing down at her legs, and I could even remember the scent of her perfume. I wasn't supposed to be losing my focus and thinking about another lady in my life. My shield was having a hard time fighting this one off.

"Sweetheart, I'm gonna have to go but call me later, okay?"

Now she was fighting unfair because hearing a woman call me "sweetheart" was like touching my sensitive spot. She just pushed my button of vulnerability and it felt great.

"Where you headed to?" I asked.

"Well, if you noticed, I'm on my cell phone sitting in traffic. I'm going to the mall to buy something new for my first day at work!"

"Oh."

"Don't sound sad. I'm not trying to rub it in, Avonté."

"Nah, it's cool."

"You're welcome to meet me at the mall, if you want."

"Nah, that's okay. I'll call you tonight, Vanessa. You gonna be home?"

"Yes, and don't feel bad, okay!"

"It's cool. Congratulations on the job."

"Thanks, sweetheart."

"Yep."

"Hey, listen!"

"Yeah, what's up, Vanessa?"

"I'm gonna put in a good word for you. I think it would be nice to work together. I hope it wouldn't present a problem, especially if we're seeing each other away from work."

"That would be cool, thanks."

"Okay, talk to you later, Avonté."

"Peace."

I wasn't sure how to take her offer, but I figured if I could get my foot in the door, then it would all be left up to me to prove my true value to the company. I could make the right connections and I'd be on my way. Maybe that old saying about who you know could finally work for me. Vanessa seemed pretty sincere about helping a brotha out. I was glad she wasn't turned off by my early hints of conceit. But, if she ever discovered the real me later on, then that was okay. I was determined to turn all my preparation from school into making my way up the ladder at this advertising agency. I was excited that it's black-owned, too. Listen to me go on and on...

A few days passed by and it took me two to realize that I was celebrating a little too soon—again. I needed to at least wait for Vanessa to give me a call and let me know I was in. My other interview didn't work out at all. The interviewer just sat there sizing me up while reading my resume and application. That's a lonely feeling when I'm sitting there waiting for someone to decide my immediate fate before I gain a little control. I started to get up at one point, but then the person ended my anxiety by letting me off in that familiar way.

"We're gonna review your resume and get back with you," I was told.

"Uh-huh, how long is it gonna take you, stupid?" I thought to myself.

"Thank you so much" is what I actually said.

Now I'm sitting here doing more research and at the same time feeling sorry for myself 'cause preparation doesn't seem to be getting my foot in the door right now. Looks like it's gonna take a lot of luck.

INA SINCLAIR

I'm on my way to work after being off for two whole weeks. It feels strange to be getting up at 5 a.m. again. Being off was a blessing because I got to sleep late and let my alarm clock rest. That damn thing gets on my nerves, but I can't wake up without it now. Must be my age or something because I can definitely remember the days when I'd wake up without any kind of help.

I guess they really missed me at work. I got a message the other day saying that I had to show some new girl the ropes. They say she's really sweet, but since she's been there for over a week it seems like they should've shown her new ass what to do by now. Why do they have to wait on me? I guess my attitude just confirms how much I enjoyed my vacation and hate for it to end. I better just be cool, get some coffee and try to be nice to this new heffa on the block. I hope they give me a little background info on the girl before I meet her. I don't want her to feel as though I'm interviewing her all over again.

I've been with Montaqua Publications for about five years now, and I never seem to get used to new people coming in at first. I always tend to treat the rookies with a cold shoulder. I'm trying to change my bad habits, but I know I'm gonna fail with this one. My girlfriend Nakia can tell you firsthand about the attitude I gave her when she first started working with us. She lives in the hood and takes the bus to work. I would be all on her and warning her not to be late. I'd tell her not to give me that tired excuse about missing her bus or not getting the kids ready for school in time. I treated her pretty bad and it wasn't like she was gonna be working under me. I was just responsible for showing her around. I eventually let up on her when I found her wiping away tears in the break room.

She set me straight about her life. She has a little girl and lives with her mother and young cousin. I call her my girlfriend but most of the time, I treat her like my baby sister. Now I'm about to meet this new girl and I'm pretty sure I'll treat her bad at first, too. In the message that was left, they never mentioned her age or background. I guess I need a little more status before they start sending me information that can actually help me do my job better. I'm not in management just yet, but I will be one of these days. Either that or I'll be working for myself.

On the way to work I was quickly reminded why I didn't miss getting up early. I had to deal with people cutting in front of me in traffic. L.A drivers just don't give a damn about anybody else being on the road. Ain't nobody going nowhere so they all might as well relax. That's why I always bring my coffee with me and either listen to the morning show or play one of my tapes that I bought recently. I'm kind of lazy right now when it comes to actually reading a book so I listen to them on cassette. It allows me to kill two birds with one stone because I can enjoy one of the latest novels and at the same time, feel like someone is reading to me. If I had a man, I might make his ass read to me all the time but until then, this is how I'm gonna do it. Sometimes I really get wrapped up in the stories, especially the lovemaking parts. I got Nakia hooked on these tapes, too. She tripped when she first heard one of them.

She asked me one night, "Girl, what are you listening to?"

"Huh? It's just a book that I'm too lazy to read."

"I'm not trying to hear that. Don't you have some DMX in your car?"

"Some DM who?" I asked.

"You need something in here to get us started, Girl!"

"So, you want me to play some of your hood-rat music?"

I guess it was strange for us to be listening to a novel on the way to a club. That was my first time partying with Nakia and I have to tell you, it wasn't my last. Girlfriend opened me up to a *New World* but it was a world that I didn't want to get *too* used to. I had so many fine men and even a few women trying to buy me a drink. I got worried about that.

I asked Nakia, "Why are they so anxious to give me a drink?"

"'Cause they wanna get with you!"

"Do I look thirsty?"

Nakia just laughed at me and we really had a great time that night. I never did let anyone buy me a drink because I just couldn't trust people I didn't know. I don't even let a man feed me unless I know he keeps himself clean. No telling what a man been digging into, grabbing on, shaking, hell, you know what I mean.

Being stuck in traffic is very soothing to me. I guess that's a strange way of looking at it but I'm always trying to turn negatives into positives. My next transformation is smiling when I see my office building. I'm gonna do my best to have a good time at work today. I'll be okay once I get back into the swing of things.

Well, parking my car and finally going inside felt like it took forever. I tried to look happy, but I really wasn't excited about returning. I got a few nice smiles and hellos as I walked to the elevator. Even the security guard winked at me. All I could give him was a hint of a smile, and he better not have called me a name under his breath 'cause I didn't say hello. I was in a slightly bitchy mood anyway so I couldn't complain too much.

I heard a familiar voice speaking in my direction. "Hey, Ina! Girl, it seems like you been gone forever!"

"Hey, Nakia!"

It was nice to see a friendly face. Nakia was dressed really great, too. Her hair was one color and she was wearing something conservative for a change. I hoped I wasn't coming back to work only to hear that she'd been promoted over me.

We both walked inside the elevator and got off at the fifth floor. Sometimes I'm really impressed when I walk in and see the big "Montaqua Publications" sign. I feel proud to work here, especially because there's so many black women in management positions. We got a lot of beautiful talented Sistahs up in here.

I asked Nakia, "What you smiling at, Girl?"

"Nothing. It's just nice to see you and I'm wondering if you knew about my promotion!"

Oh, here we go! I thought to myself.

"Promotion to what?"

"Administrative assistant!"

"Oh, okay, that's great! When did this happen?"

"A week after you went on vacation."

"And you didn't call to tell me?"

"Well, you said you didn't want to be bothered by anybody while you were on vacation."

"I know, but I'm really happy for you, Nakia."

"Thanks, Girl."

I really was happy for Nakia but mostly I felt good knowing that her position had nothing to do with me. I guess that's a mean thing to say but this is a very competitive environment and going on vacation is not always a great thing 'cause changes happen while you're away. One example is this new person that I have to show around. No telling how talented she is and what her goals and ambitions are.

"Hey, Nakia, do you know anything about this new girl?"

"You mean Vanessa?"

"Yeah, that's her name."

"She's cute."

"Now you know I didn't need to hear that, Girlfriend!"

"I know. I'm just playing with you. I haven't had much contact with her but she seems cool. I was introduced to her and then after that I talked to her, maybe twice."

"I guess I'll find out more about her today, huh?"

"I think so, Ina. There she is over there." Nakia pointed.

"That's her?"

"Yep, that's her."

"I don't like her already!"

"Why?" Nakia laughed.

"'Cause she is cute! Look at her, all tall, slender and got all that hair."

"Did you learn how to be jealous on your vacation, Ina? That ain't like you to be talking like that!"

"You know I'm hard on new people."

"Yes, I know that too well."

"What about that person standing next to her now?" I pointed.

"Who, him?"

"Yes. Is he another new hire?"

"Yeah, he's a friend of hers. She got him hired here."

"Damn, so she's just coming in and taking over already?"

"Ooh, Ina, you better wipe all that stuff off your face, Girl!"

"What stuff?"

"All that jelly!"

"Oh, I'm cool, honey. I guess I should go over and introduce myself, huh?"

"I don't know, you sure you want to? You might end up treating her worse than you treated me when I was new!"

"No, I'll be a sweetheart. Plus, I can meet her friend, too. What area is he working in?"

"I think he's in the mailroom. His name is Avonté."

"Avonté?"

"Yeah."

"He looks nice."

"He's alright."

"Looks good to me, Nakia. You know there aren't too many men around here."

"Yeah, and that's probably why he looks so good to you. To me he's just okay. Seems like a player trying to pass himself off as a regular guy."

"You think so?"

"Yeah, Girl."

"So who's being rough on the new person now?"

"I learned from you, Ms. Ina Sinclair."

"Well, I'm gonna go on over there. We on for lunch?"

"Yeah. Be nice to her. I don't care what you do to him though!"

"You're too much, Nakia."

So much was going through my mind as I approached this new girl. She was dressed really nice in her pants suit, gorgeous shoes, and not that much makeup. For some strange reason I was feeling envious of her. I guess it's because at first glance she appeared to have it really going on. But, I needn't worry because I have it going on myself. If my memory served me right, I had a lot of ambition and drive during my first few weeks on the job, too. Maybe I've lost some of that edge and gotten a little too comfortable.

That young man standing with her had a very nice body. He looked good in his light olive-colored shirt and gold tie. I started rubbing the back of my neck and straightening myself up as I got closer to the two of them. It was time for Ina Sinclair to be professional, cool and not let them see that my thoughts were leaning more toward the bedroom instead of the boardroom. Just before I approached Vanessa and Avonté, I looked behind me and saw Nakia watching. She gave me a goofy look, which didn't help my disposition at all. I guess she wanted to see how I was gonna handle myself.

I greeted Vanessa and Avonté. "Hello there!"

Vanessa immediately turned around. This girl had a gorgeous face up close. She was gonna make it hard for me to like her.

"Hi," she responded, unsure of whom I was.

"I guess you don't know me, huh?"

"No, I'm sorry but my name is Vanessa and this is Avonté."

"Nice to meet you both. I'm Ina Sinclair."

"Oh, how are you?!"

"I'm good and, by your reaction, I take it someone has told you about me?"

"Yes, they told me you were on vacation but that when you returned, you would be showing me around."

"I'm usually the one to show the new people around, but I take it you've seen everything already, haven't you?"

"I've seen a lot and it's been a great two weeks! I'm so excited about working here!"

"That's great. How about you, Avonté?"

It appeared as if he'd become uncomfortable with the fact that Vanessa and I were having a conversation that he wasn't a part of.

"I'm enjoying it, too," he responded, but not very enthusiastically.

"That's good to hear. What department are you in?"

"They got me in the mailroom but I promise that's only temporary."

"I imagine so 'cause you surely don't seem like the mailroom type."

"No, not at all. It's pretty hard to start in one of these agencies at a top-level position, no matter what kind of background you have."

As I observed Avonté's body language and mannerisms, I could see he possessed a great deal of ambition. If my memory served me right, folks in the mailroom wore uniforms. Avonté looked like he was over-dressed for his position. I also noticed that he stepped right in front of Vanessa and took over the conversation.

"So, I take it you both have strong academic backgrounds?"

"Yes, I just graduated last month with my master's degree in advertising!" Avonté said.

"Really? Then I see why you're disappointed with the position you're at right now. Perhaps we can do something about that."

"Well, I had strong competition when I came to interview for a position that suits my qualifications better."

"Is that right?"

"Yep," he responded, looking at Vanessa.

Vanessa spoke up. "Excuse me, but I have some errands to run. Can we talk later, Ina?"

Seemed like she wasn't very pleased with the way the conversation was going. Maybe Avonté was saying some things that didn't sit too well with her.

"I look forward to it, Vanessa. Stop by my office sometime…"

"Okay. It was nice meeting you."

"Nice meeting you, too."

As soon as Vanessa walked away, Avonté continued talking about himself. Seemed like as soon as his fire had been lit, he couldn't stop. It was pretty funny, but at the same time I wondered why it became so tense a moment earlier between the two.

"Is everything okay with you and Vanessa?"

"Yeah, why do you ask that?"

"Just wondering because she got so quiet while you were talking."

"Oh, she's cool. She's the one that they hired instead of me, but she's a good friend and hooked me up with this job."

"Oh, okay. Well, I must say that I find you interesting, Avonté, but if I were Vanessa, I might take your comments the same way she did."

"Just being honest."

"Well, let's talk again soon."

"You still gonna put in a good word for me?" he asked with a look of worry.

"I didn't forget, Avonté."

"Okay, thanks."

After leaving Avonté, I decided to go to the one place that always made me excited about coming to work—my office. It's like heaven to me most of the time and I guess it allows me to feel like I don't have to deal with a lot of the petty office drama that goes on. I could see right then that Mr. Avonté wouldn't be immune from the drama. The reaction he got from Vanessa really intrigued me.

"Knock, knock!"

Nakia stood at my door and it wasn't a surprise to see her so soon. I knew she would come over right away since she loves to indulge in some gossip herself. Plus the girl had truly become my best friend, even though I still had a hard time going over to her house to pick her up. She lives deep inside the hood and I live completely on the other side of town; where it's safe, I might add.

"What you doing, Girl?" Nakia asked.

"Right now I'm trying to clean off all this paperwork that everyone piled up on my desk. Did somebody write trash can on my office door while I was away?"

"No, but you were missed, Ina."

"Well, I guess so, but folks got a strange way of showing it."

I had tons of paperwork and no time to look at it. This was gonna take several days to complete, considering I didn't have anyone to assist me. Now that Nakia had her new job title, she was gonna be very busy. She didn't have an office yet but one day she would. I was proud of my girlfriend.

"What happened with the new employees?" she asked.

"Oh, those two are gonna be a trip around here. Did you know that Avonté has a master's degree?"

"No, and I don't care!"

"What did he do to you?"

"Nothing. Why's he working in the mailroom if he has a master's degree? He's probably lying!"

"Well, Nakia, that's easy to confirm; if he's being truthful about that. Why do you have so much attitude about him?"

"He just doesn't seem real to me. He only talks to people that he thinks will get him a better job."

"Well, he's ambitious and his ego is probably gonna get him in trouble, but I don't think he's a bad person. I wanna get to know him. Plus, I need an assistant, so maybe I can get personnel to give me the okay to transfer him over here."

"You mean as *your* personal assistant?"

"Yeah, why not?"

"That's on you, Ina."

"I think it would be nice. I need somebody that's really driven."

"If you say so. Can we talk about something else? What was Vanessa like?"

"She seems nice but Avonté just took over the conversation, so I didn't get to speak with her. I told her to come by my office, so maybe when she gets a moment, we'll be able to talk then."

"You don't want her as your assistant?"

"She's with Stacy in graphic design, so I don't think she'll want to be in my boring department."

"You just don't like her, that's all."

"No, I was acting silly earlier. She's really pretty, but I don't think she's a threat to what I do since I deal more with finances, and she's more into the creative side."

"Listen at you Ina, trying to be so much about business."

"Well, I'm teaching you, aren't I, Ms. Ghetto Fabulous?!"

"Oh, stop!"

I used to have a time with Nakia not too long ago. I didn't know what to expect from her because she would come in each week with some kind of new attitude or new hairstyle to make me wanna keep my distance. A case in point was when she walked in one Monday morning wearing burgundy braids. I have nothing against black women wanting to express themselves. We have a couple of black hair care companies as clients, but when I saw Nakia looking like some gangbanger's girlfriend, I wanted to run for the hills and pretend I didn't know her. I poked my head out of my office door when I saw her walking by.

"Nakia, get in here!"

I just started picking at her braids, one by one.

"What in the world is this, Girl?"

"Huh?"

"Don't tell me you lost your hearing, too, after they put this stuff in your hair!"

"Ina, what are you talking about?"

"I can't believe you came to work looking like this!"

"I look good!"

"I don't think that's appropriate, especially if you're gonna be working anywhere near me, Nakia. You've got to present yourself in a professional manner. Now if you want to look like that on the weekends, then that's your business."

I jumped on Nakia pretty hard about her burgundy braids that time. Then after a few days went by, I couldn't help but laugh because she walked in wearing her hair short and blonde.

"Oh, my goodness!" I said when I saw her.

"What, you don't like this either?"

"I am not gonna say a word."

After that, I figured I'd be tolerant with her ways of expressing herself, just as long as she worked hard. Our differences are kind of funny and she's really helped me to take risks where I normally wouldn't. Plus, showing me how to party without regretting the fun I had the next day has helped me a lot, too. I get stressed during the week but I know how to burn it off when the weekend comes.

I've also returned to going to church more often after doing a little too much booty shaking on the dance floor. I intend to do some more this weekend when I take Nakia out to celebrate her promotion. In a lot of ways, I feel like her mentor, and despite her fashion extremes, I'm always very proud of her. One weekend I even tried putting my hair in braids. I let Nakia do it for me and needless to say, I had fun with it but the style just wasn't for me.

I told her, "I am not trying to dress up for Halloween, Girlfriend."

"You are mean, Ina."

Well, my first day back from vacation was about two hours from being over. Everything seemed to go smoothly but that's probably because I spent most of the day in my office. I was still trying to sort through the paperwork. I sent an e-mail to personnel about my idea to have Avonté work for me. Maybe he'd show up one day wearing something interesting. I have a long list of things I'd like to see him wearing or possibly not wearing. I also sent an e-mail to my boss, Sharon McNair, letting her know that I thought it was a little too late for me to show Ms. Vanessa Jenkins around. I think she's already adjusted to her work environment, and since we're not in the same department, there's no need for me to mentor her at all. However, I do realize we're a team at this agency, so I wouldn't give her a hard time if she wished to discuss anything. I didn't know if I was gonna like her yet, but we would see.

The jury was still out but I thought it was gonna be fun to watch Mr. Avonté Douglas. His ego would surely make for interesting exchanges between him and his victims as he went along.

A voice interrupted my thoughts. "Excuse me, are you busy?"

Nakia never did close my door when she left a while ago. Now it looked like I was finally gonna have that chat with Vanessa after all.

"Hi, Vanessa!"

"I hope it's not too late in the day for us to talk."

"No, not at all. I was just getting caught up with paperwork. It's gonna be a while before I read through all of this."

"I can imagine! Did you go anywhere for your vacation?"

"Oh, nowhere special. I can't admit to those finding-my-groove-back stories or anything like that."

"No? Everyone told me that you were a party girl."

"I don't think so! You should probably meet Nakia because she's the true party girl around here."

"I'd like that very much. I want to get to know everyone around here if possible."

"That's a good thing, Vanessa. How do you like working for Stacy?"

"Oh, she's great, plus it's a very creative environment where I am."

"So you have no interest in the financial aspect of the advertising agency?"

"No, why do you ask?"

"Just wondering."

I'm glad she didn't pick up on my obvious sigh of relief. Vanessa really did appear to be the type of young lady that would advance in her career because she seemed so intelligent. I wasn't really concerned about her career choices, and I guess that sounds kind of mean.

I couldn't help but be curious about her relationship with Avonté. It wasn't that I wanted to date him, but I could use a little fun every once in a while. He could become my latest "trolling" companion, if he played his cards right. That's a term that all my Sistafriends are familiar with. I'd probably hear from personnel tomorrow about my idea, I hoped.

"I really hope I'm not disturbing you, Ina," Vanessa said.

"No, you're not," I said, though for a hot second, I did forget that she was sitting in front of me.

"Thanks, it just seems like you're preoccupied with something."

"No, I guess I was anxious to receive an e-mail response about a request that I made but it's not here yet. Other than that, I'm dreading more paperwork to come in. I have people to answer to myself and I know that somewhere under this pile is a request to do something urgent or important."

"Wow, I can imagine. Would you like any help? My day is just about over since I've completed the latest project we're doing."

"Oh, well, congratulations. You should be at some happy hour celebrating or winding down."

"I don't really drink or anything like that. I did want to hang out with my friend after work but I was kind of put off by his all-about-me behavior earlier today."

"We're speaking about Avonté?"

"Yes."

I watched Vanessa as she adjusted herself. She was visibly disappointed by what Avonté did earlier. Part of me wanted to smile but the other part understood where she was coming from.

"Are you two dating?"

"Kind of hard to say because we just met when we interviewed for the job that I have now."

"Oh, but you're somewhat interested in him?"

"Yes, there's something about him that I really like. He can be so cocky sometimes but it's in a subtle way. Then if you just look at him, that's reason enough to want to be with him."

I was almost afraid to respond to her last comment but I instantly had a mental picture of Avonté walking by wearing nothing that needed my imagination's help. I had to clear my throat before speaking.

"Are you giving up on him? What he did was wrong but you seem truly interested in him."

"I don't know. I'll probably just watch and wait to see what he says to me. Maybe he'll apologize, and then, who knows!"

"Well, Girl, I don't think you should write him off just yet, but at the same time, you shouldn't let him consume your mind either!"

"Okay! Thanks for talking with me, Ina. I didn't expect the conversation to become so personal, but it feels nice to talk with another woman for a change."

"You're welcome, Vanessa. Come by anytime."

"Thanks, I should go now but I'll see you tomorrow Ina!"

"Take care, Vanessa!"

It wasn't so bad speaking with her. She seemed really nice, even though I felt guilty in that I'd like to enjoy a little personal time with Avonté myself. Maybe I was just being mean like Nakia always tells me.

"Oh, well!"

NAKIA DAVIDSON

I don't know how many people in the world can use their job as a means of escape but each morning when I get up, I can't wait to get to work. I almost feel guilty about it because I'm always rushing my little girl to school. Her name is Tanisha. She's my motivation for wanting to make something of myself. After me and her father went our separate ways, I became determined to find a better life for us. I had to move home with my mom and little cousin, and I don't regret that decision at all. It was either that or remain in a situation that was gonna cause me to hate myself even more.

When I unloaded my stuff at home for the first time, it definitely felt like baggage. My mom gave me a big smile but I had a hard time smiling back. I felt a little bit like a failure so I went to my room and just sat there by myself for a few hours. Tanisha had to smile for both of us and when I wasn't lost in my thoughts, I could hear her playing outside with her cousin Trent. That made me feel a sense of relief at times, but for the most part I'd keep returning to my thoughts. The heaviest question on my mind at the time was, *What am I gonna do now?* I had no clue then but I knew I'd made the right decision in coming back home.

It's been so good for my daughter, even though our surroundings aren't the best. My former boss and now friend, Ina Sinclair, would have you thinking I lived one step above hell but it ain't that bad. She hates being anywhere near the so-called "Hood." We have some really good families on my street and that makes up for the occasional bad person around the way or hearing that helicopter every thirty minutes. I'm still trying to get Ina to spend the night over here, but the most she'll do is pull up and blow her horn. She's a trip sometimes but I really like her.

I didn't think we'd ever hit it off at first 'cause I thought she was just somebody that I could never relate to. I'd just look at her and kind of brush her off as some type of sellout. I learned eventually that she's a sweetheart that never looks outside her safe surroundings, that's all.

When I first started working at Montaqua Publications, I used to pass Ina in the hallways. She'd look right through me instead of at me. Sometimes I'd see her staring at me from the corner of my eye, and I'd feel like she wondered about my life but didn't know how to introduce herself to find out.

At that time, I was running errands and getting coffee for everyone and they mama. My job was only temporary and I felt blessed to get it. My mom gave me the phone number for this job agency and that led me to Montaqua. I celebrated every week because for whatever reason, they kept calling for me to come back. I felt like my life was slowly getting back on track and all my dreams were coming true. On Friday nights I could buy some Taco Bell for my daughter without worrying that I might not have any money left to give her for school the following week. I still don't make enough, but it's a lot better than not making anything.

I've seen those kinds of days all too often. Even living with my ex was hard 'cause I'm not the type to really ask a man for money. I can't just say, "Can you give me something so I can feed your daughter?" I shouldn't have to say that anyway but it got to a point where I was asking for money and that took so much out of me. My self-esteem dropped like it had a ton of bricks tied to it. Now that I can look back on how I used to feel about myself, it's like I'm looking at a completely different person. Now my ex is the one calling to see how we're doing and most of the time he just gets on my nerves. He's always trying to find out if I'm seeing somebody new. I usually remind him that right now I'm all about taking care of Tanisha and making sure she's got the best that I can give her.

He asked me, "Yeah, and who else is buying her things?"

I lashed back in frustration. "I ain't seeing nobody, damn!"

I've hung up on that man so many times it ain't even funny. He always knows how to catch me when I don't feel like being bothered. That's a feeling I get about twice a week because that's how often he calls me.

Today, I got my hair "did." That's how my girlfriends in the hood say it. I got it done because Ina promised to take me to this club downtown called Unrestricted. That place is like a meat market for the young and not so young urban America. Working at an advertising agency has made me become more creative with my descriptions, though most times I just be clownin'.

After I got my promotion to administrative assistant, Ina promised she was gonna do something nice for me. I'd been hinting at going to this place for days. I think she was getting tired of me repeating how much I wanted to get my groove on and see if some fine ass black man would step to me with a little intelligence and a heavy dose of sex appeal.

Ina said to me, "Nakia, you are too much!"

I told her, "And you need to learn how to have some fun, Girl!"

"I think I'm picking up all your bad habits. You probably gonna hear about me turning into a freak pretty soon, too!" Ina had said.

"I ain't no freak, Ina. At least, not yet!"

I think she and I both haven't been with a man in a very long time. I don't really plan on changing my situation but I have a feeling that Ina is after her a little piece. She called me last night and told me that on Monday, Avonté is gonna be working as her assistant.

I reacted with disbelief. "No you didn't!"

She just smiled and said, "Yep, I sure did."

Then she told me that he might be at the club tonight. I didn't really care to hear that. It almost ruined me looking forward to it, but I keep hearing such good things about the place that I can't wait to go. Plus, Ina is paying for everything. She also told me that Vanessa might be there, too.

I asked her, "Why?" and gave her a frown that made my whole forehead crinkle up.

"'Cause I told Vanessa she should get out more often."

"You're just inviting everybody and they Mama when you supposed to be doing this for me!"

"Don't you want to have familiar faces all around you?"

"No, not really!"

"You're crazy, Nakia!"

"Listen, Ina, I want to be able to make a fool out of myself without worrying about some new girl and that fake ass Avonté spreading rumors about me the next day at work."

"Damn! And here you are always telling me I'm mean?"

"I'm just being real with you, Girl!"

After I heard myself giving Ina all that attitude, I felt ashamed of everything I'd said. I eventually apologized and then began preparing myself for some all-night booty shaking. I still think Avonté is fake but since I ain't the one who invited him, that means I don't have to say a word. I can just smile and pretend like he's saying something interesting, which is a stretch for both of us.

Now, it's time to keep an eye out for Ina. One thing I don't have to worry about is her showing up late. She's usually pretty good about that, especially since she doesn't like being over here after dark. I've already made sure my baby is okay, and Mama has been really cool with watching Tanisha whenever I go out. It's been a long time since I've left my baby overnight with my mother. In fact, the last time was when I brought her here so that me and my ex could spend a romantic night together.

Those were the days because he was so good to me back then. For the life of me I don't know what happened but I guess people change. I used to wonder if I was the reason because I can remember him being so sweet in the beginning. He always had a little ghetto in him but Terence was so cool and would crack that beautiful smile of his in a minute. That night of romance we had was the bomb and after it happened, I spent many days and nights reliving it. Those memories would make my pussy wet in a second. I can't believe I just said that…

I can remember another night in particular when I really got lost in my thoughts. I never heard Terence come home that day and I think Tanisha was playing in her room at the time. There I was, thinking and touching myself. I imagined a moment when his body was moving back and forth against mine. We were all sweaty. I looked down and saw his face rubbing against my breasts. My nipples were so erect and just popping right back up every time he rubbed against them.

Then, as these thoughts raced through my mind, causing my heart to beat faster and faster, I could feel the wetness of a tongue licking me on my inner thigh. It scared the shit out of me! When I opened my eyes, it was Terence, just smiling like crazy, still dressed in his UPS uniform after coming home from work.

"What you thinkin 'bout, Lady?"

He didn't give me a chance to answer verbally. Instead he kissed me softly before I could say a word.

He told me, "Don't stop what you were doing."

He was talking to me so sweet, damn. I kept touching myself as he kissed me on the lips. Then he ran his tongue slowly around the outside of my bottom lip, down my chin, and then to my neck so gently. It was hard to stay focused on touching because I just wanted to grab him. But he kept whispering "Keep touching yourself" over and over in a very seductive way. I was on fire at that point.

He was talking to my body. He said, "I love the way your heartbeat sounds, baby."

At that point I felt like I was reaching the point of ecstasy because even though I was still touching myself, Terence was the one who had complete control. He had my body and soul locked inside this room of passion. At this point, I couldn't take it any longer. He was seducing me in such a sensual way while kissing my breasts and running his tongue all over me. I arched my back slightly and then, oh, my goodness! I wasn't sure how much more I could stand.

"Nakia!" a female voice shouted, snapping me back to reality.

"Oh, shit!"

"Nakia! What are you doing, Girl?"

"Sorry, Ina. How long you been there?"

Damn, Ina just ruined that moment.

"Long enough to get an attitude!" she shouted from inside her car.

"Don't start, Girl, here I come."

I'm a little embarrassed 'cause she drove up and I didn't even notice, but it's nice to have something good to remember, no matter how much I can't stand my ex right now.

"You okay, Girl?" Ina asked.

"Yeah."

"What were you thinking about?"

"My ex..."

"Oh. You want to talk about it?"

I answered her question with silence. I hid my sad eyes by looking out the window as Ina drove off. My eyes filled up with tears, but I began to smile because Tanisha was in the window, waving goodbye to me. I don't know why I'm so sad now since I know I'm better off without Terence.

Ina hit my shoulder and said, "Nakia, you're supposed to be excited right now!"

"I know."

"Then come on, Girl, I still got that DMX tape you gave me!"

"I ain't ready for him yet, Ina. Put on some D'Angelo."

"Thank God!"

"You're too much, Ina."

"You okay now?"

"Yeah."

This time I answered with a smile.

It was cool riding with Ina, especially because she didn't talk that much. We were no more than about five minutes away from the club when I remembered something that I wasn't looking forward to.

"Were you kidding when you said Avonté was gonna be coming to the club, too?" I asked.

"No, why?"

I shrugged my shoulders and looked the other way.

"It won't be that bad, Nakia. Plus, you're gonna see so many other fine men that you'll forget about Avonté."

Once again I shrugged my shoulders and didn't say a word.

"Don't give me that look!"

I looked at her and said, "Right now I'm wondering what you're gonna do with him since Vanessa might be there, too?"

"Oh, I can make it look real innocent on the dance floor, honey. She won't know what I'm thinking about or trying to feel on."

"You're already turning into a freak, huh, Ina?"

"I'm thinking about it. Hold on, Girl, let me turn in here."

Ina pulled into the parking lot of the nightclub. I just watched that devilish grin she had on her face. I couldn't help but wonder what was going through her mind and just how far she planned on taking her curious desires. It was a trip to see her biting her lip as she thought about tonight and her possible encounter with Avonté. Speak of the devil. I could see him standing in the parking lot so I guess she was about to enjoy her first opportunity.

"Ain't that him over there?"

"Where?"

"Right there. Look where I'm pointing, Girl!"

"Oh, it sure is. Damn, he looks good in that suit."

I responded with no enthusiasm, "If you say so..."

Actually, Avonté did look good in his black suit, dark gray shirt and shiny tie to match. He saw us pull in and park because he kept trying to wave to get our attention. I don't think Ina can see that far at night, and I didn't feel like saying anything to her about him waving at us.

"He's still fake to me," I told her just before getting out of the car.

"Be nice, Nakia!"

As I waited on Ina to finish checking her makeup, Avonté approached. I wasn't really interested in entertaining him until Ina got herself together, but I guess I had no choice. I was mostly feeling the music coming from a car that parked close by. They were playing one of D'Angelo's slow jams and I couldn't resist swaying a little to the beat. I don't see how anybody can stand still when that man sings.

"Hey, lady, I guess you like that song, huh?" Avonté asked as he came closer.

"Yeah, that man sounds so good to me."

Avonté whispered, "Nice..."

I could feel his eyes all over me but I wasn't trying to respond or inspire him to keep looking. Ina was the one that wanted his ass, not me. I folded my arms and leaned against the car. Avonté was still undressing me with his eyes so I guess it didn't matter what I did.

"Ain't you ready yet, Girl?" I shouted.

"Yeah, in a minute!"

I beat on the window a couple of times and that seemed to do the trick 'cause having this man look me up and down had me feeling seriously violated, in a way. I could see Ina putting her stuff in her purse really fast and dropping things on the floor.

Ina tried to play off her clumsiness. "Nakia, I'm just trying to fix myself up, Girlfriend!"

She finally got out of the car and not a moment too soon. I had the feeling that Avonté was gonna find the courage to step closer to me, not realizing that my being nice was only a temporary thing.

"Oh, hi, Avonté!" Ina said.

"Hey, y'all ready to go inside?" he responded while trying to play off his flirtatious behavior toward me.

"Yeah, but remember I'm just treating Nakia, so I hope you don't think that just because I invited you, I'm gonna pay your way inside."

One thing about Ina, she's always serious when it comes to money issues. It was nice to see her set some ground rules for Avonté to be conscious of. She had me worried for a second there because she's always looking at him like he's all that.

I followed both of them inside and just kind of watched until my vision was interrupted by the lights reflecting off some fine men standing around holding their drinks. I guess they were just trying to see which women they'd end up making eye contact with. It's always funny to see how men just stand around moving their heads to the beat and trying to be cool. The women in the club are the ones that truly react to the music. They had a song playing right then that I was really feeling. The crowd of people chanted "Party everywhere!" and I couldn't resist getting in on the fun.

I knew I was looking good, too, shaking my booty, but no man had approached me yet. I wasn't about to dance with Avonté. I just took matters into my own hands and started getting my party on by myself. Ina was too busy talking to Avonté and sipping on some drink she got when I wasn't looking.

I was just too through with Ina standing there trying to fan herself, acting like her conversation with Avonté was so hot. I needed to go back to focusing on having a good time by myself because Ina was so preoccupied, and I knew she would do that to me. Somebody must not have told her the true meaning of "Girls' night out" yet.

Time flew by once I danced to a couple of songs and had a drink. I wasn't sure where Ina and Avonté had disappeared to, and I hadn't seen any sign of Vanessa in the club either. Okay, I wasn't looking hard for her but I knew she was supposed to show up that night. I'd been enjoying myself, even though the first guy I danced with was on the short side. I could see over his head and it was even more embarrassing when he went down on the floor trying to do some kind of dance that I wasn't familiar with. He must've made that shit up before he came.

Then the next guy was kind of tall and basically had just one dance move. He probably lined up in the back row when they used to do the Electric Slide. I shouldn't talked about these men too bad since it'd been a while for me, too, as far as getting my groove on. It's just so much you can do dancing around the house with your daughter. Then, watching *Soul Train* don't teach you nothing but how to wake up when you know the camera is on you and make your booty jiggle up and down. I forgot how much fun I used to have dancing in places like this and working up a little sweat. It was time for me to head to the ladies' room and then come back and get another drink. There was still no sign of Ina. I knew she'd better be around to give me a ride home though.

As I made my way toward the bar after returning from the bathroom, one of those fine men holding a drink caught my attention, but this time it felt different. He wasn't looking me up and down. Instead, he was focused on my eyes. In a split second, I couldn't tell if he was shocked or pleasantly surprised. I just knew it felt like an instant attraction moment for me. Now I was starting to show my feminine side because all I could do was smile ever so slightly and pray that he approached me. Even though I can be bold sometimes, I'm still a little shy when it comes to first meeting men, especially those that I'm attracted to like this one.

This man was standing in a black turtleneck and a beautiful light-green shirt and black pants. His vibe from a distance read smooth with a hint of player but I didn't want to label him just yet.

"Can I have a rum and Coke?" I asked the bartender.

"Coming up!"

A voice spoke from behind me, "Excuse me, Miss…"

For an instant I got really nervous, but I cleared my throat and turned around.

"Thanks, I just wanted to get one of these napkins," the person said.

I thought that sexy fine man had approached me, but it was some dude who spilled a drink on his shirt.

"Rum and Coke!" the bartender shouted.

"Thanks," I responded.

I just had to stand there for a moment and collect myself. Maybe I should've approached that guy because after scanning the room, I didn't see him anywhere. If it weren't for the music keeping me company, I would've been feeling really sad and lonely.

Somebody sure must've turned up the bass in this club because my whole body was vibrating. To be honest, I was getting a little turned on by the feeling. I had to laugh about that and hold my drink to my forehead. Here I was standing all alone, keeping company with my own damn thoughts 'cause I got deserted by my girlfriend. If my night didn't get better, I was gonna be really mad at Ina the next time we talked.

A soft but deep voice caught me off guard, "Hey..."

I turned to my left but felt a strong body brush against me on my right.

"How you doin'?" the deep voice asked.

"Huh?"

I could barely hear him but I knew what he'd said.

I responded nervously, "I'm fine."

My brain was having a hard time clicking in so I was all late with my response. He just smiled and I didn't know what to do or say next.

"Is it alright if we talk?" he asked.

This man looked twice as good up close. He was the same one in the turtleneck that I was hoping would approach me. He touched my arm and stepped to the side. I felt his presence so strong that it seemed like with one smile and a hint at his direction, he parted the crowd of people, and I had no problem walking to the lounge area. I was so nervous that it felt like I was walking in slow motion. I looked back only to be met by his warm eyes and sweet smile. The man had me feeling like I was in a dream being led to a final destination of bliss. I couldn't snap out of that shit at all.

"This is more like it, don't you think? Now you can hear me and I can appreciate you better," he said.

"Uh-huh."

"You okay?"

I had to take a deep breath and ease my nervousness with some laughter.

"What's funny? I like your smile, by the way."

"Thanks. I'm just laughing at myself because no man has ever made me feel this nervous before."

"I don't want to make you nervous."

"It's not you, it's me, I- I guess."

"Okay, just as long as it doesn't prevent you from seeing me again sometime?"

I started acting like Ina had a little earlier. This man had me fanning myself and feeling faint.

"You sure you're okay?"

"Yes, I'm fine. You mind if we sit over there?" I pointed to a nearby booth.

"I was gonna suggest the same thing since you seem a little tired. Maybe you danced too much out there. I saw you earlier."

"You did?"

"Yeah, but at that time, my prayers weren't working too good."

"What do you mean?"

"I kept praying that you would feel my eyes on you and somehow turn and look at me."

I just smiled and blushed.

"I've never heard anyone say that before."

"I've never said it before."

"Are you sure? Be honest."

"Okay, I'll admit to thinking or experiencing that feeling before but no, I've never said that to anyone."

"Uh-huh. I'll bet if you pulled out your wallet, I'd find a Platinum Playa card somewhere in there!"

"I knew you had a little fire in you."

"A woman has to be careful."

"True and if you should feel threatened by anything I say, feel free to walk away."

"You're a confident man, huh?"

He just smiled and I saw a hint of bashfulness in him. I thought that was cute, but I felt like this was too good to be true. The funny thing was that I also felt comfortable with this ultra- fine, sexy brown man and yet, I still didn't know his name.

"So, you gonna show me that playa card now?"

"I don't have one but I can give you my business card."

"Okay..."

He reached for his wallet and pulled it out. I kept looking at his face and the smoothness of his skin. He licked his lips gently and left them...slightly wet. I had to cross my legs under the table because his every move was so seductive to me. When he found one of his business cards, he placed it on the table and slid it in front of me. When I touched the card, I never took my eyes off his. Our fingertips made contact and we both smiled with delight.

He asked, "You have a card?"

I shook my head no.

"But you're gonna give me your number, right?"

I just smiled.

"Orlando Duncan, hmm...," I said.

He had a nice little business card. It appeared that this man had something going for himself. Tall, sexy, fine and professional, too!

"Ooh, a black man with more than just a job, hmph!"

"I've been blessed while at the same time never knocking the steps I had to take to get where I'm at."

I just kept smiling and listening to this man talk.

"Are you for real?" I asked.

Orlando started laughing.

"I'm aight!"

"Well, you don't fit the image that you portray on your business card, Orlando."

"What image is that?"

"I mean, investment banking, portfolio manager, master's degree from Howard University."

"As I said, I've been blessed. I should've put on there that I worked at Burger King, too! Those were some good foundational years."

"How old are you, if I may ask?"

"Yeah, it's cool. I figured you would get around to it."

"And?"

"I'm 37."

"Oh, really? I would've never guessed that until I read your card because you would have to have some experience to accomplish all this."

"That's very true and I'm not done yet, but at the same time it doesn't mean I have to subscribe to how others think I should look."

"Hmm, I think I should give you my number."

"Is that right?"

"Yes, but not because of what you do."

"Well, that's good to hear."

"No, don't you get nervous thinking I'm a gold digger. It's just nice to finally talk to a man who has something going for himself and is possibly reaching for some kind of deeper meaning in life."

"You see that from across the table, huh?"

"I do...kinda..."

"Maybe once I know your name and get that phone number, I can tell you what I see."

"You don't have to tell me but I will give you my name and number. Give me something to write it on."

Orlando gave me another one of his cards. He had such beautiful hands. They didn't really appear manicured, but still they were well taken care of. He didn't have a lot of flash about him, although I imagined he could definitely afford it. Maybe that would come out later. That is, if he was really serious about seeing me again.

I handed him back the card. "Here you are."

"Nakia Davidson."

"That's me!"

"Sounds nice..."

"I can be, sometimes."

"I imagine you can be a lot of things at different times, Nakia. I see a woman that I could enjoy challenging conversations with."

"Yes, I will debate you on some things!"

"What happened to that shy girl?"

"She's here, too..."

Time went by in a dream-like setting as I talked to Orlando. I found myself holding on to his card as though I had a piece of him. At times I even held it to my nose hoping to breathe his scent. He just smiled when I did that and paid really close attention every time I spoke. I'd never had a man watch me so closely without feeling like he wanted to have sex with me. Orlando was actually interested in what I was saying. He still flirted with me from time to time and I didn't think he'd turn down a chance at my booty. But he seemed so sincere that I thought he would blush if I kissed him on his cheek.

"Hey, Nakia," Orlando said softly.

"Yes?"

"Since we didn't shake hands when we first met, you think we could right now?"

"You want to shake my hand?"

"Yeah..."

"Okay."

We both reached slowly forward and made contact with each other's fingertips. I thought he wanted to just grab and shake hands, but it felt like he was creating a new kind of foreplay because I got turned on by his gesture. Our entire hands connected and locked. I had to take a deep breath and close my eyes. When I opened them, he was smiling.

He spoke softly, "I hope you don't mind..."

"Mind?"

"Yeah. I just wanted to hold your hand for a moment."

"No, it feels nice."

"Thanks."

Orlando was killing me with his seductive way of communicating. He probably knew what he was doing, but I had a hard time fighting off the fact that this felt so damn good. I don't like for a man to be able to do this to me. To have this effect on me is kind of scary but still, Orlando was a different kind of man. I figured he was too old for the games that I was used to. If anything, maybe he'd just come at me with some new game. That might even be scarier than the typical shit that I encounter. One day I might end up screaming, "Give me a man with regular issues anytime!"

Time passed by and I started to realize it was getting pretty late. Orlando was like my introduction to *Black Man Heaven*, but reality was beginning to sink in. I needed to find Ina so I could get home 'cause riding the bus wasn't an alternative I'd look forward to, especially this late at night.

"You okay?" Orlando asked.

"Yes, why do you ask?"

"I can always tell when something grabs your attention away from us. I guess I'm already spoiled by the connection we've shared thus far."

"Oh, really?"

"Yes."

"It's not easy thinking about other things when I talk to you, Orlando."

"Well, that's a good thing, Nakia."

"It's scary to me!"

"Nah, you shouldn't be scared."

"It's natural for a woman to get scared when she feels herself being swept away..."

"Okay."

"You giving up already?"

Orlando seemed to rest his thoughts as though he didn't want to cross a certain line with me.

"No, Nakia, I just don't want you to feel threatened in any way. If I'm doing any kind of sweeping, I want it to feel like a feather so that this experience will linger in your mind when you go home tonight. Maybe it'll cause you to think about me and perhaps call me sooner than either of us expected."

"Well, I think you should call me, too. Maybe I'll be the one sitting around thinking that this was a one-time thing and you're never gonna call."

"Oh, I'm gonna call."

"You sure?"

"Yep…"

"You're not just saying that?"

"I'll call you tonight, or should I say this morning…"

"Yes, it is late and that's what took my attention away from you, Orlando. I came here with my girlfriend Ina and I haven't seen her since we got here. I'm afraid my ride home has disappeared."

Orlando asked carefully, "Would it be too bold to ask you to let me take you home?"

"Yes, but I'd probably say it was okay."

"You need a ride home Nakia?" Orlando asked with a boyish grin.

"Yes…" I sighed.

"Wanna leave now?"

"If you don't mind."

"No, not at all. I should get going, too."

"You have kids, Orlando?"

"No."

"Ever been married?"

"Nope…"

"Engaged?"

"How come you didn't ask me these questions earlier, Nakia?"

"Making you nervous?"

"Nope."

"Be honest…"

"Nah, not at all. It's just that questions like those deserve some kind of explanation sometimes. You know, we all got stories behind the reasons why we are who we are. I've never been married or engaged, but there was a time when I stayed up all night trying to come up with a special way to propose to somebody I was seeing at the time."

"Oh, what happened?"

"Well," Orlando paused for a moment. "Maybe I'll share that with you another time."

"Bad memories?"

"Good and bad. Not ready to shed that part of me just yet."

"Okay."

"So, let's make our way through this club and I'll take you home."

"Okay."

I couldn't believe that Miss Ina left me behind. This was supposed to be a celebration for my promotion. I know messing around is kind of new for her, but damn, that shouldn't make her forget who she is. It might be better for me to blame Avonté for the change because I'd really hate to think badly about my girlfriend.

Walking with Orlando felt so nice, though. It was a welcome surprise when he reached for my hand as we stepped outside the club. My ears felt so numb from that loud music inside, but my heart was still pounding to the beat of this new discovery.

Someone shouted in the distance, "Nakia!"

Orlando asked, "Is that your friend coming this way?"

"Yeah, that's her."

I had to hold my breath 'cause I wanted to yell out a few not so kind words to Ina as she walked toward us.

Orlando asked, "I wonder where she's been?"

"I'm wondering the same thing 'cause it don't look like she's been in the club dancing."

"Maybe she had an emergency?"

"I don't think so..."

Ina finally made it over to us and she could instantly see that I had a serious attitude. Wasn't much she could've said to me that I would've understood or appreciated, but I did want some kind of explanation from her.

"Are you ready to go, Girl? I'm sorry for leaving you in there," she told me.

I looked at Orlando and I thought he could read my mind before I said anything. I wasn't against him taking me home but I felt uncomfortable about it since we had just met. Then at the same time I wanted to hear what Ina had to say about leaving me alone like she did. Avonté wasn't that damn fine to be acting like she was in love.

Orlando grabbed my hand and said, "It's okay, Nakia. Just let me know that you got home safely, okay?"

Orlando looked so disappointed. He didn't even try to speak to Ina. He started walking away before I could introduce the two of them.

I spoke up before he could walk away completely. "Orlando, let me walk you to your car…"

"Okay, it's right over here."

"I should've guessed that you drove a Porsche."

"Yeah, I'm proud of it. Something I always wanted."

"I'm scared of you, Orlando."

"Why you say that?"

"Just playing. I'll call you when I get home."

It felt so nice to wrap my arms around this man's neck. He stood so tall and smelled so delicious. I couldn't recognize the scent, but I would from then on. That scent belongs to him only, damn!

I let out a big long sigh even though I really wanted to scream. To be honest, I really was scared of the man. At first sight he appeared to be the kind of man that every woman dreams would come knocking on her door. Well, that night my dream came true, and this was the first time I'd felt like I was wearing glass slippers. Orlando was such a gentleman and had me intrigued every second I was with him. My heart sank when he started up his car engine. I just stood there watching him back out and then drive away. I was scared that he might be feeling really disappointed in me. He'd probably just throw my number out the window and then turn his phone off for the next few days once he got home. I probably should've had more faith, but I really felt bad because he was so excited about taking me home. As I turned to look at Ina, I gave her a disgusted, mean look.

"Look what you made me do!"

"I'm sorry, Girl!"

"Where the hell you been anyway?"

"I was with Avonté. He convinced me to go outside and sit in the car with him. I found out a lot about him and he's really nice."

"You two have been sitting in the car all this time?"

"Well, no."

"Humph…"

"We got something to eat."

"Did you have sex with him?"

Ina instantly got quiet and started to walk away.

"I'm parked over here, Nakia. Can we go now?"

"Yeah, I ain't gonna ask you anything else."

I was so disappointed, mostly because I look up to Ina. She's the one that should be attracting a man like Orlando. She's got the great job. She's single and drives a nice car. I couldn't understand why she was acting like sex and flirting with men was such a new experience to her. Maybe she missed out on something when she was my age but I can't see myself acting like she does in a few years. I want to have my shit together and be able to live somewhere nice with my daughter. It would be great to have a man but I'm not gonna act like I'm guaranteed to have one. I better just keep my mind on what I have a little bit of control over. These men have too many issues for me to deal with; especially since I got rid of most of mine a long time ago. I named my issues Terence and I'd hate to think that they've returned with a brand-new name called Orlando.

Right now, as far as I'm concerned? I'm through with Ina for a while. I'm glad I don't work for her anymore cause that's gonna make it easier to avoid having to go to lunch with her every day like we've been doing. She needs to give me a few days before I can forgive her; especially if Orlando ends up not calling. If that happens, I won't be biting my tongue like I'm doing right now. I can tell you that much.

GOOD HABITS DIE HARD

I am so tired of dealing with Avonté lately. Yes, that's coming from my own lips after I've spent a month being something that I'm not. It's been about that long since I've even spent time with Nakia. I didn't realize she was so angry with me that night at the club but I understand her feelings completely—now. I've also been trying to understand my own behavior and at the same time deal with the tension that this has caused at work. Before all this happened, I could speak to Nakia in the hallway without wondering why she had an attitude.

I said to Nakia earlier today, "Hey, Girl, you busy?"

She just walked by and left me feeling so empty. If she were anybody else, I'd be like "Fuck her!" But, she's not just anybody else. I've tried my best to put it all behind me and move on, but I have to admit that I really miss talking to her.

Lately, if I want to know what's going on with Nakia, I have to listen to gossip. I'm sure she can say the same thing except that what she hears about me is probably not so appealing.

I've heard really cool things about her—not only professionally—but also with that man she met at the club. She has all the women around here feeling envious of her because he seems so sweet and attentive. I lost count on how many times he's sent her flowers. That man must have a special account at the flower shop just for her.

I caught a glimpse of him the other day when he came by the office to pick her up. Orlando was sitting out there in the lobby looking too fine as usual. He was dressed in this black suit with a blue dress shirt and a really nice tie. That man had it going on and here I was chasing Avonté's booty instead of out there finding me a real man like Nakia did. I actually tried to speak with Orlando, but I didn't get very far. I walked in his direction and sort of pretended like I vaguely remembered who he was.

I said to him, "Hey, we've met before, haven't we?"

"Yeah, Nakia introduced us in front of Unrestricted."

"Yeah, that's right…I guess it was an awkward situation then, huh?"

"Yes, Ma'am. Actually it's still kind of awkward since I'm aware that you and Nakia aren't really speaking."

I didn't know what to say after that so I wished him a blessed day and walked away. I returned to my desk feeling pretty bad. Then seeing Nakia walk by my door looking so excited that her man was here didn't help matters either. I'm not a bad person but I really felt like one.

Things have been interesting, to say the least, with Avonté around. I'm putting through the paperwork on a transfer request that he asked me for a couple of days ago. That man has really been something to deal with. He seems to know how to take a woman through a whirlwind of issues in a short amount of time. I feel like I've known him for years when it's only been a little over a month.

That night outside the club I guess was my downfall because to be honest, I had a really good time with him. He had me excited like I was in high school again, doing something that I knew I shouldn't be doing. I got so worked up on the dance floor bumping and grinding and feeling his thigh between my legs. Then when he suggested we go outside, I grabbed him tighter and told him intensely, "Let's go," like I was the one in charge rather than my sex drive kicking in and making me do something that I'd regret later.

Avonté was shocked that I didn't hesitate, but then he flashed that devious smile and we both walked outside feeling the heat. Once we got to the car, we just started kissing like we were trying to put a fire out, burning on our lips. I can't say it was romantic, but it was definitely hot.

"We ain't supposed to be doing this!" I told him.

But it wasn't like I was preventing him from pulling my panties down. I got even more excited when he did just that because we were still standing outside his car. The kissing got even heavier and then I made him walk around to the back of the car where I turned around and lifted my dress. I was into this moment like I don't know what! It drove me wild to finally be penetrated after going through so many nights of imagining what it felt like. Nakia and I both used to talk about how long it'd been for us. We would have all-night discussions about the subject. But on that night with Avonté, it was both passionate and a little nasty which turned me on even more.

When the following day came, unfortunately, Nakia wasn't speaking to me but Avonté had plenty to say. I have to admit that at that time I was acting like he was the hottest thing on earth. I would close my office door, talk about business for ten minutes with him, and then we'd start laughing and joking about our interlude in the parking lot.

"You got some fire in you, Ina. I didn't think you would be so bold."

"I didn't think so either, but I'd definitely do it again."

"Oh, really?"

"I sure would."

"How about lunch then?"

Avonté had that devious smile again and, at that time, it wasn't hard for him to say things that would turn me on. I was getting what I thought I wanted and he was doing his "thang," which I wasn't sure at the time what that really was.

On that day, I'd met him for lunch in the parking lot of our office building, but this time we indulged inside of this SUV he was driving. I wasn't gonna be so bold this time, but I did enjoy myself.

After a few more days of office flirting and phone conversations filled with sexual innuendo, I'd gotten a little tired. I wanted to see what Avonté was all about—as a person. I began to notice that we never talked about his desires in life or his future in the company. He made it very clear that he wanted to succeed and have the money to sustain a good lifestyle, but his methods seemed a little shaky. He's very professional and has a way with getting his ideas across without being demanding, but...I've had to remind him several times that he's basically my secretary, which I could tell didn't sit too well with him. I've also noticed that he's stayed clear of Vanessa and hasn't mentioned her at all. At first I thought I was the reason for that but when I asked him if he was still seeing her, he just looked at me and smiled.

I asked him, "Is that a yes or no?"

"She served her purpose."

"Excuse me?"

"You know how sometimes people come in and out of our lives for reasons that we usually find out later?"

"Yes, I understand that."

"Well, Vanessa hooked me up and was sort of that bridge leading me here. I didn't think things would move along so fast, but I knew I had the potential to make things happen once I got my foot in the door."

"I see a lot of potential in you, Avonté, even though I think you use it in the wrong way."

"What do you mean?"

Our conversation was interrupted by a phone call so I didn't continue my thoughts with him. I was really taken back that day by his comments about Vanessa. I almost forgot she was still around because he never mentioned her. I don't deal that much with her department so there was hardly any reason for us to chit-chat.

Avonté's motivations were just becoming all too clear to me, but for a few weeks I really became spoiled by his get-things-done mentality. I would only find out later that he used that to his advantage as well. Gossip travels kind of slow around here, depending on your position or relationship with the office workers. When the stories about Avonté got back to me, they would always be about him wanting to do his time with me and then move on.

I recently heard about him putting together two financial reports for my boss, Sharon McNair. One report was the one I authored while the other one was something based on what I'd done but claimed by Avonté as being a representation of his ideas. I don't know what Sharon's response was but nevertheless she kept the report and didn't discuss anything with me. My attraction for Avonté quickly faded once I got wind of his underhanded moves. Now his devious smile actually *looked* devious to me.

The gossip just kept traveling to my office a lot faster once people got wind of me being upset with what I was hearing. I guess others wanted to fan the flames and perhaps see me go off on him or something. I was beginning to think that maybe Avonté had developed some enemies in the office pool. My suspicion was proven wrong though, once I'd heard about some new lady in the office that he sparked the interest of. This little piece of news came to me when I had lunch with Sharon inside her office.

"How are things working out with Avonté?" she asked.

I almost reacted to her in an angry way because I thought she was speaking personally, but I caught myself before I fell into that hole.

"I'm not too sure if he's happy in his position, but he's definitely a go-getter type," I responded.

"Yeah, I can see he's a thinker and makes his agenda known."

"Yep…"

"He's already introduced himself to the new girl from our Texas office. She came to me once asking me if he was a part of management," Sharon said.

"Oh, really? Did he tell her that?"

"No, she just said that he had a really strong grasp of the business."

"Oh, well, I hope he's not passing himself off as management. Who's the new girl?"

"Jolie Thompson."

"And you said she's from Texas?"

"Well, I'm not sure if she was born there, but she comes highly recommended out of our Texas office."

"Oh, okay."

I wasn't sure if I was feeling jealous about this new girl or what, but I did have a strange feeling in the pit of my stomach. Maybe it was this cold seafood salad I was eating.

"Is she working with us permanently?" I asked.

"No, this is a temporary assignment for her. From what I understand, it's only been three days so far and she's already homesick. She really seems nice."

"Oh, I'll have to meet her later then," I said with forced enthusiasm.

"Her office is not too far from here."

"Her office?" I interrupted.

"Yes, something wrong?"

"No, I'll visit with her soon."

This new temporary girl had an office already and it took me forever to get mine. I'm feeling like I need to have somebody point out to me what I did wrong in my past life. It seems like it's all coming back to haunt me now. I'm probably overreacting but I'm vowing right now to start with a fresh new attitude tomorrow. I think my first positive move is getting rid of Avonté, and then maybe my next move should be apologizing to Nakia for my behavior at the club. I'm just hoping she don't say "Whatever!" and walk away from me. I've seen firsthand how stubborn she can be sometimes. Her stubbornness makes me feel like we're sisters because I'm exactly the same way. But, I have to admit that she's the one who is truly making progress in her life.

This day was pretty long for me but it's finally over. I had so many thoughts about Nakia and our friendship. I've also had to deal with my own jealousies throughout the day. I looked out the window and saw her going home early. Her man picked her up and she looked so happy. There he was, waiting for her while leaning up against his Porsche. I really had to wonder why I didn't have someone like him waiting for me. I can remember having long talks about men with Nakia and usually someone like Orlando was exactly the kind of man I'd describe. Then Nakia would tell me that she didn't want any man coming into her life because it would only ruin her focus and perhaps take time away from her and her daughter. I wonder if she still feels that way. My guess is that she's learning pretty quickly that finding a good man can only enhance her life.

As I watched her approach Orlando outside and give him the biggest hug ever, she had the sweetest smile on her face. I removed my jealousy then and thought about how happy Nakia must've been feeling right then. I feel very proud of her and I sincerely hope we can get past the distance that we've created around us. We need to be friends again!

As for Avonté, it seems like he got the hint that I was no longer very fond of him. He didn't even stop by to thank me for putting in his request to work in another division. He keeps his distance from me and I'm not really sure why. I know I haven't spread any rumors about what I think of him or what I wouldn't mind doing to him. Maybe the expressions on my face speak louder than any words I could use. I'm not really sure, but I'm hoping to have a conversation with him just to confirm my feelings about him being a jerk.

Our recent conversations have truly blown my mind. His attitude and ways that he expresses himself are something that I never noticed before. Nakia could see right through him but I never did. Just the other day I sat with him in the lunchroom with a look of astonishment on my face.

I kept asking him, "Are you serious?"

"Yeah, why you trippin'?"

"Excuse me?"

"Nothing…"

Our conversations seem to have no true connection except the motivation to start arguing over his egotistical ideas. I've begun having no recollection as to why I liked him so much in the first place. Nakia might tell me it's because I was horny and had never been pursued in the way that Avonté did. He was aggressive, yet he was very sweet and had a gentle quality about him. I've had to stop myself from smiling so hard a few times because I felt like it made him think he had me in the palm of his hands. Actually, one night he did pull my strings like a master puppeteer.

I invited him over and he brought my favorite bottle of Merlot, a Will Downing CD, an arrangement of tulips for my new crystal vase, and a grocery bag full of stuff that he'd planned to cook for me.

When I opened the door, I was like, "Oh, my God, what is all this?"

I was shocked, surprised and my heart was skipping by leaps and bounds. Avonté had romance written all over his face, and his whole vibe that night spoke of sincerity and even maturity. He was a master story-teller that night. In between the moments when the food was simmering in the kitchen, he'd come out and tell me stories about his family. He painted images of a sweet little boy that touched my heart and made me want to hold him, but when he stood up and looked at me, he was all man. He fed me some little appetizers that were nice but when he let me taste his grilled Portabello mushrooms smothered with onions, shrimp and some sort of special sauce, I was in heaven.

"Is this an original recipe?"

"It's something I experimented with the other day and thought I'd try it again on you. How you like it?"

"You see me over here devouring every bite, don't you?"

"Glad you like it, Ina."

"I'm very impressed, Avonté."

After that he smiled and gave me a very sweet kiss on the cheek. I couldn't believe the way he was catering to me that night. He didn't eat with me right away. Instead, he cleaned up the kitchen before sitting down to eat a small portion of what he'd made.

"I can't believe you did all this for me tonight."

"I enjoyed it. I sort of planned it all in my head today at work, so it was just a matter of pulling it off. The only trouble I had was finding that CD. I went to two stores and found the last one."

"The 'Invitation Only' CD is my favorite. I think you're just trying to get me in the mood…"

"Is it working, Ina?"

I just smiled and took another sip of wine. Yes, Avonté was pulling my strings all night and before I knew it, his fingertips discovered how to loosen the straps on my dress. He took control of me and it wasn't that bottle of Merlot or the sounds of Will Downing causing me to surrender so helplessly to his touch. It was the foundation of sincerity and a sweet sensuality that he'd lay before me. Avonté had me dancing on top of him all night. I didn't have a care in the world until I screamed so loud that I feared the neighbors might've heard me. I think Avonté got a thrill out of that.

Now, as I sit and think about how beautiful that night was, I can't help but be totally confused as to how quickly a man can change. Maybe Avonté's emotions are attached to his ego rather than to his heart. He seems to be able to distance himself quite easily and walk away from anything he shared with someone. It's kind of scary and I'm trying to do my best to act like none of our intimate moments ever happened. That's been a struggle for me because I feel almost like I've been lied to.

I've watched him all day talking and laughing with others, and it seems like he has completely wiped me from his system. Sharon was right in that his attention is now fixed on that new girl from Texas. I think Sharon said her name was Jolie but at this point, I don't really care. I wish her luck if she's gonna get involved with Avonté because women are only temporary stepping stones for him. I'm just glad I woke up. I'm no longer influenced by his calculated acts of kindness and I can't believe I fell for his shit. Actually, who am I kidding; it wasn't hard at all. He got that combination intelligent brotha slash bad-boy act going for him and it works. I told him he needs to show more respect for women, and a little honesty wouldn't hurt either.

He had the nerve to ask me, "What for?"

"Because it's no fun being taken advantage of," I told him.

"It's not like you've been handcuffed while I'm making my moves."

"No, you're right about that, Avonté, and I imagine your conscience is clear, huh?"

"As a matter of fact, it is."

"Well, good for you..."

He had himself convinced that being a disrespectful jerk was a good thing. I keep playing back this one particular night in my head because it reminds me just how much of my time was wasted. From now on I'm gonna listen to all warning signs when it comes to men and get the hell out before it's too late.

Well, my nightly ritual continues. It's been the same for the last three weeks. I've been bringing my work home so that I can get something accomplished. That's been the only way I could finish certain projects and stay ahead of my now departed assistant, Avonté. I usually end up cooking something easy and then spreading my work all over the dining room table. I never pictured my single life to be like this. I thought men were the only ones to fill up their refrigerators with microwave meals and frozen vegetables. I haven't had a meal cooked from scratch in so long. The worst part about everything right now is that I have too many memories of that jerk being over here. Since he stays with his mom, I would invite him over all the time. A few weeks ago you might've seen me spread across this table instead of a bunch of graphs and charts. I've got to find me another man so I can erase those memories, too. Either that or I need to move into a new condo. But that can be expensive if I do that every time I'm done with a man.

I really miss talking to Nakia, but I can't imagine her missing me right now. I'm glad that I've been forced to think about myself so I can realize what needs changing. These microwave dinners ain't doing me any good. My stomach is sticking out a little bit and I feel like I'm getting lazy. All I do when I get home is eat, work, read a little bit in bed and then fall asleep. That's been my life lately. I haven't been very active at all except for those moments when I drove down to the Ben and Jerry's ice cream shop. I'm gonna miss my favorite flavor, triple caramel chunk. Just saying that makes me feel like I'm going through withdrawal. Seems like we just go from one addiction to another. Before the ice cream, it was probably Avonté. Now I hope my addiction becomes self-improvement. That would do my mind and body some good.

After a couple of hours going through paperwork, it was time to relax my mind a little. I fixed myself a Tequila Sunrise and got in bed. I've been keeping company lately with this book about men being from another planet. I can't say it's helping me figure them out, but I've discovered a few interesting tidbits. Sometimes I end up laughing, especially when I see similarities between the men I've known lately and what I read in this book. Ten minutes into it and I'd receive an interesting surprise.

"What's up Ina? How you doing tonight?" Avonté inquired.

He had called and it was a total shock. His voice sounded very relaxed and smooth just like usual over the phone. He always did have a nice voice and right now I hate that about him because I'm not supposed to be feeling good about hearing from him.

I responded after a brief sigh. "I'm fine, and you?"

"I'm good. I want to apologize for not stopping by to say anything to you today. I felt like it might be uncomfortable if I did, you know?"

"I can't really say. It felt pretty strange to me that you didn't say anything, Avonté. I mean, from the start since you've been climbing the ladder at others' expense..."

"What you trying to say?" he interrupted.

"I'm saying that you definitely don't hide the fact that your only priority is *you*."

"Hmm, maybe so..."

"You don't see it that way?"

"No, not really."

"You must be in some kind of denial then, Avonté."

"If you say so, Ina...Listen, I just called to see how you're doing and to apologize for not stopping by your office. Maybe we'll talk later."

"I don't know. Maybe, Avonté."

After moments of silence, Avonté whispered, "Take care," and we both hung up the phone simultaneously. I wasn't able to return to reading my book. He ruined all my motivation to do anything so I drank the rest of my Tequila Sunrise and drifted off to sleep.

"Motherfucker…"

Forgotten Girl Talk

Today I walked into work feeling so good. I had just spent the weekend with Orlando before he left town on a business trip. That man showed me so much, and I'm not even talking about sex, although that was the bomb, too. He got me feeling so good right now to where I've been thinking a lot about Ina. I hate to say that I miss my girlfriend, but I really do—all those lunchtimes we spent together telling each other crazy stories about men or our lack of sexual satisfaction. Well, that ain't the way I used to describe it, but I guess my vocabulary has expanded in the past few months. Ina would be real proud of me right now with her sometime proper ass. I remember how she would say she ain't been satisfied in a *long ass time*, and I would smile before saying something that I knew would shock her.

Something like, "I ain't had no dick inside me either, Girl!"

She would tell me to be quiet and then look around to see if somebody heard what I'd said.

I'd tell her, "Nobody can hear me!"

"You never know, Nakia. People pick up on words like that."

"Okay, I'll try not to say it like that anymore."

"Uh-huh…"

Ina would just look at me like she couldn't trust anything coming out my mouth. I really miss those looks, too.

First thing I did when I came into work this morning was check to see if she was here. I was surprised to find out that she hadn't come in yet. Ina usually beat me to work, especially on a Monday. It's always her thing to start the week off right. Her motto is to do as much as possible so things won't catch up to you toward the end of the week. That's one of those "Ina Sinclair" lessons that I learned when I first started working here. It's too bad she isn't here right now because I was really focused on saying hello and breaking the ice between us. One of us is gonna have to start speaking to the other so we can become friends again. I think we've gotten too used to not speaking, and that only creates a lot of negativity.

I guess I've really grown 'cause I ain't never cared about saving a friendship after I'd felt someone did me wrong. Ina treated me badly that night at the club, but it's been so long since then that it's time to forgive and forget. Besides, I think she learned a lot about herself from that experience, too. I've already heard through all the gossip that she and Avonté don't see each other anymore. I told her to stay away from that fool, but I can't really tell if she's been hurt or not by him. She seems to have returned to just being Ms. Sinclair, the kind of woman who's totally about business.

I almost had a talk with Avonté the other day when I saw him walking around like he was all that. I wanted to tell him to kiss my ass because I was already mad at him and he ain't even said a word to me yet. I kept my cool because it didn't make sense for me to defend someone who I no longer spoke to myself. Now, once me and Ina start talking and hanging out together again, then I'll have the right to curse Avonté out. But for now, I'll let him have his little fun. I was sad to see his friend Vanessa leave the company two weeks ago. She seemed nice, even though I didn't get a chance to hang out with her away from work. I definitely think she was a victim of Mr. Avonté. I want to make damn sure that Ina don't end up being his next. She better not let that fool break her heart or make her feel like less of a woman.

Two hours went by and I was really getting worried. No one had said that Ina called in sick today and I knew she wasn't on vacation. I was afraid to try to call her at home and I didn't really want to leave a message on her office voicemail either. I kept thinking she might not return my call since I'd been ignoring her in the hallway when we'd pass each other. I often wonder if she speaks about me to anyone else. I've had talks at night with Orlando about Ina. He understood in the beginning why I wasn't speaking to her but after a day or two he was ready to forgive. He kept telling me that his reasons were selfish because Ina's mistake allowed us to meet each other that night. I thought that was so sweet of him to say.

Sometimes I have to pinch myself when I talk to him, and other times I try to remember my past experiences just so I don't set myself up for more heartache. I don't believe Orlando is the kind of man who would hurt anyone, but he's so fine and carries himself so well that I know he gets hit on every day by other women. I worry about having to compete for his attention should he come across a woman more experienced than me.

I feel so young and naïve most times when he shares stories with me. Those beautiful trips to the Caribbean or the memories that he can just pull out of the air have such deep meaning to them. That man just sends hot flashes through my body when I listen to him speak. I sometimes wonder if I'm truly able to visualize the images that he describes. I usually don't say anything when I'm not able to relate to what he's talking about. I just smile and listen. I'm only 26 years old but he got me wishing I were over thirty just so I can say, "I remember that, too!"

One night when we talked on the phone for hours, I could hear some music playing in the background.

"What you listening to?" I asked.

"Just a bunch of CDs. I don't feel like watching anything on television and plus I'm talking to you, sweetheart."

"So I have your full attention, huh?"

"You sure do, Nakia."

He sounded so good. He said he had the lights off and was lying on the couch in some silk pajama bottoms but nothing on top. He had me rubbing my thighs and wishing I were there with him in person.

Orlando asked, "What you wearing?"

I responded bashfully. "I'm not gonna tell you..."

"Oh, yeah, why not?"

"'Cause you ain't gonna get me to have phone sex with you!"

"Phone who?"

"You heard me!"

"So, you psychic now?"

"No, but I can tell you trying to get me all hot and bothered."

Actually, Orlando had me feeling very aroused. His laughter was so sexy and his voice felt like he was slowly massaging every inch of my body. I really didn't want to admit to him that I secretly wanted to indulge in some stimulating talk over the phone. I noticed that the music in the background influenced the way he spoke to me as well.

"What song is that playing?"

"That right there?"

"Yes, what is that?"

"Just a little Bobby Womack."

"I never heard that before."

"You haven't?"

I felt bad about not recognizing the music he was playing. I want so much to be everything to Orlando and to be able to relate to all of his experiences. I became quiet as he told me the name of the song.

"This is my favorite song by him, Nakia. Something about the whole vibe of it makes me think about my life, you know? It kind of takes me back but at the same time makes me feel really good about just living and making it to this point in my life. Kind of hard to explain but memories attached to songs can be really powerful."

"What's the name of the song?"

"'That's the Way I Feel about 'Cha'..."

"Oh," I responded, having absolutely no clue.

I'd never heard the song before, and my response had me sounding even more like a naïve little girl.

"Don't feel bad, sweetheart. I don't expect us to have the same taste in music. Plus, I'm over here trying to get you horny!"

"You are?"

"Yeah!"

"I would've never guessed! Thanks, baby."

"For what?"

"For being so sweet and making me feel good."

"You're more than welcome, Nakia."

Well, in the middle of all this reminiscing I'd been doing this morning, I did manage to squeeze in getting some work done. A couple more hours passed by and still no sign of Ina. I guess she ain't coming in to work today or maybe she's meeting with someone away from the office. She's advanced a little bit herself in the last few weeks. I've heard she's taken on a couple of projects that keep her busy. She told me a while back that she wanted to make about eighty thousand this year and it looks like she's well on her way. I notice when she gets disappointed in a man she usually works harder in her career. I'm trying to enjoy both worlds myself. I don't see any reason why I can't make the money and still be in love, too. Orlando encourages me all the time and that makes me feel really good.

"I can't believe they gave you an office already, Girl! Have we not been speaking that long?" Ina said through my open door.

"Hey! I've been looking for you, Ina."

"I know."

"How did you know?"

"Honestly, I didn't know but I was hoping you were because I've been wanting to apologize for the longest time now..."

Ina walked farther inside my office and closed the door behind her.

She took a deep breath and had this huge smile on her face.

"I am so sorry, Nakia, about how I acted. We have got to start talking again because I can't take it anymore!"

"It's okay, Ina, I forgave you a long time ago. You know me, I'm just as stubborn as you are."

"I know that's right!"

I just looked at Ina like she was crazy but in reality, I was so happy to be talking with her again. Now I had someone to share my happiness with and also someone to go to when I'm feeling insecure. Ina has been where I am now so I definitely could use her advice. I'm speaking both professionally and personally.

She settled in the chair in front of my desk and asked, "So, what's been going on with you and Orlando?"

"It's been so great..."

"That's good to hear!"

"It's kind of scary, too, Ina, because there's so much to this man. I'm afraid of not being able to relate to the things he's been through."

"Don't even try to, Nakia."

"Don't try?"

"No, appreciate him and share your own experiences. It seems to me like he cares about you a lot."

"Yeah, but I guess I'm just waiting for some kind of drama or disappointment to happen like it always does when things are going right between me and some man."

"Don't even go there. Let me tell you about this young man that I went out with not too long ago. I'm gonna show you that you are blessed, so you better hold on to your man!"

"Okay."

"I think he comes from the same neighborhood you come from, so you know I started to change my mind about going out with him."

"Where you meet him at?"

"The grocery store..."

"Then you must've been attracted to him, huh?"

"I can't lie, Girl, I was. His vocabulary almost turned me off but I'm learning to be more patient, thanks to you..."

"What did he say that was so bad?"

I started laughing at the expression on Ina's face before she could even begin telling me about this guy. His name was Shaun. She said he had a hard time pronouncing the word "strategy." Then when it came time to use words like "nothing" and "something," he was really struggling.

He was saying stuff like "I ain't got nuffin' to say except you fine, lady!"

Ina said she pretended not to hear his destruction of the English language so she just stood there smiling. Ina kept telling me she reminded herself to be patient and not be so judgmental. I was having a hard time believing that.

"So what did he do to ruin his chances with you 'cause I know he made a mistake somewhere!"

"I ain't that bad, Girl!" Ina responded.

"Yes, you are!"

"Okay, I did lose my patience when we went out."

"Uh-huh..."

Ina told me about how the date never really got off the ground. She'd met Shaun at his house and from there he was gonna drive her to a restaurant that he said was really nice. Ina said she was curious to see what Shaun's idea of a "nice restaurant" looked like, but they'd never get that far. For one thing, Ina said she really hated leaving her car behind but said she felt better when she saw that Shaun had a garage.

Shaun had one of those typical ghetto rides, an old burgundy Cutlass Supreme. That's how she described it to me. Ina said she took a deep breath and reminded herself once again to be patient 'cause she's definitely spoiled when it comes to the kind of transportation she rides in.

Then as they drove off, she said she noticed her seat made a funny noise. Of course, with her constant attitude on the rise, she questioned him about it. And she didn't even have to tell me that part 'cause I could definitely picture it for myself.

"What did he say?" I asked.

"He told me it comes loose, sometimes."

She said she looked at him with one eyebrow raised and kept her hands on the seat. She said it was already bad enough that she had to smell his strawberry air freshener, let alone have to endure his runaway passenger seat. Ina had to keep herself from laughing as she told me what happened next. She said that when he stopped at the next traffic light, both their seats moved forward.

"Oh, hell no! I wasn't about to be sliding back and forth in his ghetto ride, Girl! Can you picture two grown folks sliding back and forth at every stoplight? Girl, please!"

I just sat there laughing at Ina and all of her *I'm-too-through-with-him* expressions and hand gestures. I didn't blame her getting a little angry because once again she had gone through another bad experience with a man. My guess is that she felt like she wasted her time—again.

"You never heard from him after that?"

"Nope, and don't want to either!"

"I thought I was the one having crazy experiences..."

"To be honest, I've been very envious of you, Nakia. You've been making positive changes in your life and here I am doing God knows what with my life."

"Ina, I think you have it all together. Maybe you just wanted to try something different."

"It ain't working, Girl!"

Ina and I hugged each other and it felt really good. I noticed a difference in her as we sat in my office sharing stories. She seemed to be so sweet, almost humble to a degree. It was like she really wanted to talk with me about her life and show that she's here for me as a friend. We almost shed a few tears, but I was guilty of laughing a little too much at her story about Shaun and his "ghetto ride."

Well, after listening to Ina's latest experience and clowning with her the whole time, I couldn't help but think about Orlando. I wondered what he was doing and if he'd been thinking about me, too. I know Ina could read my thoughts because she looked at me with a very curious expression. She had a combination of happiness and concern written all over her face. I guess it was obvious that my heart was missing someone. Before Ina and I had our little drama episode, we'd always been pretty close and could tell if something was wrong. She's the only girlfriend that I've had in my life that could read me so well. I'm usually surprised because of our backgrounds being so different. I believe that what we share is one of those meant to be friendships and I ain't mad at that.

I'm pretty sure that no amount of drama will keep us apart forever. I know I was pissed at her for a while, but I felt really good talking with her.

Ina asked, "You okay, Nakia?"

"Yeah, just thinking."

"Must be thinking about Orlando, huh?"

"You can tell?"

"Oh, please!"

"I guess you can tell, huh?"

"I know I've been really silly lately when it comes to my choices in men, but I remember what it feels like to adore somebody."

"Does it show that much?"

Ina just shook her head and I couldn't believe it was so obvious that I was missing Orlando. I don't remember feeling this way before, even though I did love my baby's daddy very much when we were together. This time feels so different because not only am I in love with Orlando, but I also look up to him as if he were my hero or something. He's like one of those men that you find in those old romantic movies except the difference is that this is a fine and handsome black man.

I keep thinking to myself that I should be extra careful because any amount of disappointment would probably tear my heart apart. I've created in my mind an aura of perfection with this man, but I'm sure he ain't perfect. Nobody is perfect, but it feels like he comes pretty close to it. Then, on top of that, I worry about myself not measuring up to his idea of the perfect woman.

"Girl, you got some issues over there, huh?" Ina said.

Ina spoke so loud she startled me.

"Why you say that?"

"'Cause I've been talking over here for the last five minutes, and you ain't responded with any clear answers!"

"You said something? What did you say?"

"Nothing, Girl, you just tell me what has you drifting away like that."

"Just afraid that things won't work out."

"With Orlando?"

"Yeah."

"They won't if you keep thinking that way. Just focus on the time you spend together instead of worrying about the end."

"How can I not worry?"

"What you worried about?"

"I'm worried about him meeting someone like you, Ina!"

"You lost me, Girl."

"You know, someone older, more experienced, and beautiful."

"Don't worry, you gonna get old too, Nakia!"

"I'm serious!"

"I know but just try to be careful that you don't let things go sour just because you're worried about something that might happen."

"I know you're right, but this kind of man is so new to me."

"He just got you wide open, Girl...You sprung!"

"And you been hanging in the hood too much, Ina!"

"Don't even try to go there!"

Some things never change. Ina still does her best to avoid her ghetto roots and fascination. She was probably a hood rat in her former life.

I told her, "You know you love it over there!"

"Nakia?"

"What?"

Ina's hard glare answered that question.

I said, "Okay, I'll stop."

Time went by and neither one of us got any work done. I'm glad the environment at this agency is very laid-back. As long as we get things done on time, we're allowed to relax and have a lot of freedom. Talking to Ina for so long made me feel a little guilty, that is, until I looked outside my office door and noticed Avonté standing and talking to somebody.

"There goes your former friend," I told Ina.

She glanced and said, "I don't even want to talk about him."

"Well, you know what I think about him but he must not be that bad since you did spend a lot of time together."

"Can we not talk about him right now?"

"Okay, I won't pressure you."

"Good, let's talk some more about Orlando."

"I don't want to get sad all over again…"

"Then tell me the good stuff! Those flowers he sent you the other day showed me that he's very romantic. That man got taste, Girl."

"Yeah, I've never had someone spoil me like this and it's not really in a material way. It feels like he puts effort into trying to surprise me with something nice."

"You got me smiling over here, Nakia but now I want to hear about you getting your freak on with Mr. Romance!"

"See Ina, you have been hanging in the hood too much!"

Ina gave me another one of those mean looks.

"Okay, Ina. I mean, Orlando and I have had some beautiful nights together. You ever been kissed and held so tightly that you didn't want to let go or be let go of?"

Ina sighed and said, "It's been so long, Girl, I can't remember."

"The other night I almost didn't, but then Orlando whispered something that made me laugh so I had to let go."

"What did he say?"

"He told me that I better let him go so he could put on one of his glow-in-the-dark condoms!"

"Oh?"

"He was just kidding but I think he could sense me getting carried away and if he didn't say anything, he could've easily been intimate with me and not use a condom. Men in my past would've been like, 'Hey, I thought you was gonna put it on me!'"

"Yeah, I know what you mean, but maybe with Orlando that wouldn't have been such a bad thing."

"No, I couldn't go there. Plus, the next time I get pregnant, I want to be married and have no doubt that the man is mine forever."

"Yeah, well, sometimes I feel like my luck has run out."

"Oh, please, Ina."

"I know, but you said it yourself!"

"I never said that!"

"No, but you did say I was more experienced and more beautiful than you, so where's my Orlando?"

"You crazy, Ina. Can I go back to work now?"

"Okay. Talk to you later!"

"Bye, Ina."

As Ina walked out the door, I took a deep breath and a quick look at all this work I needed to be doing. My guilt set in even more when I realized that Ina and I had been talking for almost three hours. God only knows who been walking by and hearing us get loud, although Ina was the only one really raising her voice. She was never that loud before so I know she been hanging in the hood and probably listening to those CDs I gave her a while ago. She still ain't returned my DMX tape to me.

I guess I better make it look like I accomplished something today at work or I might get in trouble for the first time. Usually I'm harder on myself than anyone else could ever be. I like that change in me because a long time ago, I never cared about holding a job, but now look at me. I'm really proud of myself.

Time went by and I managed to complete a few things. I had to make a couple of long distance phone calls for my boss, and it really felt good to be trusted with so much responsibility. One of those calls I made back East was to someone who had me blushing. I wondered if he could sense it because he lowered his voice as though he were listening while talking. He sounded so much like Orlando that I wanted to change the subject from buying advertising to lovemaking. He really threw me for a loop when he asked me a question that instantly made me laugh. I was so embarrassed.

"Excuse me, Ms. Davidson, but are you flirting with me?"

I responded nervously. "Oh, my God, does it sound like I am?"

"Maybe it's just me but I have to admit to enjoying it a little too much. My wife might not like that."

"I'm sorry but I have to be honest and say that you sound so much like someone very special to me."

"Oh, okay, that explains what I'm hearing in your voice then."

I had little beads of sweat on my forehead 'cause I definitely didn't want this to get back to my boss that I was flirting with clients over the phone. I'm gonna have to get a handle on my yearning to be with Orlando so much.

I feel so strange in this position of wanting to be with someone so badly. So far I haven't put my life on hold, but still it feels like my every thought is about him.

A familiar voice spoke from my doorway, "Hey, Lady, you think we could talk?"

When I looked up, my first thought was, "Oh, hell, what does this fool want?"

"Can I help you, Avonté?" I asked in a professional tone of voice.

"Just wanted to peep in and say hello. I sure wish we could talk sometime, Nakia."

"What about?"

"May I?"

Avonté respectfully gestured to see if I'd allow him inside my office. I let him know it was okay but just for a moment.

"Seems like we never really talk, Nakia. I think that perhaps you already feel a certain way toward me, but I've yet to be given a chance to prove that I'm a decent guy."

"It's kind of hard, Avonté, especially with the way things turned out between you and my girl Ina."

"I guess that's true in a way but still I'm hoping we can put that aside and get to know each other."

"You're not trying to come on to me, are you?"

"No, I think you'll give me a really hard time if I did."

"I'm glad you can sense that."

I just looked at Avonté and the one thing that struck me was the sincerity in his eyes. Plus, he seemed truly uncomfortable and unsure about talking to me. I liked having that upper hand and at the same time I couldn't see any reason not to talk to him. First, I was gonna talk to Ina about it because I have to be loyal to my girl. I was curious to see what kind of person Avonté was when he wasn't putting up this front that he always has around the office.

I told him, "Maybe we'll talk another time but I've really got to finish up this last little bit before I go home."

"Oh, okay! Well, let me know when."

"I will."

"Thanks, Nakia."

Before I could tell him he was welcome, he had already walked out the door. He was genuinely nervous about talking with me and I found that kind of cute. No, I would never fall for that man but I like seeing a positive change, even in jerks like him.

"Hey, Girl, I'm about to leave! How late you staying?" Ina asked after peeking her head inside my office.

Tomorrow I'm gonna keep my door shut so I won't have all these surprise announcements coming in.

"I'm gonna stay a little longer so I can finish this," I responded.

"Don't stay too late. I was hoping we could leave together."

"You gonna wait for me?"

"No, you heard me say I'm gonna leave now, didn't you?"

"Whatever!"

"I'll call you tonight, okay?"

"Okay, Ina."

Ina is something else. I guess I should've told her that her ex friend just dropped by but I was afraid it might make her mad. Maybe I'll tell her about it tonight if she's not out getting her party on.

I'm not going anywhere this weekend. I'm just gonna take some work home, rent a couple of videos, and stay near the phone just in case Orlando calls me. Yeah, he got me "open," as Ina remarked today. Maybe I am getting a little carried away with my thoughts of him, but the time we spent together was so beautiful that I think I have a right to keep him constantly on my mind. My only fear is that maybe he's not feeling the same as me. I wish I could be a little less attached emotionally, but it's beginning to feel like it's too late.

I was really happy to finally be leaving work. I thought Ina had left me behind like she said she would but there she was, waiting outside. I was very happy about that, too, because I didn't feel like taking the bus or spending money on a taxicab. I've gotten truly spoiled by Orlando coming to pick me up every day. On the way out of the office, I ran into Avonté, again. Actually it was me who approached him this time because I noticed he was carrying a book on Cajun cooking.

"Now, what are you doing with that book? You got some Creole girl you trying to impress?"

"No, I'm actually doing this for me…," he responded. "Well, you remember Vanessa?"

"Yeah, that girl that worked here for a short time."

"Uh-huh. Well, she's coming over tomorrow night so I'm trying to learn a couple new things."

"Oh, really? I didn't know you had it in you!"

Avonté was walking proud with his little cookbook in his hand. It sounded nice to hear him speak about doing something for someone other than himself. I was always under the impression that he was done with that girl Vanessa after he got what he wanted.

I asked hesitantly, "So, you're still seeing Vanessa?"

"Not really. I mean, I haven't seen her recently, but a few days ago I took a chance on calling her just to see how she's doing, you know."

"Oh, a booty call!"

"Nah, it wasn't like that."

"Uh-huh."

"Trust me, it wasn't."

"I see a look in your eye, Avonté, saying that you wouldn't mind if things were to go in that direction."

"Well, can any man really deny some booty when it's right there in front of him?"

"So, it was a booty call then, huh?"

"No, you putting words into my mouth now!"

"I'm just reading the expression on your face, Avonté. We in the advertising business so it's pretty easy to read what you wish to sell tomorrow night."

Avonté just started laughing. I could see him releasing all kinds of nervous tension. I was making him sweat but I wasn't serious. I was just playing with him. It's not my place to be concerned about his intentions with that girl. I hope he treats her with respect and isn't bringing her back into his life because he needs something from her. I definitely think he used her when she was working at Montaqua.

I reassured him. "It's okay, Avonté. I'm just messing with you."

I could still see him struggling to respond to what I'd said.

"I'm glad you let me off the hook, Nakia, 'cause I'm probably guilty of wanting a little sex with Vanessa. But at the same time I think it'll be cool to hang with her again. The other night I found myself reminiscing about when I first met her that day we interviewed for the job. We had an immediate connection that felt really good. I'd like to pick up where that day left off rather than the way I ended up doing her."

"Oh, really?"

"Yeah..."

"I'm impressed and really happy to hear you speak that way. I hope you're being sincere though and not just trying to say things that you know I'll like."

"No, I'm being for real with you. I hear the gossip around the office about my using folks and my never-ending motivation to move up the ladder. All that is true to a certain extent, but I'm ambitious and I want to achieve something in life."

"I understand ambition, but…"

"You don't understand why I did what I did," Avonté interrupted.

"No, I don't, especially in the way that you moved from Vanessa to Ina. And now I'm just wondering if you discovered something that you needed from me?"

"Yeah, I did."

"Excuse me?"

My hand was beginning to form the shape of a fist because I wasn't about to be next in line to be used by this potential fool.

"Just want friendship," he told me.

As I relaxed the frown on my face and looked at Avonté struggle to maintain eye contact with me, I could hear Ina blowing her car horn in the distance.

"Listen, I have to go."

"Is that Ina over there?"

"Yeah, she's gonna give me a ride home."

"Okay. So, you think that could ever be possible between us?"

"Friendship?"

"Yeah," he responded.

Avonté looked like a little school boy anxiously waiting to find out if I'd say yes to his question. He was cute although I wished he could display this kind of respect and gentle charm all the time. Because of my initial impression of him, it's really hard to just brush it off and begin trusting him so easily now.

"I guess anything is possible, but you can't expect me to give you a definite answer now," I told him.

"No, I guess I can't, but I'm just trying to hold on to this moment 'cause it feels like my assumption about you and I is really true."

"Your assumption?"

"Yeah, I always assumed that you and I could have conversations that felt really good. You might even feel like you didn't want them to end."

"Oh, well don't get too confident in your assumptions. I have to go now, Avonté, but I hope you have fun with Vanessa."

"Okay, Nakia, take care."

"Bye."

I must admit that it was nice to see that side of Avonté even though there were subtle hints of him being a little overconfident with himself. One thing that I knew I had to prepare myself for was Ina and what she might say to me. I knew she probably watched me talking to Avonté like a hawk, and I was sure she was gonna want to know the details of our conversation. As soon as I opened the car door I prepared myself. She instantly made me feel like I had psychic abilities because I guessed right.

I'd never seen Ina's mouth open so wide. "Girl, it's about time! What were you two over there talking about for so long?"

"He was just trying to make conversation, that's all."

"Didn't look like that to me!"

"Well, Avonté is trying to get me to become friends with him but, of course, I have to consider your feelings about that first."

"I'm over Mr. Avonté."

"Sounds to me like you still angry with him, Ina."

"I guess so but if you want to be friends with him, then I cant stop you, Girl."

"Well, I still don't trust him, but at the same time I've seen sides of him that seem really cool. I can't just put up a wall and tell him that we can never be friends or be cool with each other."

Ina got quiet and focused her attention on the road. Her silence let me know that me being friends with Avonté could potentially hurt my relationship with her. I didn't want that to happen so I figured it might be best to maintain the distance I have with him, for now.

I broke the silence. "So, how was your day?"

"It was okay," she responded with very little enthusiasm.

My attempt to change the subject didn't seem to work too well.

"Listen, if it makes you feel better, I won't become friends with him. Now, let's talk about something else, okay?"

"Okay. I hope you don't think I'm being silly, Nakia."

"Yeah, I do, but I also understand why."

"You think I'm being silly for real?"

"No, I'm just playing. Relax, Girl, damn!"

"Uh-huh. So, you think Orlando will call you tonight?"

"I hope so! I can't wait to talk with him again. Ina, I have never missed a man this much before in my life. One day without speaking to him feels like ten days…I'm glad I can go to work every day 'cause I know I'd drive myself crazy thinking about him. I don't like this feeling, but it's like I can't stop it."

"Nakia, you gonna make me have an accident talking like that!"

"Huh? You crazy, Ina."

"No, I just haven't been in love like that since high school and that feels like a million years ago!"

"Oh, well it's been a while for me, too. I'm not sure I even felt this way before, although I know I've been in love."

"Well, I'm happy for you, Girl, but just be careful of your heart."

"I will or at least I'm trying to. I just have to hear his voice soon 'cause I'm getting nervous not being able to speak to him. I hate feeling like this. It's almost like the less I hear from him, the more I think he's drifting away—not only physically but mentally. I can't imagine he's thinking about me as much as I think of him. Do you think he is?"

"I don't know, Nakia."

"I almost feel like a fool that I've let myself get this way. It's almost like I can't stop this runaway train from happening. I just hope I don't crash into something!"

"Yeah, you're right, Nakia."

"What's wrong with you, Ina? Are you listening to me?"

"I'm listening."

"Then why you acting like what I'm saying isn't getting to you? Like you got your mind on something else."

"I'm just trying to focus on the road, Girl. You see where I am, don't you?"

"Yeah, we almost to my house."

"That's right. We in the ghetto right now, so I don't want to have somebody approach my car and try to rob me. It ain't been that long since the riots so you never know, somebody might start having flash-backs while I'm driving over here..."

"Oh, brother, I thought you changed, Ina? You still got your little ghetto fears, huh? You're too funny."

"Don't laugh, Nakia, I can't help it!"

"Uh-huh. Maybe you need to throw away that tape of 'Boyz N the Hood' and just spend more time seeing it for yourself."

"I don't think so! Where's your street at, Girl?"

"It's coming up right here on the left."

"Thank goodness and it's still light outside. I'm gonna just drop you off, okay?"

"I know, Ina. Thanks for giving me a ride and for listening."

"You're welcome, Girl. I'm sorry for being jealous earlier. If you want to be friends with Avonté I won't let it hurt us."

"I hope not but I can't say for sure that he and I will be friends. But I'd like to feel comfortable if I happen to be talking with him and you're around."

"I understand. I hope Orlando calls you so you can relax. Let me know what happens tonight, okay?"

"I will. See you tomorrow."

"Okay, bye."

I was so happy to be home, mostly because my little angel greeted me at the door. My little reminder always wakes me up to reality. I need to stop acting like some lovesick little girl before I end up losing my mind.

"Hi, Mommy!" Tanisha said.

"Hi, sweetheart, how was school?"

"Fine."

"Did you finish your homework?"

"Yes."

"Where's Trent?"

"He's outside playing. I was helping Granny make dinner."

"You were?"

"Uh-huh..."

My little sweetheart was looking so shy and adorable. I remember when I used to look like that twenty years ago. It feels like an eternity now. I can also remember being in a hurry to get older. Too bad we can't switch it around and be in a hurry to get younger. One thing I'll never regret is having Tanisha. She is so sweet and I know I'm a good mother, just like my own.

As I walked inside the kitchen holding hands with my daughter, I couldn't help but smile when I saw my mother. I was feeling sentimental then. I've always been so proud of her because of the way she accepted Trent into her life so easily. He's our cousin but because his own mother wasn't able to take care of him, my mother didn't hesitate to bring him into our immediate family. He went from being my distant cousin to being my little baby brother. He's really close to Tanisha and I know one day he's gonna make us all proud 'cause he's already so smart. It's such a blessing to be able to take care of family when they need it. That's probably a Southern tradition that my mom picked up from her own childhood. She's very unselfish with her love...

I told Tanisha, "Why don't you go get Trent so we can all eat together."

Before she started to run outside, my mother informed me that all three of them had eaten already.

"I'm sorry, baby, but I didn't think you were gonna come home until late," she said.

"Oh, okay."

"Are you hungry, Nakia?"

"Yes I am, Mom."

Mom just smiled and started fixing my plate. I told Tanisha it was okay to go outside and play. It was so good to be at home that I almost felt like I'd been working harder today than I actually was.

Mom asked, "How was your day, baby?"

"It was nice. I actually made up with Ina."

"Oh, really?"

"Yeah, we finally did."

"It's about time, too! How is she doing?"

"Crazy as ever. She just dropped me off."

"Oh, I thought maybe that man brought you home."

"Who, Orlando?"

"Yeah, unless you ain't told me about somebody else?"

"No, it's just that you sounded as though you didn't care for him very much."

"You haven't really brought him around so I don't know him, honey."

"Yeah. I was meaning to but he had to leave town. I promise to bring him around when he comes back."

"Okay, but I hope nothing is going on that you haven't told me about. You know how you always wait until things are crazy before you tell me."

"Everything is okay right now, Mom, except for me missing him a lot."

"You sure?"

"Yeah, I'm sure."

"I won't have to loan you any money 'cause you done bought this man something you can't afford?"

"No, Ma'am. I only made that mistake once!"

"Twice."

"Okay, twice, Mom."

She never hesitates on reminding me about how freely I spend my money. I guess I've yet to understand what makes mothers feel like they have the right to nag you about how you spend your own hard-earned cash. And, my mom be all over me about my credit cards, too! She sees something in the mail that even looks like it's a new card, and she'll question me about it. She'll start off with one of those speeches about how concerned she is about me, but I usually have to cut her off 'cause the only thing she found was a piece of junk mail. I know I spend a lot of money, but I ain't trying to be the fool holding the most credit cards. Four is enough for me right now. Still once again, Mom couldn't resist reminding me of that second time I spent a huge amount of money on my ex.

"How much did you spend again, Nakia?" she'd ask me.

"You ask me this all the time, Mom!"

"Yeah, and I think it was something like four thousand dollars for some foolishness!"

"Well, at the time I wanted to do something special for my man, but, of course, now I feel like a fool cause we no longer together. I really don't need to be going over this with you, Mom."

"I'm just concerned, that's all, sweetie."

"I know, but you just gonna have to trust me."

"Uh-huh."

"Please, Mom. And by the way, I haven't bought Orlando anything."

"Well, that's good."

I was very happy that my mother left me alone to eat because she was getting on my nerves. I believe she's concerned about me, but she needs to find a less vocal way of showing it. But, who am I to stop her since this is her house?

I'm trying desperately to save right now so I can get a really nice apartment for me and Tanisha. I can't wait until that day comes because then I'll have plenty of freedom, but I know I'm gonna end up missing Mom a lot. I'm spoiled by the fact that she's really good with my baby, and I'm not sure how it's gonna affect Trent when we're no longer around every day. I'm hoping to bring Orlando over so he can meet both Trent and Tanisha. I wonder how he'd feel about that or if he'd have a strange reaction to me introducing him to my family. Men sometimes trip when you bring kids into the picture. I hope that's not the case with Orlando. I'm kind of shocked that he doesn't have kids, or so he says. Maybe he's with them right now and just doesn't want me to know about that part of his life.

I remember asking him if he had any kids and he answered by saying that he hadn't been "blessed that way yet." I really shouldn't second-guess him but right now my anxiety is getting the best of me. I need to talk with him soon before I lose my mind. I ain't used to this feeling at all.

After I finished eating, Mom told me that she was feeling too tired to do much of anything for the rest of the night. I picked up that she was hinting that I should do the dishes and lock up for the night. It was finally dark outside and both Trent and Tanisha were in their rooms worn out from a long day of going to school and running around out-side like they had no sense. I remember when I was young like that. I did the same thing that they're enjoying now. Mom didn't warn me it would be like this when I got older. I often wonder if I should warn Tanisha or just let her find out on her own that she's gonna one day wish she were still a child.

As I stood there doing the dishes, my mind wandered all over the place. Of course, I thought a lot about Orlando. Not too much time passes without me thinking of him, but my thoughts this time were mostly on Ina and her crazy self. I needed to smile while I cleaned all those dirty pots and pans. I remember before our fallout how Ina kept teasing me about not going out enough and not trying to date that often. She thought that maybe I sat over here behind closed doors either glued to my television all the time or maybe I was doing something that she confessed to indulging in quite often. Actually she didn't confess until I happened to ask her where she was going that night.

She told me, "I've got to go buy me some double-A batteries for this little gadget I have."

It sounded like she was laughing about it.

I asked, having no clue, "What kind of gadget?"

"You know, Nakia."

I actually sat there for about thirty seconds trying to figure out what she could be talking about before a lightbulb came on in my head.

"Oh!" I shouted.

"Don't act like you never used one before!"

"Well, when I lived with my ex, he brought one home because he wanted to watch me using it. That was a while ago."

"You might want to get you another one if you didn't keep that one,

Girl, 'cause it looks like you trying not to be with anyone for a while."

Ina was too funny that day but she did have me considering the possibility of getting some kind of vibrator, but I never did. In fact, I left the one that my ex gave me at his place. My guess is that he found someone else he could enjoy that with, and I hope he washed it, too.

I decided back then to just do without sex and try to focus on other things. It worked for a while or at least until Orlando came into the picture. Now I was wanting to get me some all the time, but only from him though.

After I finished cleaning up the kitchen and picking up clothes everywhere, I sat down on the couch and started watching TV. There was absolutely nothing on tonight and my attention span wasn't too strong anyway. I felt like I couldn't sit still. Tripping, I guess. I could hear the usual helicopter sounds overhead and sirens in the distance. I've become so used to that sound that I begin to miss it when it gets too quiet around here. I start to hear all those little noises around the house too clearly and that makes me feel really restless. So, here I was unable to get comfortable and fall asleep while everyone else was probably in dreamland. Maybe I should follow Ina's advice and get me one of those little gadgets, as she likes to call them. That might relax me and put me to sleep. Right now I don't think anything could relax me but Orlando.

Well, sometimes when you're feeling restless and can't get to sleep, you often remember things that you need to do but been putting off for a while. I just remembered that I needed to call my ex because he's been bugging me about seeing our daughter. I'm not trying to keep him from seeing her but I just feel a little suspicious about it since he's never expressed so much desire before. Lately he's been leaving me messages and even calling me at work telling me he wants to come by and spend time with Tanisha. When I asked him to pick her and Trent up from school last week, he asked me if I thought he was some kind of taxicab service.

"I don't have time to be driving a bunch of kids around like some housewife," he told me.

"Well, it'll give you a chance to spend time with your daughter and keep me from having to leave work early."

"You probably just have a date with some dude."

"Whatever, Terence. I'm just giving you a chance to see your daughter, that's all."

After we had that little argument I figured he would stop bugging me about seeing Tanisha, but he hasn't. I'm getting a little tired of him ruining my day at work when he calls. I know I shouldn't let him get to me, but he does. Right now I'm thinking, *Do I really want to call him?* It's getting late so maybe he'll be too tired to talk for very long.

Terence can really wear me down whenever we do talk. He starts trying to reminisce and then asks me if I miss him. That gets on my nerves. There was a time when I did miss him, but when I look back on those feelings, I realize I was being stupid. How could I ever miss what he put me through that last year of being together? So much emotional abuse, and I know he was messing around with this girl he was working with. I guess things didn't work out and lately he hasn't been too lucky with women or his finances. I know about his money situation because as soon as I mention helping out with Tanisha, he'll make up some excuse and ask me to go ahead and pay for it. Then he makes promises to reimburse me, but I don't sweat him about it. That would only end up being another thirty-minute argument.

I think it's great when a man takes care of his child, but Terence lacks sincerity when it comes to truly being a father. One moment he's calling all the time and the next moment he disappears and can't be found. When he calls, he only speaks with me and never asks to speak with Tanisha.

I'd shout, "Tanisha, your father is on the phone!"

"Oh, wait, Nakia! I just wanted to say hello for a second," he'd respond nervously.

"You can say hello to her, can't you?"

"No, I'm walking out the door right now."

"Okay, Terence."

Sometimes I would feel like calling him right back to see if he truly was walking out the door. I'm willing to bet he was lying, but I think it would be a bad thing if I confirmed my suspicion. I'm trying to give him the benefit of the doubt by not losing total respect for his ass. Oops!

All this thinking about Terence and my hesitation to call him has made me tired. I'm even a little bit sleepy now, which made me smile.

I'll just call him tomorrow! I thought to myself.

As I went to make sure the front screen door was locked, the phone began to ring. I dreaded answering because I just knew it had to be Terence bugging me again. After a couple rings, I decided to take a chance and answer.

"Girl, are you still up?" I asked after I realized it was only Ina.

"Yeah, I couldn't go to sleep without knowing if Orlando called you or not. Did he call?"

"No."

"He didn't?"

"No, Ina, he hasn't called me yet."

"What's wrong with him?"

"He just hasn't called. Why you have to remind me when I was just about to go to sleep?"

"I'm sorry, Nakia."

"That's okay, although now you woke me up!"

"Maybe you need to find you someone else and make Orlando jealous. Then he won't be going on these long trips where he doesn't call and let you know what's going on."

"Yeah, I'm surprised I haven't heard from him, but it's not like we're a serious item or anything."

"Maybe for him, Nakia, but who are you fooling?"

"What you mean?"

"I can hear it in your voice that you love this man a lot."

"Don't say that!"

"But I'm right, huh?"

"I have feelings for him, Ina, but I knew someone like Orlando would get bored with me."

"Oh, stop it, Girlfriend!"

"Why else hasn't he called?"

"I don't know but I don't think you're to blame. You just need to move on and if he comes back, then you make him work hard to get your attention again, you hear me?"

"Yeah and I know you're right, but it would be impossible for me to try to ignore him. All I have to do is hear his voice and I melt."

"At least try, Nakia!"

"I will."

Talking to Ina didn't help this time but I know she means well. Trying to be strong and act like I can get over Orlando so easily is gonna be tough. I wish I had the money to just go on a long trip and forget about things, but I don't even have enough vacation time to take a short trip to San Diego. I want to have the same kind of freedom as Ina so I can take some Caribbean trips or go to Hawaii. I've never been anywhere except to Las Vegas and a couple of times I went to Arizona with Terence to see his parents.

Well, if I can't go anywhere then I'd sure like to be able to send my mother on a cruise or something. She's never been anywhere either. It's not like we don't live a good life, but sometimes I think we're missing out on a lot of experiences. I believe that if I had been exposed to more things in my life, then I wouldn't feel so much like I have nothing to say when talking to Orlando. He says things to me that I truly can't relate to but it sounds so beautiful when he describes something. Guess I should just stop doubting myself and do as Ina says. I'll make him work at trying to be with me so I can know for sure that he's truly interested.

Who am I fooling? Let me just take my butt to bed! she thought.

ORLANDO DUNCAN

Lately my favorite line has become, "Let me introduce myself."
It seems like I've been on a hitting streak lately and knocking
home runs with either hand. The women are lined up everywhere,
falling for my smile. I hate to sound like a brotha with an ego bigger
than his intelligence, but opportunities are coming when I least
expect them. Right now I'm on a business trip that I was really looking
forward to because of the financial opportunities. Never in my wildest
dreams did I expect to run into my old college sweetheart, Nadia
Franklin. She was a freshman when I was a junior, but we were reaching
for the same Snickers bar in the campus bookstore and hit it off
immediately. Now jump ahead one hundred years later and there we
were ordering the same cocktail at a jazz club in Miami.

When I first saw her I gazed upon her with smiling eyes and lustful
thoughts. To be honest, I didn't know who she was at first. I just
thought she was this really fine, honey-brown sistah with a beautiful
short haircut. Then when my eyes traveled from her sexy grin to her
beautiful hazel eyes, I realized the face was familiar.

I looked at her as if I could barely make out her face and said, "Nadia?"

She didn't answer at first so I thought the moment was about to be
filled with embarrassment.

"Excuse me?" she responded.

"Nadia, that is you, huh?"

"Hey, Orlando!" she shouted.

Just seeing her enthusiasm gave me a rush. I know I expressed that feeling by the way that I embraced her so tightly.

"This is so unreal," she said softly in my ear.

I remembered that expression so vividly. Nadia used to say that all the time especially when she had trouble studying for something.

"You still using that expression huh," I told her.

"And you still remember that I used to always say it."

"Some things never change, Nadia."

I finally loosened the embrace but I continued to hold both her hands.

"Yes, like you still being so fine, Orlando. You must have a wife somewhere missing you, huh?"

"Nah, I'm still single. You know how it is, concentrating on the career, building the portfolio, and all that good stuff."

"Well, the years have made you more handsome, sweetie. Look at you with a little bit of gray, but it looks like you keep in good shape. I always knew you would get better with age."

"Thanks, Nadia. What can I say about you though?"

"What about me?"

"You fine, too, and got me wishing I had never said goodbye on graduation night."

"Yeah, you broke my heart on that night, but I understood eventually and got over you."

Nadia started laughing because I guess she could sense my ego stand up and take notice of the last part of her comment.

"You got over me, huh?"

"Yep, that's what we ladies must do in order to get on with our lives."

"I know, and it looks like you did just that."

"I try, sweetheart."

Nadia's words began to linger in my mind. Her smile was a welcome blessing that I never imagined I'd experience again. This reunion felt as good, if not better, than our old college moments gazing into each other's eyes in the hallways around campus.

"So, I guess I better ask this question," I told her.

"What question?"

"Are you married?"

"Yes, and I have two kids."

"Damn."

"Huh?"

"Well, I mean to say, congratulations."

"I know what you mean to say, Orlando, and it's okay. As I said, I had to move on, but there were times when I wished that you and I had created the beautiful children that I have."

"Thanks for saying that, Nadia."

"I mean it."

"I know."

"You wanna see pictures of them? I just adore my kids."

I took a deep breath and had to swallow not only my pride but also try to calm the fires of my excitement, too.

"Sure, let me see."

Hearing the news of Nadia being married and seeing pictures of her kids made me step back a little. I had to be cautious about what I was feeling while at the same time it was great to see how happy she was about being a mother. Some brotha out there was really lucky and to think, it could've been me.

"Any regrets?" I asked.

"Where did that come from?" Nadia responded.

"Sorry, I guess I should ask myself that question."

"Hmm, and what would your answer be?"

"Yeah."

"Well, I'm flattered and you are still so very sweet. I know that you had to follow your heart's desire and being in a relationship wasn't what you desired. Still, I'm shocked to find out that you're not married or in a relationship now."

"As I said before, some things never change."

"Maybe so, Orlando, but that's one thing that should change because I know a woman would make you her world if you gave her the chance to. I could see that, even though we were so young back then."

Nadia's comments really took me back. She had me struggling and trying to find the right words to say. I couldn't even come back with something cute to make her smile, but as always she commanded my attention.

"I better go but here's where I'm staying," she told me.

"Okay. So, I guess the next time we run into each other, I'll get to meet your husband, huh?"

"No, I'm actually here alone. This is my birthday present. A chance to get away from being a mom for a week, all expenses paid and nothing to do but pamper myself."

"I heard that…"

"So, give me a call later, okay?"

"I will, Nadia. I promise."

"Okay. It was really great seeing you again Orlando."

"Thanks…you, too."

As I stood there watching Nadia walk away, all kinds of delicious thoughts and memories went through my mind. That lady has matured in all the right places. One thing that will never go away is the magic between us. After all these years, I can still feel a certain energy there. It's like back in the day when we were in school, we never hesitated to kiss each other. The energy was always so strong that we had to touch all the time. Now, years later, that same energy is still there but it has to smolder under the surface. It's like we're both very aware of the time that has passed in between seeing each other last. We have to keep a slight distance, if you will. I kept mine because I knew that there could be no way that she wasn't involved.

Nadia is the kind of woman that is only left by fools or ambitious men with no time for relationships. Seeing her after all these years makes me wonder what side of the fence I stand on. She got me still standing in the same spot in this club just watching her every move. Right now she's near the entrance having a conversation with someone at the door and I'm just checking her out from head to toe. Yes, I'm having lustful thoughts again, but I'm also thinking, *Damn, she has become so beautiful!*

Visions that beautiful usually come to an end, and this one was no exception as Nadia finally left the club. It was time for me to leave, too, but I felt pretty good knowing that I had her number. I'm not sure if I should call her or not and besides, I'm supposed to be here on business. I have to wake up at seven in the morning and attend a few conferences. I guess I do have time to contact her since she said she would be here for the entire week. Maybe she and I could get together sometime and keep it totally innocent by simply having lunch. I don't think she'd mind that too much.

Well, one thing that I've been neglecting to do since I've been on this trip is call Nakia. I'm not sure why I haven't been in touch with her. She's a real sweetheart and I definitely enjoy her company. Sometimes it feels kind of weird having that young lady look up to me so much. I feel like one mistake and I could damage her idea and image of what she looks for in a man. I know she's been through drama in the past so I don't want to add more ingredients to her plate of bitterness, if you will. I guess I'm not helping much by not calling her either so I better do that when I get back to the room.

I start to smile every time I think about Nakia. Meeting her in club Unrestricted that night was a lovely experience. I know she likes to remind me quite often about how she never connected with anyone like that before. It's always been the usual *why-don't-you-let-me-have-your-number?* kind of thing. Never did she actually sit down and have a great conversation with someone she'd just met.

I told her that conversation is so important and in most cases can be the best aphrodisiac in the world, especially if the connection is strong. Looking at her I find it hard to believe that she's never experienced that kind of chemistry before. Then when I talk to her, I can hear the innocence in her spirit come out. I can see so much that has been missing in her life, and I can tell that she's a young woman who has yet to be appreciated with respect for who she is as a person. I love talking to her and just bringing out her spirit. It's almost like watching a child open up presents on Christmas Day. Nakia's smile and the reflection in her voice just light up with so much enthusiasm. I hope my absence hasn't taken away from that. Yeah, I better give her a call soon.

It's funny how a moment ago I was lost in my thoughts about Nadia and now here I am speaking so fondly of Nakia. It's a trip that both of their names are so similar, too. I'm wondering if that means anything? Cupid must be sending me a message. Either that or God is about to put me through an interesting test. With both ladies, there is such a huge difference in who they are as women, yet I'm fascinated by both. Nadia is probably at a place in her life where Nakia is trying to be some day. I wasn't there to watch Nadia's growth, but I have seen some beautiful changes in Nakia. Maybe I shouldn't assume that I had something to do with it, but I'd like to think that I've inspired Nakia to do great things for herself. She's an incredible lady in the making. When we talk late at night, I can't help but marvel at her growth as the conversation progresses. She's usually worried about something or another, but then after saying things that allow her to look at herself through her own eyes, she begins to see the truth behind her worries. I'm beginning to really miss Nakia after thinking about those moments. I hope I don't get an ear full of her nagging me about why it took so long for me to call. She doesn't seem like that kind of lady and besides, we haven't made a serious commitment with each other. I'll have to be careful about using that "C" word in her presence. Seems like she might jump at the chance since she's used to long-term relationships.

Hey, I'm thirty-seven years old and the only long-term relationships I've had are my career and financial pursuits. With regards to love, I can only confess to always thinking about Nadia but even that hasn't prevented me from pursuing others. I never thought I would ever run into her again, and I can't really say I was hoping to either. It's also been a long time since I've been drawn in by the spirit of a woman and there's no doubt that Nakia does just that. From the first moment I laid eyes on her, I was drawn in and now I feel compelled to call her and let her know that she's been on my mind. I just hope that my revelation will bring a smile to her heart. Worrying about what a woman is thinking has become brand-new to me—again. Perhaps I should say it's been a while and I have to admit that it feels pretty good.

When I got to my hotel room, the light was flashing on my phone. I was debating for a moment if I really wanted to call the front desk to find out who had left me a message. It could be good news in that they cancelled tomorrow's meeting so I decided to go ahead and call downstairs.

"Hello, this is room twenty-one twelve. Do I have any messages?"

"Yes, Mr. Duncan. Let's see, you have one message from a Mrs. Nadia Franklin who wants you to return her call."

"Okay, anything else?"

"No, that's it."

"Thank you."

I instantly smiled when Nadia's name was mentioned. She must've been anxious to hear from me since I'm the one who was supposed to be calling her. Those lustful thoughts hit me again, but I knew I'd be wrong to put off calling Nakia. I just couldn't keep doing that to my girl, so I turned on my portable CD player and started dialing her number back home in L.A. I always like to have some music playing in the background when I talk to her.

"Hello?" she answered on the second ring.

"Hey, stranger, you remember me?"

"Who is this?"

"It's me, Orlando."

"Huh?"

"What you mean, huh? Guess I'm not missed as much as I was hoping to be."

"No, wait! Hold on, okay?"

I could hear Nakia click over to the other line. I must've caught her while she was talking to someone else. She's over there sounding so innocent, like she don't know what to do.

"Okay, I'm back."

"How's the weather out there?"

"Is that really what you want to know?" .

"No, just trying to start a little conversation and see if you over there mad at me."

"I was worried but I'm not mad—yet."

"Well, I've just been busy with all these conferences. As soon as I got in they had me attending every meeting under the sun. I've had very little time for personal issues. You understand, don't you?"

I usually ask if a person understands in order to detect whether or not they can tell that I was lying. I mean, I have gone to some meetings but to be honest, I haven't been too busy where I couldn't make some phone calls. This is the generation of the cell phone, and I always got mine right next to me. Nakia seemed to buy my little explanation.

"I miss talking to you, Orlando. I bet you out there getting spoiled by female attention, huh?"

"I haven't really noticed."

"Yeah, right!"

"Well, maybe I might notice a smile but I really can't sit here and recall the face or anything like that."

"Okay, Orlando."

"Well, you sound like you believe me a little bit so I'll leave it at that."

I didn't like the way the conversation was going between Nakia and myself, but it was really nice to hear her voice again. I guess she had some uneasy feelings, and I was probably a little too sensitive about her responses. I could tell that deep down she wanted to question why I hadn't called sooner. She was trying to act like it didn't bother her, but I knew it did.

My favorite girl from the hood is just trying her best to put up a front. She sounds like she got a little coaching from somewhere. It must've been her friend Ina. That lady is a trip sometimes. I'm talking about Ina. One day when I delivered flowers to Nakia personally, I ran into Ina in the hallway. She was all up on me looking at the flowers and smiling like she had other things on her mind. I think she did but I kept her at a distance with my just-being-polite-but-don't-want-to-be-bothered attitude. But, despite her flirtatious ways, she seems to be pretty close to Nakia.

Well, a strange vibe in the air caused the conversation between Nakia and I to end sooner than I'd expected. That kind of bummed me out and I'm having a hard time getting to sleep. Maybe it's just my imagination that Nakia was mad at me, but she seemed to be a little more quiet than usual. I guess I have some mending to do when I get back to L.A. For now, I'll just enjoy and see where this trip takes me. It's actually been pretty good and I'm not saying that because of running into Nadia. I've been doing some serious networking out here and making contacts that could very well set me up with a nice position. I've never considered living somewhere else other than Los Angeles, but right now Miami is looking really good to me. Maybe I need to experience one of those hurricanes and see if it still looks good to me.

Laying back and flipping through the channels really doesn't help my disposition right now. Just like back home, I'm finding too many channels with nothing to watch but my own reflection on the screen looking back at me. This is not the way I'm supposed to be spending my nights when in a tropical setting.

The phone began to ring just as I was boring myself to sleep with my thoughts. The room temperature was just right and I was lying in a really comfortable spot in this king-size bed. I wish I had the strength to turn the ringer off but my curiosity wouldn't let me do that.

I answered, "Hello?"

"Hey, sweetheart," a voice responded.

My voice recognition skills didn't click in so I played it safe by not attaching a name to my response.

"Hey, you," I said softly.

"You know who this is, don't you?"

"Of course I do."

I laughed in a seductive way, hoping that I could buy a little more time.

"Were you asleep?" the female voice asked.

"Almost…"

"I'm sorry, want me to let you go?"

"Never…"

"Careful what you wish for, Orlando."

"Why you say that?"

"'Cause then you might not be able to get rid of me and that's not a good thing."

"Could be good for me."

I couldn't believe the fog hadn't lifted and allowed me to figure out whom I was talking to. I was seriously tripping and getting nervous that I might slip and say the wrong name.

"So, what's bad about not getting rid of you?" I asked.

"'Cause I'm married, sweetheart, that's why! I can't just leave my husband because we happened to bump into each other. I don't think our college days could carry over into our adult days after not seeing each other all these years, do you?"

I started to laugh for a moment. All the nervous tension was releasing from my body. I'd finally discovered whom I was talking to. I was glad I didn't say the wrong name because to be honest, I was thinking this was Nakia on the phone.

"Why are you laughing?" Nadia asked.

"Just feels so unreal to hear your voice again, Nadia, that's all."

"Uh-huh. I'm starting to feel like you didn't recognize my voice. Is there someone else in your life right now that you're not telling me about?"

"Nobody serious…"

"But a potential?"

"Hmm, I don't know yet."

"Sounds like you haven't changed, Orlando. You still breaking hearts and choosing career over love, huh?"

"Yeah, it's worked all these years, so why change?"

"'Cause you need somebody in your life. You need to have a family. I have been so happy being a wife and a mother and I wouldn't give it up for anything!"

"Not even me?"

"Well, sweetheart, you bring back many memories and make me truly think about being unfaithful for one night, but no, I wouldn't give up my life, not even for you."

"So, you thinking about one night with me, huh?"

"You'd like that?"

"I ain't gonna lie, it's been on my mind."

I could almost sense Nadia smiling on the other end. Her voice started to sound a little different—like she was getting comfortable under the sheets while listening to me speak.

"You always did have a way of making me want to be bad," she told me.

"Yeah, I remember how bad you used to be!"

"I'll bet you do."

"Yeah, you remember in the park that night?"

"Well, I remember you being a very horny young man and not caring that the area was so dirty!"

"Yeah, but you still got turned on yourself."

"I did."

"I think I got some splinters in my behind from sitting on that park bench and having you ride me, lady."

"You're bad, Orlando."

It sounded like Nadia was blushing on the other end of this conversation. That was a very welcome sound. It was nice to know that a certain innocence about her hadn't gone away after all these years.

"What's on your mind now?" she asked.

"Mostly memories of you and me."

"You know you have me over here smiling, don't you?"

"That's a good thing?"

"Yes, it is, sweetheart."

I began to recall another time when I'd asked Nadia to meet me at the university on a Saturday. I really didn't think she would come that day. I mean, I was very straightforward about telling her that I wanted to have sex. I told her to meet me where the piano practice rooms were. The room number escapes me, but I do remember waiting for an hour after the time that we agreed to meet.

"I can't believe you forgot the room number!" Nadia said as she listened to me recall that moment between us.

"Yeah, I confess. So, you remember it?"

"I'm just playing. No, I don't remember either."

One thing I do remember about that day was waiting forever and being nervous about it. This wasn't gonna be our first time or anything like that, but just the excitement of doing it on school campus had me very anxious. I felt like I was still in high school because I kept looking to make sure I had a condom with me. I was pacing back and forth nervously looking around. After about forty-five minutes, I got so angry that I ended up ripping the condom package open and throwing it in the trash.

"That made me laugh when you told me and then showed it to me in the trash that day," she said.

Nadia resumed her laughing. I remember how embarrassed I felt about it because she finally showed up fifteen minutes after that, and I had major attitude written on my face.

"Where you been?" I shouted in sort of a half-whisper.

"Trying to get here! You don't know what I had to go through to get here today," she told me back then.

I just looked at her for about five minutes, and then I pointed out what I did with the condom because of the frustration I was feeling. That's when she just laughed at me and couldn't stop until she felt sorry and began hugging me.

"I remember that, Orlando. I thought you were too cute that day because you didn't stay mad. I remember you as being the ultimate sweetheart because instead of getting on me about what didn't happen, you turned that day into something really special."

"Yeah, I do remember how I made you smile a lot that day."

"You did because most guys would've still tried to have sex with me, but instead you bought some snacks from the vending machine and then we had a junk food picnic on the grass."

"Yeah, that ended up being a lot of fun. Shoot, you impressed me that day, too, Nadia!"

"I did?"

"Yeah, 'cause when we ran out of chips and candy, you used some of your change and bought some more! I had never been with a lady that shared, financially speaking."

"You're funny, Orlando. I can't believe you remember that day. I think that's got to be one of my favorite moments between us because it showed me that we were good friends and that you weren't gonna treat me bad or walk away because we didn't have sex."

"Thanks, Nadia."

"You're welcome. I just hope that gentle side of you hasn't changed or disappeared."

"I believe I'm still the same."

"I hope so."

After sharing so many memories, Nadia and I found ourselves having moments of silence where all we did was smile and reflect. We kept asking the same question of each other, over and over again.

"What you thinking about?" I asked.

"I was gonna ask you the same thing."

We both eased the suspense by just laughing and returning to silence. I was actually beginning to think about Nakia. Those thoughts came about because of the praise that Nadia was giving me about being a gentleman. That made me feel guilty because moments earlier, I was thinking nothing but lustful things. My motivation was to try to get Nadia to invite me to her hotel room. But now I was more focused on appreciating this talk I was having with a friend.

"So, tell me about your girlfriend."

"What are you...psychic?"

"No, but I just wonder if you're holding back on how you really feel about her."

"In all honesty I was holding back so that I could possibly make something happen with you tonight."

"I already knew that Orlando, but I also know that no matter what, you always speak your honest feelings."

"Yeah, I guess I do, huh?"

"Yep, that's why you remain so dear in my heart."

"Thanks, Nadia, that's a nice place to be. Well, since I'm guilty of being a sweetheart, I don't imagine we'll be indulging in some sex anytime soon, huh?"

"Nope."

"I was afraid of that."

"Besides, your heart is somewhere else and you know I don't like coming in second!"

"So true."

"Plus, I really love my husband. I felt guilty just thinking about you in a sexual way. I almost couldn't get a hold of myself, but I have special memories of my man that serve as a really great foundation for our marriage."

"He's very lucky."

"Yes, he is, and someone will be very lucky because of you one day soon."

"You think?"

"I can feel it, Orlando."

"Then you are psychic."

"No, I just know you and what a good man you truly are."

"Thanks."

Before our conversation ended, I gave her my phone number and address back home in Cali. I wanted to keep in touch with her because it felt really good to talk with her again. She definitely reminded me of what it felt like to be young and still a gentleman. Plus, I was gonna need her shoulder to cry on if things didn't work out with Nakia.

"Don't you hurt that girl, Orlando!" Nadia told me.

"Me hurt her?" I responded innocently.

"Uh-huh. I'll talk to you soon. Enjoy Miami, sweetie!"

"I will. Take care, Nadia."

As I hung up the phone, I wondered if Nadia was smiling. It felt really good to have that conversation with her. Now I feel like I'm lying in a bed of contentment because I'm not trying to pursue a moment of passion with her. Instead, I'm thinking about how I'm gonna hook up with Nakia next week. My focus has cleared with respect to a potential connection that could turn into something really deep. I was never one to juggle different ladies so why start now? Besides, having a sexual encounter with Nadia would only cause her to walk around in guilt. I don't want to be responsible for bringing her down or causing her to lose the beautiful family that she's blessed with. That lady has come a long way from the days when I knew her. I'm blessed to have her back in my life in the best way possible—as a dear friend.

Always A Catch Somewhere

Another Monday morning had come. This one was a real struggle because I'd been beating myself up all weekend long. Thinking about Orlando mostly. And then Ina came over and we talked for hours about men, love, marriage, you name it. I was happy to have someone who could share in my disappointment and frustration. But now I feel like I have a hangover from all that talking. Not to mention, I don't know how many Tequila Sunrises we had so I'm sure that's also why my head is still spinning. This little get-together happened on Saturday. Then on Sunday, I just spent the whole day being depressed, hung over, and avoiding the world. I even shut my little angel out for a moment, but all her loud talking just begged for my attention.

"Would you keep it down out there!" I shouted.

She and little Trent were doing their usual running around and driving me crazy, a weekend routine. I had very little patience for what usually doesn't bother me. But yesterday, everything bothered me. I wish I could say that Ina helped me get over what I was going through, but time is the only medicine for me right now. I'm going through that same old thing again, being disappointed in a man. I thought Orlando would be so different from all others. He *is* different, but I'm still seeing the same ending to what I believed in my heart would be so special.

Ina chipped in with her wisdom. "Well, men are all the same, Girl!"

I wanted to agree but I couldn't really. Then after talking about Orlando some more and drinking two more glasses of those Tequila Sunrises, out of nowhere, I said the same thing.

"You know, Ina, men are all the same!"

"And you just figured that out?"

I don't know what we called ourselves doing by drinking so much and drowning each other with sad stories about lost love and dreams about marriage. Thinking about it the next day made me feel so depressed. In fact, thinking about it now is no picnic either.

Saturday was really a trip, though. Ina called around 10 in the morning. I had just woken up five minutes before that, and she was sounding like she'd been up for hours already.

She asked, "What you doing today, Girl?"

"Nothing, you?"

"Oh, maybe sit around and look stupid all day."

"Oh, stop, you probably got a date or something."

"With who?"

"I don't know!"

"I don't even want to see a man today, Girl! I might just cuss him out 'cause I didn't get a chance to cuss out the one that did me wrong."

"I know that's right!"

Ina and I spent about an hour and a half talking about men and that kind of set up the day's events for later. I didn't feel like going anywhere or seeing anybody myself. There's enough folks out there with angry stares and bad attitudes already. I didn't need to add to that madness.

"You wanna come over?" I asked.

I didn't think she'd accept my invitation. I know how she is about spending any length of time in my neighborhood.

"Yeah, we should spend the day together, Girl. I'll even pick up some videos and bring some Mexican food over. We can make some Tequila Sunrises, too!"

"Wow, you surprised me..."

"What?"

"Nothing. I'll go around the corner and buy a few things, too," I told her.

"No, you don't have to. It'll be my treat, Nakia."

"Okay, but what videos you gonna get?"

"I was thinking about some of those old movies with Cary Grant or something like that."

"What! You better get some '*Love Jones*,' Girl. I'm not trying to watch some old black and white flick."

"Nakia, you need to see something different. You gonna watch that movie and probably start thinking about Orlando."

"I'm already thinking about him so that don't matter. I still don't want to see those old movies you talkin' 'bout."

"I'll tell you what, I'll get one for me and one for you."

"But the VCR is in my house."

"No, you didn't just go there, Ms. Selfish one!"

"Uh-huh."

"Okay, Nakia, since you gonna be like that I'll pick up only what you like."

"I'm sorry Ina, you can get one of those old ones, too. You gonna stay all night?"

"No!"

"Just playing, Girl. I know how you are."

"That's why I'm coming over early so we can have plenty of time before it gets dark."

I love Ina. I don't know what I'd do without her crazy self. I've probably said those words a few times before, even after she gets on my damn nerves. I guess our friendship must be special or I might get offended by her always putting down where I come from. Heffa...

I was so happy to have the house to myself on Saturday. My mom took Trent and Tanisha to San Diego to Sea World. She planned on staying the night and would be back Sunday. That made it even better for Ina and I to do some serious girl-talking. Ina finally came over a little after 1 p.m. and I was so happy to see her. She looked like a bum in her sweat pants but I didn't look any better in my raggedy jeans and T-shirt.

"Girl, neither one of us got makeup on today, huh?" Ina said.

"What you trying to say?"

"Trying to say you look as bad as I do!"

We just laughed and put all the food on the table. Ina bought a lot from this place called Baja Express. I always go there to get these chicken quesadillas that just melt in your mouth. I could eat those things every day if I didn't mind my ass getting bigger.

"Damn, Girl, how much did you buy?" I asked.

"I want us to enjoy ourselves...Forget about your ass getting big, Girlfriend...".

Before I knew it, the whole dining room table was filled with Mexican food. I just looked at her as if she had lost her damn mind.

"We gonna eat all this stuff?" I asked.

"I don't know about you, but I'm gonna try."

Complaining about so much food didn't stop me from nibbling while Ina was setting up the table. I love me some hot salsa, and nothing goes better with that than some delicious Tequila Sunrises. I stopped nibbling for a second just to make some. And when I took my first sip, I just smiled and started laughing at the expression on my face. I could see my reflection my glass.

I was really happy to have Ina come over. At that very moment it felt like Saturday was gonna be nothing but fun. The day was probably more interesting than anything else. Revealing, sad, and funny at times, Saturday was a trip.

All that food on the table made me full just looking at it. At first I just stood there but then Ina threatened my life and told me I better eat it up or else. Then after ten minutes into getting our eat on, Ina broke the ice, so to speak, by talking about that man she tried to go out with once.

"You talking about that guy with the broken car seat?" I asked.

"Yeah, Girl! I've been so desperate that I thought about calling him again."

"Calling him for what?"

"To go out!"

"Why?"

"I told you, I've been feeling desperate!"

"Then just go to a club or something."

"Yeah, but then I'd have to get all dressed up, play that trifling game of trying to meet somebody and then have a conversation…"

I interrupted. "Wait a minute!"

"What?"

"You trying to tell me you just want to get your freak on?"

"Uh-huh! That's why I was gonna call that brotha with the slip-and-slide car seats and take him to a motel. I definitely wouldn't bring him home with me 'cause then he'd know where I live. I just want some dick *once* before I die!"

"No, you didn't just say that! What happened to you, Ina?"

"Huh? What do you mean what happened?"

"You just a big ol' freak, Girl."

"Well, Nakia, it's been a while and I do have needs. Plastic ain't getting to that spot no more."

"You crazy, Girl. Who knows what you gonna tell me next."

"You not so innocent yourself, Nakia, so I don't know why you trying to act like you're so shocked. Plus, you got you some not too long ago with Orlando. That's why you not able to sympathize with me."

"Now you're just being silly, Ina."

"I know but it would be nice to be in a man's arms—sometime."

"I'm sure you will but I don't think you need to settle for someone that you're not really into."

"Isn't that strange how things change?"

"Change?"

"Yeah, 'cause I can remember when we first used to talk about personal stuff. I was the one giving you advice and telling you to be patient. Now, here you are, Girl, all this wisdom and telling me what to do!"

"Yeah, yeah. But either way, I'm feeling just as bad when it comes to men."

"Well, stand in line and don't give away your number again so fast!"

"Okay!"

"Men are a trip."

"I will drink to that, Girl..."

Ina and I were in full agreement as we continued drinking and stuffing our faces. We had a really good time together Saturday, and now I'm hoping all that talking we did will serve as a Band-Aid to help me get through this week. My heart is still bruised and my strength comes and goes with each sigh. I feel like I'm on life support right now. I hope nobody makes me mad today because that might set me off. I really need to get a grip and get past all of this 'cause I feel like if someone were to pull the plug on me, the monitor would read "Orlando" instead of the usual flat line.

It took me an hour to get to work today. The buses were running slow or maybe I forgot what it felt like to ride one since I'd been getting rides most of the time from others. Ina couldn't drive me to work because she had to meet with clients. She told me to call Avonté and ask him for a ride, but she sounded like she was trying to see what I'd say. I didn't think she was serious. To be honest I was tempted because I really didn't want to be bothered with sitting or possibly standing so close to a bunch of strangers on the bus. This whole Orlando situation has given me a serious attitude. I get upset about the smallest things now. All my familiar routines have become a pain in the ass and even my heart sometimes palpitates. I don't like feeling like this. One thing I do enjoy about getting to work early is that my boss doesn't come in until late. I'm able to take care of the routine phone calls, messages, and the all-important coffee-making duties.

Not too long after I'd settled into my leather chair behind my desk, Avonté stuck his head in the office for a moment to say hello.

"Well, hello!" he said.

Something about him makes me smile now and it ain't a crush or anything like that. He just seems more real to me than...you know who.

"You here early, Nakia."

"Good morning to you, too!"

"Oh, sorry about that. Good morning."

"Yes, I'm here early."

"Who brought you here?"

"The bus."

"Oh. Well, you should let a brotha take you home then."

"I just might."

"Really?"

"Yep."

"Damn."

"What's wrong?"

"Nothing. You just caught me off guard 'cause you know all you ever tell me is no."

"Well, Avonté, I guess I trust you now."

"Thanks, I'll leave you alone then. Don't want to push my luck!"

Avonté left me with a smile even though my attitude was simmering beneath the surface. It unveiled itself as soon as I heard that same voice that once reminded me of Orlando. I remember last time I spoke with this man he thought I was flirting with him. This time he could tell right away that I didn't want to be bothered, and I know that wasn't very professional, but it was real.

"Did I catch you at a bad time, Ms. Davidson?" he'd asked.

I didn't answer his question directly. Instead I spoke to him in a professional manner with very little emotion behind the words that I chose. Needless to say, the conversation didn't last very long and I felt guilty about taking my anger out on an innocent man. I've seen better mornings than this one. It was time for my break.

Fifteen minutes felt like two seconds to me. I don't always have Mondays that turn out this bad, and I don't usually complain this much either but today deserved my bitching. I waved to some of my co-workers in the office and forced my smile each time while walking back to my desk. I ran into Avonté again in the hallway, and he seemed pretty excited about taking me home this evening. He better not get too excited 'cause I probably won't be the best company to have sitting in his car.

Ina must've been having a really good meeting with those clients. I poked my head into her office to see if she was there and she wasn't. That didn't help me. I could sure use a pep talk from her right now.

"Nakia, what's up?" a familiar voice said as I walked into the office.

"What are you doing here?" I responded.

"I was hoping for a sweeter hello from you, for one thing. I couldn't wait to see you so I thought I'd surprise you at the office."

"Well, you could've waited."

"Is there a problem, Nakia?"

"Orlando, you can't expect me to just jump in your arms after not hearing from you for so long."

"You right."

I just stood quietly with my arms folded. I was pretty hot under the collar as I looked at this man. Even in my simmering, angry state of mind, I'd noticed that he looked really good. He had on a black and gray turtleneck, some black slacks and gorgeous shoes, which were probably Italian. My intense focus was finally interrupted when I heard footsteps behind me. I realized that my door was still open so I turned around to close it. I didn't want anyone overhearing me if I happened to lose my cool.

"I don't know what to say, Nakia, except that I'm not used to having someone in my life. You know, someone that I have to call when I go away on trips or someone that's back home worrying about me. This is all new to me."

Orlando made sense, but I wasn't allowing any bit of understanding to enter my heart just yet. He caused me to feel so much disappointment, which made me turn off any belief that I'd finally found a good man to give my heart to. That's a feeling that if I think about too much, I'll start crying right here in the office. I'm tired of crying and feeling bad because of a relationship with a man.

"You gonna talk to me, Nakia?"

I just stood there in silence. My eyes were starting to fill up with water. Orlando tried to touch me, but I backed away.

"Well, I bought these flowers for you. I remembered how much you liked those orchids I bought you last time."

Orlando was trying really hard. The flowers were gorgeous but right now they were just as blurry as the confusion in my heart. I kept my arms folded, and he was forced to place the flowers on the desk.

"I guess I'd better go then. I care about you a lot, Nakia, and that's why I was anxious to see you. I wanted to tell you everything about my trip and to somehow begin repairing the trust that I know I've broken. I'll be at home most of the day and you have my pager number. I hope you'll call me."

Orlando walked past me, opened the door and walked out of my office. When the door closed, the tears finally fell from my eyes and I began to feel bad for not saying more. Somehow I had to get myself together because it wouldn't be good for someone to walk into the office and see me crying. This was gonna take a moment so I locked the door. I sat quietly staring at the flowers on the desk before throwing them in the trash. Then I took them out and placed the flowers on a chair in a corner of the office. A big part of me wanted to run outside and stop Orlando from leaving, but my pride forced me to stick with my decision to stay in the office.

The day went by really fast after that. I had about ten minutes left before Avonté came walking through the door. I've probably seen him more times today than I've seen him in the past two months. He seems really anxious to take me home. I can already hear the alarm inside my head going off. I think he's gonna try to ask me out on a date. And if he does, I hope I don't sound too mean when I tell him, *No, thanks!* It's nothing personal, but I can't just jump from one man to the next, even if it is just an innocent date.

"Hey, Nakia, you ready?"

Avonté startled me. He's getting a little too comfortable popping his head inside my office.

"I'll be ready in a second."

"Cool."

"Let me just staple these papers together and then get my keys."

"Okay. So, how was your day?"

"It was nice."

"Nice? I saw you had a visitor today, Nakia. Then after that you got kind of quiet."

"Yeah, I don't know if I can talk about it right now."

"I understand. That was someone important to you, huh?"

"I guess so. I'm not sure how important I was to him, but maybe it doesn't matter any more."

"Sounds like something I shouldn't ask too many questions about."

I just shrugged my shoulders and tried my best to hide my emotions from Avonté. I know I wasn't very successful, but all of his questions were causing me to think too much about Orlando. I was emotionally drained so right now it was best for me to just remain quiet.

Avonté continued trying to keep a conversation going as he drove me home. Most of the time I would try to smile or utter a sound just to let him know I was listening. I remember Ina telling me that Avonté loves to talk about himself, and he did a lot of that, but he also showed me that he was genuine in his concern for what I was feeling. I still wondered how long it would be before he would ask me out.

"Hey, Nakia, let me ask you something," he said.

Here it comes, I thought.

"Does Ina ever talk about me? I know I did her wrong..."

"No, she doesn't really, at least not lately."

I answered Avonté with no enthusiasm at all. In fact, I really didn't know what I had just said to him. My mind was a million miles away. I just wanted to get home, hug my child and forget about this day. I was gonna listen to Tanisha tell me about her day at school and avoid any kind of memory that made me think about Orlando. I wished I could forget about him now.

"This your place?" Avonté asked.

"Yeah."

"Cool. You want me to pick you up in the morning?"

"No, I think Ina is gonna come get me tomorrow."

"Okay. Well, let me know if she can't and I'll come get you."

"Thanks, Avonté, that's sweet."

"No problem."

"Bye now."

"Later."

Avonté drove off and I watched him until he turned the corner. I'll have to make it up to him one day for being so sweet. Not to mention, he didn't ask me out on a date, which is a good thing. He seemed like a really good friend today. I could actually confide in him and that was a nice change.

Before I could turn and face the house, I heard a very welcome sound. "Mommy!" Tanisha screamed from inside the house.

She was standing inside the screen door and instantly made me smile. Right there was my reminder why I get up and go to work every morning. I wish she could stay a child forever so she wouldn't have to go through all the trials and tribulations that I have. Then again, dogs do come in all sizes. Oh, let me stop.

"Hey sweetie, how was your day?"

"Fine. Somebody called you, Mommy."

"Who was it?"

Tanisha shrugged her shoulders.

"Did you eat dinner already?"

"Yes."

"Did you do your homework?"

"Yes, Trent helped me do it."

"That was sweet of him."

Once again she shrugged her shoulders. I'm trying to teach her not to do that so much, but at the same time she looks so cute when she does. It's hard to stop her from developing bad habits because I just enjoy watching every little thing she does.

"Where's Grandma?" I asked.

"She's resting. She said she was really tired today."

"Oh, okay. Have you been letting her rest?"

"Yeah."

"Where's Trent?"

"He outside somewhere."

"Okay, well, you come tell Mommy about your day while I fix my dinner."

"You hungry, Mommy?"

"Yes, I'm starving."

Tanisha started laughing and melting my heart.

"Why are you laughing?"

There she goes, shrugging her shoulders again.

An hour went by and Tanisha got tired of talking to me. She went to her room to watch TV, and little Trent finally came inside looking like he'd been digging ditches. I made him take a bath and wash off all that funk.

It was nice and peaceful around the house and I felt pretty good. After I clean out the bathtub I plan on sitting in there myself for a long time and just relax. I wanna clear my mind completely of this day. Maybe later I'll try to call Ina and see how her day went. I really missed her today and I know she's gonna give me an ear full. I can only imagine how she'll react when I tell her that Orlando stopped by the office. She knows how I'm feeling right now about him, although I don't think she'd agree with me not talking to him. That moment at the office today felt so intense that it gave me a serious headache.

Right now my shoulders and my neck are aching. I was about to have my baby give me a massage, but her little hands can't do nothing for me right now and Mom is just too tired. I know how she is when she gets off work so I'm not gonna even try to knock on her bedroom door. I hope I don't end up being the same way, but I guess we all get a little grumpy when our days don't go too well. Today was one of those days and I didn't want to be bothered either. But, when you have a young child you have to smile and be happy, even when you don't feel like it.

Well, five minutes into my bath and the phone started ringing. I just knew that my mother wasn't gonna answer it so I yelled out to Tanisha to get it.

I sat still in the warm water hoping that it was a wrong number. The temperature of my bath water was perfect and I had some candles going, too. I mean, this was what I'd been waiting for since my day started going so bad. One day I hope I can have a house with one of those really large bathtubs in the center of the floor. Then I'll probably be in there for hours upon hours, unlike this bathtub where the water seeps out after a while. I hate when that happens, but I've gotten used to it

"Mommy, telephone!" Tanisha shouted.

"Well, bring it to me!"

"Okay."

Tanisha pushed the door open and walked inside. I only had the door halfway closed anyway. I can't have too much privacy around here.

"Is it Ina?"

Tanisha shrugged her shoulders.

"What I tell you about shrugging your shoulders all the time? Okay, give me the phone, sweetheart."

Tanisha handed me the phone and ran back to the bedroom. I was wondering if I really wanted to say hello or not, especially if it wasn't Ina on the other end.

I answered hesitantly. "Hello?"

"Nakia," a male's voice responded somberly.

"Orlando." *My second guess*, I thought to myself.

There was silence for a moment after I said his name. I guess he wondered what my reaction would be. Part of me was happy that he called, yet I was still angry with him. My feelings were so confused right then because I wasn't sure how I should react.

"Nakia, I guess I called because I really want a chance to explain. I'm hoping that you'll listen and truly hear my words because I care about you."

"I'm listening."

"On the flight back home from my business trip, I realized the harm I did by not calling you. And then when I saw your face and looked into your eyes today, I realized how much you believed in me as a man. I remembered that first time we spoke at the club and you were so fascinated with me. I felt really strange about that, but at the same time it was a big ego boost."

"I had never talked to a man that could make me think and feel the way you do, Orlando."

"I realized that and in a way I had moments where I wanted to run from you, Nakia."

"Run from me, why?"

"Because what happens when you see I'm just a regular guy? You'll then move on and look for someone else that fascinates you."

"The way you disappeared makes me think you are just a regular guy. It really hurt not hearing from you. I've been the one who's scared of losing you to someone that fascinates you."

"So, maybe we were both worried about nothing."

"I don't know, Orlando. Did you see anyone while you were gone?"

"I ran into an old friend, but she's married now."

"Disappointed?"

"What do you mean?"

"Do you wish she wasn't married?"

Orlando didn't answer right away. I felt that if he'd been true to wanting to be with me, then there should be no hesitation in answering that question.

"Bye, Orlando."

"Huh, wait!"

I hung up the phone, disgusted and ready to scream. But, instead of wasting the air inside my lungs, I just closed my eyes and sank deeper into the bath water and into my disappointment in a man that I'd thought had it all together.

Sistas In Need

It's now the holiday season and I don't have a man to spend it with. I'm tired of feeling disappointed and thinking every man is no good. Nakia isn't helping out with her disgusted attitude about men. I thought that if I said something bad, then she'd counter by telling me the positive side. Boy, was I wrong. Now all she does is agree with me and then says something even worse about men.

My response would always end up being, "Damn, Girl!"

She finally told me about what happened with Orlando. She'd been keeping the details to herself, but I always knew something was up. All of a sudden she just completely stopped talking about the man and that seemed so weird to me. Whenever I'd ask her if she'd spoken to him, she would brush me off or say that they were just friends and occasionally exchanged emails.

I'd say to her, "Tell me anything, Girlfriend."

Nakia finally confessed that there were no emails exchanged and that she cut off all communication with Orlando.

"I just want a man who knows he wants to be with me," she said with a sigh.

"I know, huh!"

"I mean, it is so disappointing to go from believing in someone to learning that they're no better than the rest," Nakia cried out.

"Don't give up, Girl. I know I've been hard on men, but I also remember how happy I was for you being with Orlando. Shoot, I thought I was responsible for getting you two together."

"Thanks, Ina. I guess it'll just go down as another important lesson in my life."

Nakia was so sad during that conversation. It seemed like every day, from that point on, she'd been that way. I almost want to choke her because of the way she's changed. Then I remember that she's gone through two disappointing relationships back-to-back. First, with her baby's father, Terence, and now with Orlando. All I can do as a friend is keep reminding her not to give up, especially on herself.

I told her, "Girl, that special man is gonna walk into your life when you least expect it."

"Yeah, I know and look what happened." One could easily see the disappointment written all over her face.

All I could do was look at her and shrug my shoulders. I'm gonna pray that God brings a good man in her life 'cause I'd hate to see her succumb even further into her newfound bitterness—though I can definitely understand where it comes from.

Well, I can't say that I've been faring much better in my pursuit of a good man. Actually I haven't been pursuing anyone, but I did happen upon a man recently at work. His name is kind of funny to me for a black man. Or maybe I'm in denial about being ignorant.

I asked this brotha, "What's your name again?"

"Sebastian," he responded.

"You black?"

He just started laughing as though I caught him off guard with my somewhat silly question.

"Yes, I am, why?" he asked.

"Just teasing you..."

I came off as slightly rude that day, but he didn't seem to notice too much. Sebastian was visiting our office from Chicago where he's an advertising executive for another company. He was lending us his expertise on various projects. I was impressed by the way he spoke in the boardroom. Hell, he had me daydreaming about other rooms he could take me to. Once our meeting was over, that's when I played the fool and revealed the ignorance that I mentioned a moment ago. After my stupidity, I figured that I blew off any chance of speaking further with Mr. Sebastian. Actually, his full name is Sebastian Turner. He's a very well-groomed and well-spoken man. He reminded me of Orlando. I guess in a way I've always had a secret crush on Nakia's friend. Ex-friend now. I know I've been wishing that I could receive the same kind of attention that she received when they dated. All the beautiful flowers and hugs waiting for her when she got off work? Shit, that's a welcome way of life for any sistah.

I'm different from Nakia in that I'll approach men, but then sometimes I might say things that get me in trouble or perhaps turn the man off. She just plays the cutesy role and then takes over later. I could learn a few things from her, and I have, to some degree.

When I arrived at work, Sebastian approached me. I did as Nakia often does. I let the man do all the talking until I could see it was time to speak up. I learn fast. Especially when I know I messed up the first time.

"Hello, Ms. Simmons."

I just smiled and turned to give him my full attention.

"I was hoping I could catch you this morning so you wouldn't plan your day and not allow time for me to see you," he told me.

I was shocked and surprised. "Plan my day?".

"Yes, I'd like to take you to lunch, if possible."

"It's possible."

"Sounds good…You are a fascinating lady. I heard great things about you, and I can see there's perhaps some other sides to take note of, too."

I caught Mr. Turner taking a quick glance at my body. I couldn't resist smiling ever so slightly. "How so?" I asked.

I was looking at this man with one eyebrow raised out of curiosity. I became anxious to hear what sides he was referring to.

"Hmm...Yesterday you approached me with such confidence whereas today you seem more reserved and almost shy. I could be wrong but I do notice a difference in you."

"Thank you."

"No, thank *you*. So, are we on for today?"

"Tomorrow."

"Fantastic, I'll see you at noon?"

"How about one?"

"I do like your confidence. Okay, see you then, tomorrow at one."

A girl has got to have some kind of control over her situation. I loved the fact that Sebastian was so excited about seeing me. I smiled as he walked away, and then I turned red 'cause Avonté noticed me looking at Sebastian's butt.

"Hey, Ina, haven't seen much of you lately," Avonté said.

"Yeah, I know. How are you?"

I had no enthusiasm at all, but I had to speak with him because I'd heard that he and Nakia had been spending more time together.

"I'm doing great. Work is going really well and hanging out with Nakia has been the bomb! I never thought that I would develop such a cool friendship with her."

"Is that all it is?" I asked, feeling borderline jealous.

"Yeah, why?"

"Just curious, that's all."

"Oh, okay."

"Well, take care, Avonté. Say hello to my girl if you happen to see her before me."

"I will."

Once again, I was guilty of being rude, but with Avonté, I didn't mind. As Nakia often says, "I just wasn't feelin' him at all." I didn't even turn to watch him walk away. I went inside, closed the door and thought about how sexy Sebastian was. At that point I began looking further into the man beneath the business-like exterior. He has a certain sexiness about him that's very subtle, but I like it. I found some information on the company he represents in Chicago and noticed an interesting coincidence. The company is called Turner Enterprises. Then as I looked further into the file I noticed Sebastian's name at the very top.

Brotha got bank! I thought to myself.

Then I thought about how sweet he was when he approached me and wondered if that was sincere or maybe he's just really good at getting what he wants. A man has to have special talents in order to achieve what it appears this man has. My curiosity was sparked even more. As a matter of fact, the fire had damn near been ignited to a point where it could burn the building down! Nakia made me feel guilty about that later on when I gave her the 411 about Sebastian.

She told me, "I always knew you had that gold digger mentality in you!"

"It's not like that, Nakia."

"Uh-huh."

"Okay, his money excites me, but his gentle personality makes me let my guard down, Girlfriend. It's almost like he reminds me of Orlando in a way, or should I say, how Orlando was with you."

My comment instantly brought silence to the room. At that moment I'd touched a nerve with Nakia even though she didn't get mad or say anything to me. She did look at me strange though. I probably should've never let it slip that I talked to Orlando after they broke up.

"Sorry. I didn't mean to mention his name..." I said.

"It's not your fault. I'm still not over him, I guess."

"I thought maybe Avonté was keeping your mind off Orlando. I know he and I don't get along anymore, but I don't hate him."

"Avonté has been sweet. In fact, I honestly believe he's learned something from what happened between you two."

"Oh, really?"

I tried to be sympathetic to Nakia but forcing myself to believe that Avonté was somehow different from the selfish non-romantic jerk that I once knew was stretching it for me.

Nakia asked, "Why you looking like that?"

"I'm okay, Girl. So, how is Avonté different now?"

"He listens."

"For him, that is different."

It wasn't hard to pry myself away from Nakia because she was talking a little bit too much about Avonté. I just didn't want to hear it, and I couldn't see myself trying to pretend like I cared about his emotional growth. Asshole.

This day that I had been anxious to see came pretty quickly. I didn't need my alarm clock, the traffic didn't bother me, and I didn't need any coffee to jumpstart my energy level. I am excited! Right now I'm looking forward to seeing that tall delicious man, Sebastian, walk through my door. I got to work early just so I wouldn't miss any opportunity for him to come and talk to me. I love listening to his soothing voice, *Hmm!*

As I walked down the hallway, I was surprised to see Nakia at work so early, too. Albeit, was a nice surprise. That girl is still looking all melancholy even though she claims to enjoy her friendship with Avonté so much.

"How about we do lunch tomorrow," I said.

"What about today?"

"Nope. Got Sebastian today!"

"Oh, yeah. Let me know what happens."

"You know I will!"

Now I'm sitting here reading more about Sebastian like he's coming here to interview me. Maybe I shouldn't know so much about his company or he might think my motives lie somewhere else. Actually, for the first time in a long while I was nervous about seeing a man. That's a unique feeling for me, but it's a nice change.

Well, thirty minutes went by, and the man that I had been waiting for caught me completely by surprise.

"I see you're getting familiar with my company, huh?"

My head was buried in the folder when Sebastian walked into my office. I never locked my door so I guess it's my fault and now, I was embarrassed.

"I knocked but you didn't respond. The lady outside told me you were expecting me," Sebastian said.

I guess my hearing must be bad, too, 'cause I heard no knocking.

"Shall I wait for you or do you want to go now?" he asked.

"It is kind of early, Sebastian, very early, but I'm flattered that you're so eager to see me."

"Well, I've seen you in action, Ina, so I want to see if you're that way in everything that you do."

"Hmm, I don't know how I should take that."

"With respect, I hope."

I had to take a second look at Sebastian to make sure he wasn't throwing out some sexual innuendo. Not that I mind, but I guess my early impression of him is that he excites a woman's mind before he makes any attempt at becoming intimate.

"Listen, I hope I'm gonna discover that Ina has a sense of humor, too! I'd hate to think that I need to be on guard for the next hour."

"I don't punch a clock, honey, so who said anything about an hour?" I unleashed my cockiest smile and I think Mr. Turner loved it.

He let out a "I heard that!" and then stood back to watch me get up from my chair.

Sebastian was beginning to turn me on with his bashful smile and the way he touched his lips with his finger. I could see a sparkle in his eye like he wondered just how far his efforts would take him.

"You never know," I whispered.

"What did you say?"

"Nothing, just thinking out loud."

For lunch, Sebastian and I decided to walk around the corner to this very lovely little Bistro garden-style restaurant. I love Italian food so I wanted to take advantage of this moment with such a fine man 'cause I knew the conversation was gonna be nice. As we walked I got a sense that Sebastian wanted to hold my hand. He rarely took his eyes off of mine unless he happened to be listening closely or was deep in thought, at which point he would look toward the ground. I guess he figured that making an attempt at holding my hand was a little premature so he simply kept his hands in his pocket. Things like that made me smile because it was refreshing to be with a somewhat bashful man. To me he could probably get any woman he wanted, but he has a shyness that makes him appear very humble about his blessings.

"What you smiling about?" he asked.

I guess he also noticed my moments of deep reflection.

"Just having nice thoughts."

"Oh, okay. Well, I think this is the place up ahead here," he said as he pointed.

At that moment he put his hand in the small of my back very gently, and it felt great. I took a deep breath, looked into his dark brown eyes and then at his lips. He smiled but couldn't maintain the eye contact. I thought that was cute.

"Beauty before money," he said as he opened the restaurant door for me.

"Huh?"

That comment made me skip a step for a second there.

"Lunch is on me," he said.

"Oh, okay," I uttered while letting him off the hook—slightly.

I wasn't so sure if that's what he really meant, mostly because of that discussion I had with Nakia earlier. I began to wonder for a second if Sebastian might say something else that would make me pause for a moment. Despite that one thing, he did nothing but excite my mind and make me smile. The man even smelled good, too, and I noticed the subtle move that he made to get close to me. When he opened the door, he leaned forward just enough to brush against my body.

"By the way, your hair smells very lovely, Ina."

I told you so. The man has subtle moves, and I didn't mind discovering each one of them. In fact, I was flattered by his attention to detail without being overanxious to get a feel. I had that problem with

Avonté a few times but actually, it wasn't like I was getting with him for his mind anyway.

Well, that was then and this is now. I'm gonna enjoy this man right here. Sebastian definitely has a lot of similarities to Orlando. I know I keep saying that, but he's nice and tall, handsome, well-spoken, knowledgeable, and speaks his mind when it's time. You can sense his words are thought out and chosen carefully. That shows me that this man is quick on his feet, and his mind is very strong.

"I bet you'd be a good person to have phone sex with, huh?" I blurted out.

"What?" he laughed.

"I'm only teasing you. I just enjoy listening to you speak and can only imagine a woman could get lost in an all-night phone conversation with you."

"I can't really say or admit to that, but I appreciate the compliment. As I said earlier, Ina, you definitely have different sides to you, lady! Phone sex, huh? That's something to think about."

I just smiled, took a sip of water and returned to my menu.

"Hmm, what looks good on here?" I asked softly.

I could feel Sebastian's eyes as well as his thoughts all over me. I think I was getting the best of this man.

"Indeed, what looks good...," he whispered.

"Did you say something?" I asked while placing the menu on the table.

"No, just thinking out loud."

"Oh, you do that, too, huh?"

"Yeah," he answered with that bashful smile.

Lunch turned out to be a glorious treat. It was such a pleasure to be sitting across from a man who had so much knowledge about love, life, himself. I couldn't get enough of Sebastian Turner sitting there and looking so fine. I gave him subtle hints myself, and he picked up on every one of them. When we made it back to the office building, I threw the subtlety right out the window when I saw that we would be riding on the elevator alone.

"Sebastian, would you like to kiss me?"

He just kind of grinned, looked down for a moment like a bashful little boy, and then stepped toward me like a strong passionate man. I could see so much strength in his eyes, yet I also found a certain amount of tenderness as well. He didn't answer my question verbally. Instead, he just kissed me gently before embracing me with his strong arms. Then just before the elevator doors opened, Sebastian stepped back and gave me another gorgeous smile.

"Thanks for lunch, Ms. Simmons," he said as he acted innocent.

"Don't even go there!"

For my benefit, he tried to play it off as though we were truly on a business lunch date. I appreciated his effort but I didn't mind if anyone wanted to link us together in some kind of office gossip. I can find worse things for people to say about me behind my back. When we stepped out of the elevator, I held his hand and walked him toward my office.

"I wish I could stay longer, Ina, but I have a couple of meetings to attend this afternoon," he said.

"Okay, and will I see you tonight?"

"You inviting me somewhere?"

"Is that too forward of me?" I asked cautiously.

"Yes, but I don't mind."

I smiled while still holding on to his hand. I could see Nakia standing behind Sebastian. I didn't realize she was there until now. She looked like she wanted to laugh at me or maybe she was just happy for me.

"So, Ina, call me on my cell phone later and give me directions to your place. I'll bring some champagne or something, if that's okay?"

"Okay."

"Take care, sweetheart," Sebastian said before kissing my cheek and walking away.

Nakia shouted as soon as Sebastian was no longer in sight. "Girl?"

"What?" I responded innocently.

"What's up between you two?"

"He's just a friend."

"Don't give me that…Plus, I heard you two making plans for tonight!"

"So?"

"So, I'm your friend but I can't remember you inviting me over recently for champagne…"

"That was his idea! I'm just gonna supply the takeout food and…"

"And what?" Nakia interrupted.

"And I'm gonna wear my new Victoria's Secret gown that I've been keeping a secret since I bought it!"

"Ooh!"

"Don't be acting shocked. It's been a while for me, and this man is so damn gorgeous."

"Uh-huh, but I don't think it's been that long for you, Ina. Didn't you tell me about a passionate moment with an old friend in the parking lot two weeks ago? I think you said you two went to the Marriott down the street after that?"

"Oh, that!"

"Yes, that!"

"Well, that was nice, but tonight with Sebastian could have a lot more meaning behind it."

"Who was the guy from two weeks ago?"

"Just some guy I know. That's old news, Girl!"

I had my reasons for not wanting to let Nakia know whom my sexual escapade was with. She didn't seem to push too much in trying to get me to reveal it so for now my secret was safe. Plus, I think she was just as excited as I was about Sebastian. I wanted to spend the rest of the day just talking about him, but it was time to remember where I was at the moment.

"Girl, I've got to get some work done. I can't believe I'm standing here talking to you!"

"Well, you the one acting like you can take two-hour lunch breaks…"

"Oh, please, Nakia, you know you wanted to hear about Sebastian. Plus, why ain't you at your desk?"

Nakia and I both started laughing. We always have these cute little moments where we come off more as sisters rather than close friends. I guess we've become "Sista-friends" after going through our ups and downs together. She's definitely the closest girlfriend I've ever had.

Well, ever since that great lunch I had with Sebastian today, I have been feeling wonderful. I've been smiling the whole time while doing tedious paperwork and making phone calls all over the country. Nothing could bring me down or take away this good feeling in my heart. I'm so excited about tonight that I left work an hour early. Right now I'm on my way to this really nice Thai restaurant to pick up some food. I once used them to cater an office party a while back so I know the food is delicious. I should probably make more of an effort to impress Sebastian by cooking for him, but I know my strengths and I'm aware of my weaknesses. My cooking will only make the brotha change his mind and possibly excuse himself right out my front door. No, I'm not gonna go that route tonight. And should he ask me if I cooked this delicious meal we're having, I'm gonna tell him the truth, "Just for you, honey."

No, just kidding, because he might ask me to do it again and there's only one thing that I want him asking me for repeat performances of. I don't think I need to say more because the expression on my face is loud and clear. I don't know if I can maintain any degree of innocence tonight because my hormones seem to be very anxious right now. I can't wait to tell Nakia about it tomorrow but I guess I'd better not celebrate too soon. Maybe he won't even respond to my hints or sexual advances toward him. He is, from what I've seen, the ultimate gentle-man. *Nah, he's gonna want this!*

One thing I've always been good at is setting a table really pretty. I brought out my china and crystal candleholders for this occasion. First, I had to do like my mother taught me to do. I sprayed some of that old Lemon Pledge on the table and rubbed it in until it got shiny and slippery. I hope he don't get too excited and throw me up on here 'cause we might slip and slide right off. I don't plan on slipping off of anything tonight!

I know I'm bad, but I think I've earned my right to be since it's been forever. I haven't had this kind of evening in my home in a long time. It was fun setting up everything, but leave it to me to try to do more than I should. I tried to bake some cookies, but I left them in the oven too long while I was in the bathroom doing my hair and putting on a little makeup. I've got the front door and a few windows open so I can air out this place before Sebastian arrives. I'm glad he made the decision to be *fashionably late*.

While I was in the bathroom, I heard a knock on my screen door. I knew it couldn't be him already so I took my time answering it. I wasn't about to find some unexpected visitor waiting for me at my door. Drama is not what I want to go through before my knight in sexy armor comes to screw my brains out. I can imagine hearing Nakia's voice right now talking about how crazy I am for saying that, but it's true and I don't believe in biting my words.

After a while, my curiosity got the best of me so I put on a robe and walked to the front door. I still had the door open so that my house could air out after burning those cookies earlier. When I peeked through the screen door I could see something that instantly made me smile. It was a beautiful bouquet of red roses and a card attached with my name on it. I opened the screen door immediately and grabbed the flowers. I almost ripped the card because I was so eager to read it.

Sebastian had really nice handwriting for a man. I was impressed by his creative and expressive touch. I couldn't believe he had done this for me. His card was very intriguing in that he spoke about *making tonight interesting before talking about tomorrow*. He wrote further, "I know you're gonna ask me what I mean by that. I'll tell you, eventually." He's right about that 'cause I don't do one-night stands, so he better not be thinking that's what he's getting.

The flowers looked really nice so I decided to put them in my crystal vase and use it as the centerpiece for this special dinner that I'd prepared with my own money. I'm good at making the food look like I prepared it. I already took all the restaurant food containers and threw them outside in the trash. I try never to leave evidence behind that shows I didn't go the extra mile to make a night special. Right now I'm just looking around, still standing in my robe and trying to see if I left anything out. Mr. Turner better get here soon 'cause it's already thirty minutes past the time he originally said he would be here. I get very anxious, especially when a man is as fine as he is.

One thing I need to do right now is put on this gown that's gonna inspire his dick to rise every time he looks at me. *I am so bold tonight!* Maybe I've been hanging out with Nakia too much, although she's changed and picked up some of my habits as well. Stuff like being respectful and being a lady. *I can be all that in the morning!* It's gonna be nice to have something naughty to tell her about when I see her so she can be jealous of me—for a change.

Well, more time went by as I slipped into my Victoria's Secret halter gown. It's black with thigh-high slits, and I know I'm looking good. My hair has always been easy to maintain since I keep it really short. Now the only thing that's missing is the man and if he continues to let more time pass by, he's gonna end up on my shit list, for real. He better not test my ability to forgive, especially when the men in my life lately have been one disappointment after the other. On occasion the sex has been good, don't get me wrong. But, I've been trying to listen to my sensitive side, and I know my life could be much fuller if I had a man of my own. I don't want to keep looking at Nakia's life, wishing I had what she has. That girl is younger than I am, she already got a daughter and who knows if she's gonna get back with Orlando or if she and Avonté might become an item. Either way, she's just reminding me how unfair life can be. I'm supposed to be the "Sistah" with everything going for her.

Well, another thing that I made sure to do was to find a radio station that played nothing but jazz. In my researching everything about Sebastian, I learned that he is a true jazz aficionado. His favorites are McCoy Tyner, Thelonious Monk and John Coltrane. Listening to this music by myself only makes me more nervous. Seems like this station prefers that really weird style of jazz. It sounds like the musicians are playing twenty different songs all at once. I'm trying to keep an open mind about everything, but when you're sitting here on the couch listening to music you don't understand while waiting for a man who is now forty-five minutes late and counting, it's enough to drive a woman to the edge.

I thought it was best not to light my candles 'cause by the time Sebastian gets here, they might burn all the way down. I guess I'm complaining way too much but I think I have a right to. Forget about Sebastian, I'm putting on my Gerald Levert CD and curling up on my couch. It's definitely a little chilly in here with me wearing this gown and still having the front door open. I'm too mad and lazy to get up and close the door. Besides, if I fall asleep on the couch, I don't have to worry because I got one of those security screen doors to keep the prowlers and men that don't know how to be on time out of my house!

Well, it's getting late, the food is cold and the television is watching me instead of me watching it. I look and feel like a complete fool sitting here with this gown, waiting on a man I thought was gonna rock my world tonight. I had to turn Gerald Levert off since there was no need in me having background music for lovemaking. Only sound I needed to hear was my head hitting the pillow so I could dream about the different ways I was gonna cuss Sebastian out. It seems like he would've called if he got lost. I should just stick to my decision to cuss him out rather than try to make sense out of being stood up. Unless his mother died, I ain't accepting any excuse for what he did or should I say, didn't do.

It's almost as if he knew how excited I was, got me all psyched up with the gorgeous flowers and decided he had something better to do at the last second. I called his cell phone, but there was no answer. I could leave a message, but I'd only say some things that I'd rather say in person. If and when I see that man I'm gonna give him more than a piece of my mind. He better not say the wrong things to me 'cause I might just try to kick his ass.

I'm getting angrier by the second and realizing that I didn't eat anything tonight. I'm so disappointed that I have no motivation to put food in my mouth. I wish I could sue him for wasting my time, but knowing me and the way I feel right now, I'd settle out of court if he just laid naked in my bed and let me have my way with him. My hormones are blinding me to the fact that Sebastian has truly done me wrong.

I hate going to bed angry. All I do is toss, turn, huff and puff for an hour before falling to sleep. I end up getting on my own damn nerves, 'cause that's the kind of attitude I have right now.

When I first laid down I reached over to get my little friend from on top of my nightstand. I've had many good nights using this thing, but tonight wasn't one of them. There's no motivation or desire to convince myself that plastic is better than the real thing. Sebastian had me so geared up for tonight that I almost want to make a booty call to Avonté and invite him over here. Then I would tell him, "Don't talk, just fuck and then leave."

I'm just beginning to hear what I just said, and the way I've been talking lately is really something else. I better make sure to go to church this Sunday. The worse thing about all this disappointment is that it falls so close to the holiday season. I really wanted to have someone to enjoy special times with. I don't want what I see in my living room right now to be a sign of what's to come for me—the gorgeous dinner table with candles, a crystal vase, beautiful flowers, expensive china, and some cold Thai food. If I ever get stood up again like tonight they might have to arrest me 'cause I know I'm gonna try to kill that man.

Well, just as I was finally drifting off to sleep I got a phone call. I had my eyes closed and found a warm comfortable spot in bed to spend the next few hours sleeping. I kept debating whether or not I wanted to answer the phone. I had a few more rings to go before my voicemail picked up. I made my decision and you'd think I weighed three-hundred pounds with all the noise I made trying to turn my body over so I could reach for the phone.

I answered, "Hello?"

"Ina, it's me."

"Me who?"

"Sebastian."

I had two reactions going through my mind at the same time, angry and livid. I guess they both cancelled each other out. Instead, all he could hear on my end was silence.

He asked, "You there?"

"Yes, I'm here."

"I apologize for not showing up when promised, but I had some other issues to deal with and I wasn't so sure you'd understand."

"But now you feel different?"

"What do you mean?"

"You're calling me now because you believe I'll understand?"

"Oh. Maybe I've finally got the courage to say what needs to be said."

"Sounds serious."

"Yes, well, as you know I think you're an incredible lady and I want so much to be with you, but along with that comes certain boundaries that must be discussed."

"Boundaries?"

"Yes."

"Do you have trouble with commitment, Sebastian?"

"No, it's nothing like that."

"Then?"

"Well, let me just say it. Ina, I'm married."

"You're married?"

"Yes, but before you say anything else, let me explain the situation."

"I wasn't gonna say anything, honey, I was gonna hang up on you!"

"No, just hear me out and see what I have to say. I can tell you're the type of lady that likes to know the full story, and that's what I'm about to give you."

"Uh-huh, I'm listening."

I just rolled my eyes, held the phone close to my ear and prepared myself for some long sad story that probably wasn't true. I never imagined Sebastian to be like all the men I've been running into lately. Uh-huh, full of shit.

"Go ahead, I'm waiting to hear what you have to say," I told him.

"Well, Ina, it's like this. Regina and I married for convenience, though I love her dearly."

"I'm not sure I understand that but okay, please continue."

"Well, we're great friends as well and we've reached an understanding that it's okay to satisfy our other needs elsewhere."

"And that's where I come in?"

"No, you're making this sound like I only want you sexually. It's more than that, Ina, but I just wanted you to know that I have limitations as to how deeply I can become involved with another woman."

"Have you two ever had sex?"

"Yes, but it just wasn't exciting. We learned quite early that our chemistry lies in our friendship as well as our business relationship."

I paused for a moment to collect my thoughts. I had been biting my tongue through most of his explanation, but my attitude was on the rise. I couldn't believe I was dealing with this from a man who I thought was gonna be my Johnny Rocket tonight and take me to a state of mental and sexual bliss. Just my luck, he ends up being married and now wants me to be his mistress, psychologist and freak, all rolled up into one package. Uh-huh, it was time to release some of this built-up attitude.

"Sebastian," I said calmly.

"Yes."

"You're trying to have me believe that because the sex wasn't good between you and your wife, she now allows you to go outside the marriage so you can get off?"

"Umm, I wouldn't put it that way, but yes, she does."

"And how often do you do this?"

"I don't keep count, Ina, like some playboy or traveling athlete out there on the road, going from city to city."

"Well, Sebastian, you do travel a lot and I could just end up being one of your West Coast hoes. Your motivation to even see me would be purely sexual."

"I don't see it that way, Ina. I find you fascinating, attractive, and just thought that maybe you would be open to this type of relationship that I'm offering you."

"Relationship?"

"Yes, and should you find someone, I'd understand and be willing to part ways, if necessary."

"Oh, and then you'd find someone else, right?"

"Well, I do have needs. I need a certain type of intimacy that I can't experience with my wife. I'm also a very competitive spirit and I need someone who can relax me when I crave that sort of release."

"Maybe you should consider masturbation and just work things out with your wife."

"My wife is fine with what I do."

"My goodness, Sebastian! Couldn't you have told me all this sooner?"

"No, because first I needed to see if you and I could truly relate. I'm not just after sex in the way that you seem to be thinking. To me, it's also a form of companionship, too."

"Oh, okay, well, this has been an interesting conversation but I'm not about to become involved with a married man. I've already slept with someone that I shouldn't have and that secret alone keeps me stressed and worried that I'll eventually be found out."

"You wanna talk about it?"

"Oh, no Sebastian, we've done all the talking I can handle tonight."

"How about you let me come in, Ina. I'm actually right outside in my car talking to you."

"What?"

"Take a look."

No sooner than he said that, I jumped out of bed and looked out my window. "Which car is it?" I asked him frantically.

"The dark green Jaguar. See me?"

"Yes, and I think you need to leave before I call the police on you."

"You're not serious are you, Ina?"

"Try me."

Just as I said that, Sebastian got out of his car and walked toward the middle of my driveway. He held the phone with his left hand and put his right arm out as if to show me what I was letting get away. He did look good, dressed in a black leather jacket over a light-colored turtle-neck and pants combination. That just made me hate him even more cause he was fine, and I had to kick his *married-sex-on-the-side-rich-ass* to the curb. I just closed my curtain, said goodbye and hung up the phone. Now I'm faced with the task of getting over my frustrations *and* trying to fall asleep. I better not see that man at work tomorrow, I can tell you that much.

TIME TO REGROUP

I can't believe how these people around the office been acting like they never had a damn Christmas party before. They're trying to come up with new ideas about how to celebrate. I still haven't heard anything original. Looks like they're gonna settle for a little office party slash potluck kind of thing. I'm sure it's been the same way in the past. They drew names out of a hat the other day to see who's gonna buy whom a gift. I don't really want to participate, but somebody chose my name so I have to play along with the childish game.

This is all stupid stuff to me. I ended up pulling out someone named Delores Edmonds. I have no clue who she is, so I'll probably just get her a gift certificate and a couple of lotto tickets. Shit, I don't have time for this. I'm just doing something that takes very little effort and very little thought.

I'm trying to rediscover my old self right about now, so it's not a priority for me to be sweet to strangers. Everybody been commenting on the fact that I'm a lot nicer these days, but that doesn't seem to be getting me anywhere. A few months ago I was constantly on the rise. Now all my promotions seem to be in a lateral direction. I'm getting tired of seeing all the same faces every day. Lord knows things get a little tense whenever I run into Ina. She's still acting strange behind us being together a while back. She knows she enjoyed all that wild sex we had. Plus, even though she pretends to be mad at me, I've noticed her watching me a few times when I've talked to Nakia. I can see something in Ina that others don't. I can tell she's jealous of Nakia, but she's real good at hiding it.

In the meantime it seems like the closer I get to Nakia, the more Ina starts to look at me differently. It's like she's thinking that I must not be half bad if Nakia enjoys my company. Ina even said hello to me yesterday in the hallway without being forced to speak. That gesture alone confirmed exactly what I'm saying about her phony ass.

Last week was one of those times when Ina had no choice but to talk to me. We were in a conference and it blew her mind to see me there. I guess she don't want to accept me being anywhere close to her level, but the sistah better be prepared for that time when I'm above her and making more money than she make. When we sat down at that round table, Ina looked at everyone but me. I was checking her out though. She looked really good in her light-brown jacket and short skirt. The combination was perfect against her light honey-brown complexion. She always did carry herself well even though she got so many hidden issues underneath.

I think that once a brotha is exposed to her, intimately speaking, he learns a lot of her secrets and then she becomes threatened by that knowledge. So, just like me, any brotha coming into her life is doomed to get kicked to the curb. I'm sure she'll say something different and talk about how ambitious I can be, which is true. Still, I think she and I could've worked out and probably helped each other to get further along in this company. There's plenty of room at Montaqua for us to accomplish a lot together. We could run this place!

Without a doubt, I'm trying to get back to my old self. It took me a couple of months to realize what was in my best interest, but I'm glad I finally came around. It's been really cool developing a friendship with Nakia because she doesn't hide her feelings or keep her nose stuck up in the air like she wants to avoid something—or someone. That's a personal trait that Ina demonstrates on the regular, especially where I'm concerned.

Nakia and I have had some really neat times recently. I've been trying to show her support as she gets over that dude, Orlando. He messed over her heart but at the same time I guess she's not about giving second chances to anybody. I'm lucky that she and I have become friends but that's probably because I've kept it strictly platonic, *like I really have a choice.* I check her out sometimes. It's no crime to appreciate a lady on a visual level just so long as I don't touch and get slapped for my efforts. Nah, Nakia is real cool.

I just love the way she changes her appearance so often. I don't know where she gets the energy or the courage to experiment the way she does. Right now she's sporting some shoulder-length, reddish-brown braids. A few weeks ago she had her hair in twists, and she was looking just as fine as any Ebony magazine model. I guess that's why I enjoy going to lunch with her so much 'cause I don't mind if the office gossip puts us together as a couple. I know she and I will never be a couple, but ain't nothing wrong with fantasizing a little bit.

Nakia is still hung up on Orlando and at the same time I think her old ex is pursuing her again. I ain't about to stand in line for a woman, waiting for my turn to hook up with her. I've got no time for that foolishness.

Lately I've been feeling extra pleased with myself because I finally got my own place. Yeah, a couple of weeks ago I moved into a one-bedroom apartment that I like to call "Avonté Manor." I've yet to christen the place, but I'm working on it. And when I say that, I'm talking about getting my freak on. I'm lining up potential ladies now as we speak, but I'm debating as to whether I want someone new or if I want to go with the old school, if you will.

I really think I could get with Ina if I push the right buttons and whisper what she wants to hear. That lady likes her sex with a little bit of danger attached to it. I can see right through her ass. That's probably a cruel thing to say, but that's the kind of level we at now. When I see her and she sees me, it's a struggle to speak. I'm waiting on her and she's waiting on me. If I even sound like I'm gonna say the wrong thing, she'd probably go off on me.

Well, today was a real cool day. I was working on this ad campaign for some kind of new mouthwash. They even gave me some samples of it, so I was sitting there tasting that stuff all day trying to come up with ideas for the media strategy. Every time I burp now, I can taste the spearmint flavor. I bet when I pee I'm gonna smell like air freshener. I'm keeping a couple of bottles for myself 'cause I'm about to discover what it feels like to be a true playa with his own space. No more creeping around to hotels or trying to get lucky by hooking up with a female that has her own apartment, condo or house. Now I can be the one to say "time for you to leave" and close the door behind them—instead of the opposite. What can I say? I'm just being honest and yeah, I've been thrown out a couple of times.

Right now I'm on my way to a nearby Bed and Bath store to pick up a few things. I'm trying to have my place looking really good. Nakia came over the other day and talked about my apartment because I have nothing in the living room but my television. We had to sit on the floor while we ate pizza and watched the videos that I'd rented. She tried to play it off but she enjoyed herself. I know I had a good time just talking to her and making her laugh. I have another television in the bedroom, but she gave me a mean look when I suggested going in there to watch a movie. It wasn't like I was trying to get her to watch my Millennium Shake-Off video or the "Wanda Does Er'body" tape that I picked up two weeks ago. I seriously thought she'd be more comfortable sitting on my bed, but I resolved to just be cool and not give any sort of hints that I might be attracted to her. That task was some hard shit to accomplish. Nakia had on some gray tights and a sweatshirt. Sometimes that sweatshirt didn't cover her ass when she would get up and go into the kitchen. Picture me watching her walk and saying to myself, "Oh, my God!"

Speaking of which, reminiscing about Nakia just now almost made me run a red light. I'm around the corner from this Bed and Bath store that I like to frequent since it's not too far from my apartment. I made a mental list of things I need to get, but I'm still gonna keep an eye out for something else interesting or unusual. I want to have plenty of conversational pieces around my place. You know, that kind of shit that makes a woman say, "That's cute. Where did you get that from?"

To me, enticing a woman does have an element of gamesmanship to it. If it didn't, then I could get away with having a dirty apartment and not care about my personal appearance. Nah, you got to play this game for real if you want to score and be in the championship or better yet, the Super Bowl. I'm trying to get there, and now it's definitely possible with my own place to wine and dine these Sistahs.

After pulling into the driveway and finding a parking space for my ride, I looked around for a shopping cart. I planned on buying quite a few items this time. I was about to make the balance on my credit card look scary! First thing I noticed when I walked into the store were these cool little botanical candles. *I'm about to scoop them up and get a few!*

I also noticed some silver-plated picture frames that were tight, but I don't have any pictures for those yet. Then I headed over to see about some sheets and other stuff to make the ladies want to just take off all their clothes and lay on my bed. For some reason I keep picturing Nakia's fine ass in those gray tights she was wearing. I mean, I could see the material adjust to every move she made. To say they were form-fitting is an understatement. She had me acting like Martin Lawrence in that movie, *Big Momma's House*, watching Nia Long in her lingerie, ooh wee!

"Can I help you, sir?" a saleslady asked, interrupting my thoughts.

"Yeah, umm, I need some help with picking out some bed sheets, pillows...the whole deal."

"Okay. Do you have any particular color in mind?"

I wasn't quite sure what I wanted, but I did see something nearby that caught my eye. I pointed to this mocha floral-and-diamond print set.

I told the lady, "Hmm, something like that."

"Okay. Do you want a sham, perhaps some decorative pillows, bed skirts?"

"Wow, all of that, huh?"

"Yes, it'll really enhance your bedroom, and I think you'd enjoy it, especially if you have female company."

Her last comment was like music to my ears. Maybe this lady could read my mind and figure out my motivation. That was almost too scary to know that my thoughts were that obvious, but maybe that was a good thing.

I ended up buying a comforter set as well as some Egyptian cotton towels for the bathroom and a couple of goose-down pillows for the bed. The lady at the cash register just enjoyed herself a little too much, ringing up everything that I'd bought. I didn't care because I needed all those things and I couldn't wait to get back to my apartment and put it all together.

I was thinking about inviting Nakia over this weekend since I'll have real furniture that she can sit on this time. But, if she can't make it then I just may give Ina a call. Either that or I'll head back over to Club Unrestricted and see if I can pick somebody up. Like it's that easy...

I feel a lot freer now with my own place. I don't have to hold back any more which means that by hook or crook, I'm gonna get me some this weekend. Another thing that made me smile was the cool thought of buying myself a Christmas tree. This holiday season is just gonna feel too good to be true. I can already visualize all those blinking lights and ornaments hanging everywhere. I'll have some Donny Hathaway and Temptations Christmas songs playing in the background. Turn on my fake fireplace. I'll have some wine and just chill with some lucky lady that doesn't mind getting naked on Christmas Eve. Oh, yeah, I'm looking forward to it all. I guess you could say that I'm throwing my own holiday party and inviting only one person. I'm not sure who that is yet, but we shall see.

Speaking of inviting somebody, a lot of folks around the office, including Nakia, keep asking me the same damn question.

"Whatever happened to that girl you used to talk to?"

I don't know why they try to play it off by pretending to forget Vanessa's name, but they always do. Then I hear the same tired ass response.

"Yeah, that's her name. Whatever happened to her?"

I haven't seen or talked to Vanessa since she announced to me that she no longer wished to date men. She had me wondering if I was to blame for her sudden change of stripes. That would've been a blow to my ego. She assured me that it was a desire that had been with her for many years now. I don't know if I believe her though. I'm thinking that she met someone recently who just said the right thing at the right time. Sometimes I get lucky that way, too. You know, say some shit that just touches the right nerve and turns a woman on. It's been a minute since that happened last, but as I said already, I'm gonna get me some this weekend. Fuck that!

When I got home, I saw my answering machine light flashing which means that somebody been trying to call me. Little things like that always excite me, especially when I'm in the state of mind that I am now. They say that life is what you make it, and the possibilities are endless so, umm, if I can just touch some booty this weekend, I'll be satisfied and good to go.

I'm in love with my one-bedroom apartment. I know that once I add all the extra touches, I'm gonna be the man when it comes to impressing any female company that walks through my door. They gonna be all up on me after they step inside and notice the artistic touches here and there or the subtle romantic feel of my bedroom. But, first things first...I have to go get the stuff that I brought out of the car and also see what I'm gonna eat tonight. Last night I had some crispy fish fillets that were the bomb. Tonight I might throw together a little macaroni and cheese with some baked chicken. Don't get it twisted, I'm no Emeril Lagasse, but I can microwave the hell out of some dinner combinations. Only the educated or picky eater would know the difference.

Well, time flies when you trying to figure out how to put a bed skirt on properly. I've been having the toughest time for the past hour, but it finally looks pretty good. I'm thinking about sleeping in the living room until I have company over. I don't want to mess up the bed and then have to start all over again. Look at me. I'm just having a little too much fun all by myself. I don't see why I need to put so much thought and effort into something as simple as making my bed up. Scratch that. I almost forgot my motivation so I must need to stop for a moment before I lose my mind completely. It's time to check my voicemail messages anyway.

"Hey, Avonté, this is Nakia. I just called to see what you're doing."

I saved that message because umm, well, it's from Nakia.

"Avonté, can you call me? I want to get a man's opinion on something that my girlfriend said to me. Oh, this is Vanessa, by the way."

Picture me with a not-interested smirk on my face as I listened to my voicemail options.

"If you'd like to save this message, please press 'two.' If you wish to delete this message, please press 'three.'"

I wasted no time in selecting my option.

"Thank you. Your message was deleted."

Well, after preparing my food, I decided to return Nakia's call. I don't think she'd mind if I chew in her ear. I like to think that our friendship has progressed to a level of comfort where we can pretty much do or say anything around each other. I still don't have a couch yet so I'm gonna have to sit on my freshly cleaned beige carpet. Sitting on the floor is pretty comfortable, in my opinion. I don't know what Nakia was complaining about that time she came over. Maybe her ass is just too soft. *I wish I could see for myself just how soft it is, though, damn!*

I dialed her phone number. It took about four rings before her voice-mail picked up. That instantly frustrated the hell out of me. See, Nakia has only given me her cellular phone number and that makes me feel like she don't trust this friendship completely. I want her "real" home phone number. I guess I shouldn't complain. I should be grateful that she gave me this number.

I spoke after the beep. "Nakia, where you at? See, that's why I need your home number so I don't have to be calling your cell phone and leaving messages!"

It's hard to keep my frustrations to myself sometimes.

Twenty minutes later, after finishing up my dinner and washing it down with a tall glass of Welch's grape soda, my phone started ringing.

"What you doing?" a voice asked before I could finish saying hello.

"I'm eating and watching TV. Who's this?"

"Nakia. Why you leave that crazy message on my voicemail?"

"What crazy message?"

"The one with you complaining like you lost your mind!"

"Oh, that message."

"Uh-huh. Anyway, you busy?"

"Nah, I'm not busy."

"Orlando called me tonight."

"Oh."

"Don't sound so enthusiastic..."

"I didn't think I did."

"I'm just teasing you. I can call back later if you're busy."

"I'm not busy, Nakia. What's up?"

"I think I still like him, but I just don't trust him, you know?"

"You still like who?"

"Orlando!"

"Oh, well, did you talk to him about it?"

"Yeah, we talked a little bit. Actually we talked a lot and I just wish that man didn't sound so good to me."

"Sounds like he pulled your strings, Nakia."

"What do you mean by that?"

"You sound like you got turned on by dude."

"Do I?"

"Yeah, you do."

Nakia was quiet for a moment, thinking about what I'd just said. To be honest, I didn't like hearing that she was still interested in Orlando, but I had to keep my thoughts to myself. I didn't want to chance ruining this brand-new friendship we got going. Besides, this seemed like my best shot at really discovering all that Nakia is. I mean, I could sit back, listen and learn about all her likes and dislikes. I'm hoping we can get to a point where she gives me details about her sexual experiences, too. I'll definitely hook her up by telling her about mine. I'm thinking that whatever I say to her might inspire her to wonder what it would be like to sexually indulge with me. I'm sure I'll embellish a few things, but that's a brotha's prerogative anyway. Hmm...Do I think that she'd actually tell me about her sexual experiences? Nope, but I can try.

"Hey, what you thinking about?" Nakia asked.

"Nothing, just listening to you..."

"I wasn't saying anything."

"Well, then I was listening to you think because I know you got stuff on your mind."

"Yes, I do."

"Maybe you should come over and hang out with me."

"You not trying to pull something, are you, Avonté?"

"Nah, I learned my lesson a long time ago. Plus, we've become buddies now or so I'd like to think."

"That's sweet of you to say."

"You gonna come over then?"

"Nope and you know why?"

"'Cause you think I'm gonna try something. I keep telling you..."

"No, Avonté, it's not that. I just know that you and I both have to get up early and go to work tomorrow."

"Oh, yeah."

"Uh-huh, remember we do have jobs?"

"Yeah, that's right, huh?"

"You're silly. Don't be trying to play like you ain't job-conscious 'cause I know you are!"

"What you talkin' 'bout, Nakia?"

"You still the same go-getter as before. I've been watching your latest moves. You lucky we friends or I'd be talkin' bad about you."

"Yeah, I'm still ambitious."

"Well, just be careful whose toes you step on. I'm glad you not interested in my job."

"Nah, I'm cool. I probably just suffer from not being patient because I want to do things like yesterday."

"Yes, you definitely lack patience. Well, I need to get my butt to bed, Avonté. You have a good night and I'll see you tomorrow."

"Okay, Nakia, goodnight."

As the dial tone followed Nakia's sexy ass voice, I just sat there smiling and looking down at my empty plate. I wish I had had her as my entree instead of that macaroni and cheese I just ate. I know she got to be quite tasty and hotter than the cheese that was dripping down my chin moments before she called. That lady has starred in a lot of my most delicious daydreams. It ain't hard to think about her, especially during those times when she and I get together for coffee or a movie. I guess you can say I like Nakia. I wish we could be more than friends, but I'm cool with my status just as long as I get to continue seeing her.

She promised to go with me next weekend to pick out a Christmas tree, so I'm putting that on my calendar as another opportunity to build on what we have. I'm keeping any and all personal agendas on the "down-low" so I won't blow it with her. Nakia got some serious radar attached to her heart. She can recognize game because she's seen it coming from playas as well as the intellectual types. I think I'm somewhere in between.

Getting up for work was no easy task for me. I slept on the floor in my living room. Actually, I was only kidding about not sleeping in my bed until I had company over, but it just so happens that I fell asleep while watching *Comic View* on BET. Rickey Smiley always makes me laugh but no matter how they package the show, it still looks like a freakin' repeat to me. I was trying to stay up so I could watch those uncut music videos they show late at night. It all worked out for the best since I didn't need to be staying up that late anyway.

Now here I am walking through the door, extra early for work. I don't have anything urgent today on my agenda, so this is gonna be one of those kick-back Tuesdays. Maybe it's really just the quiet before the storm because I have noticed the level of stress increase. I don't care because I plan on grabbing some of the money that comes along with the increase in stress. I got a few years to go before my hair starts to turn gray anyway. Plus, it's not like I'm some young ballplayer a few years removed from high school with the two bad ankles, walking like a senior citizen already. I got time to endure some of the pressures and stress of work related deadlines and office gossip. I'm gonna do just fine on my career path.

One of my first stops before heading to my office was to see if Nakia made it in yet. Looks like I got here before her today. I was hoping to catch a glimpse of her smile this morning since my voice was probably the last thing she'd heard before falling asleep last night. After I walked past her office, I noticed in the not too far distance, Ina's office door slightly open and the light on. I wasn't sure if I should take my chances on peeking in to say "good morning" to her. Ina got that Jekyll and Hyde personality where you never know how she's gonna act from day-to-day. I can't stand women like that, but I do give Ina the benefit of the doubt because she works so hard. I may change my mind if she keeps treating me as though I have some powerful bad breath or body odor. Lately she'll change directions in the hallway if she sees me coming toward her. That kind of behavior stands out big time. I could hear the *tsk-tsks* coming from folks that couldn't mind their own business.

As I got closer to her office, I noticed her door moving slightly. Someone's hand was on it, rocking the door back and forth. It was a woman's hand, which instantly made me assume that perhaps Nakia was in there talking to Ina. I began to hear the voices from inside the office, and neither one of them sounded like Nakia. However, I did recognize Ina's voice, but the other one remained a mystery to me. Once again I took a quick glimpse at the hand holding the door, but before I could lean my head closer to listen, the person peeked her head out. Maybe she could hear my footsteps approaching.

"Hello," I said quickly, followed by a smile.

"Hi," she responded before returning her attention back inside the office.

Damn, she's one fine sista. I found myself at a loss for words, but that didn't stop me from approaching Ina's office. I wanted to get a closer look at this never-seen-before talent. I was thinking, *Where the hell have I been recently to not see this lovely lady before?*

As I stepped carefully inside of Ina's office, I could see that she wasn't extremely thrilled to see me. No surprise there, actually.

"Good morning, Avonté. What brings you here?" Ina asked, only slightly appearing to be interested in my response.

The lady near the door looked at me with a half-smile.

"I just stepped in to say hello. It's not often that I get to work this early. Plus, I saw your door open so I thought I'd say good morning," I replied.

"That was nice of you, Avonté. Have you met Delores?"

"No, I haven't. Nice to meet you."

"Nice to meet you, too. I've seen you around the office before, but you didn't notice me," Delores said.

I just paused for a moment as I collected my thoughts. I feared if I spoke, she'd probably hear me stuttering. I knew Ina would've loved to watch me make a fool of myself in front of this beautiful young lady.

"You know, I have a confession to make, but I fear that I might be breaking some office rules here," I told them.

"What office rules?" Ina asked while sitting behind her desk like a Supreme Court judge.

"Well, I've always wondered who Delores was because I pulled that name in the drawing for Christmas gifts. Your last name is Edmonds, isn't it?"

"Yes, it is..."

Seems like Delores could pick up on the slight tension that existed between Ina and me, but she remained very friendly and cordial toward me. I was rethinking my decision to buy her a gift certificate and some lottery tickets. Delores was way too fine to be getting her something so simple. With her long silky black hair, Asian eyes, and beautiful brown skin, I needed for my imagination to kick in because she had me standing there with a platinum smile. I could tell that Ina wasn't too thrilled with that either. No, I needed to find something really nice for Delores and who knows, maybe she'd accept an invitation to come over for dinner one day.

Delores started rubbing her hands together and took a deep breath. "Well, I better leave you two alone and try to get some work done today," she said.

Ina smiled in Delores's direction. "Okay, Girl, we'll talk later."

I stood for a moment waiting for Delores to say something or perhaps wish me a good day, but it didn't happen. She just turned to look at me briefly before saying "bye."

"Take care," I responded.

I closed the door after Delores walked out and then I turned to look at Judge Ina, sitting behind her desk with a blank expression on her face.

"Damn, how long she been working here?" I asked.

"Delores?"

"Yeah!"

"Oh, please Avonté, if you want to know then you go ask her yourself..."

"What's wrong with you, Ina?"

"Nothing at all."

"Something must be wrong since you acting so cold toward me."

"Avonté, this is neither the time nor place to have what is beginning to sound like a lover's quarrel."

"I wouldn't call it that."

"What would you call it?"

"I'm trying to find out because I'm not the one with the problem."

"Why did you step inside my office anyway, Avonté? I was talking to somebody and you pretty much just interrupted the conversation. I could've been having a meeting with Delores, but you don't seem to care. You just barge in because everything has to always be about you."

"You finished, Ina?"

"I have a lot to say, but this ain't the time nor place as I've already said."

"Yes, you did say that, Ina, but I'm trying to figure out why we have to have all this animosity between us."

"You figure it out, Avonté. Just think back to how things transpired between us. You seem to have a very short memory when you do people wrong."

"Wrong?"

Ina glared at me as she sat back in her chair getting agitated.

"Wrong, Ina?"

"I really don't need this right now, Avonté."

"Seems like we need to clear the air, and this could be the perfect opportunity, Ina. Whatever you need to say to me, you should just get it off your chest."

"There's really not much to say to you, Avonté. We had our little fling; you got what you wanted…"

"Oh, so now you're the innocent one trying to act like you haven't done some sneaky shit yourself, huh?"

"I think you should leave, Avonté, before this gets really ugly. I'm not playing with you."

"I will, but be careful of who you accuse of doing things to get what they want. Try to remember some of the things you done, even behind your best friend's back."

"You can leave now," Ina insisted.

"Thanks, I will…I will…"

After I walked out of Ina's office, I left the door open. Moments later, I heard it slammed shut behind me, and a few people nearby turned around suddenly. I'm pretty sure they wondered what that commotion was all about. The embarrassed look on my face instantly allowed others to put two and two together. They could tell that I was the inspiration for that door being slammed so hard. I could already see myself being on the front page of the office gossip when it circulated today.

One thing good about all the promotions that I've received lately is that just like Ina, I have my own office door to close behind me. I didn't slam mine shut, but it's a big relief to have a place to go to so I can get over my momentary embarrassment. I wasn't gonna stress about it for too long though. One thought about that fine ass Delores instantly brought me back to my own reality. Or perhaps I'm fantasizing since I don't know the lady yet. I intend to change that real soon. I could see that she liked me, but she had to keep it on the DL, what with Ina and all her attitude so close by.

Before I settled into some work, I wanted to see if I could possibly find an email address for Delores. Maybe if I say hello to her this way, she'll respond and be interested in getting together later. I'm not gonna even beat around the bush about how fine I think she is. I'd even consider canceling any weekend plans I had with Nakia to hook up with Delores. That alone says a lot for me because Nakia is real cool to hang out with. I'd just like to have some sex before this month is over, and I know Nakia ain't even thinking about me in that way.

With just a few clicks of the mouse and typing in "Delores Edmonds," I found what I was looking for, her email address. I clicked on the email icon and found myself excited, yet once again at a loss for words. I've got to stop freezing up when I'm about to make my moves on a lady. I must be losing my touch and still experiencing the effects of my recent nice-guy transformation. Well, for my first email to Delores, I decided to write something simple.

Hey, Delores,

Forgive me for this personal email but I really enjoyed meeting you. I'm hoping that we can talk really soon and get to know each other. I don't usually approach women in this manner, but they say nothing comes to those who never try so here I am, giving it a try.

Avonté Douglas

It took me two more minutes to click on the send button. I guess I'm worried about what Ina may have said to her. I wouldn't put it past Ina to try to get all these people to turn against me, especially someone that I'm potentially interested in.

No sooner than I mentioned trouble, my recent favorite lady came walking through my door, without knocking, I might add.

"Avonté, I haven't even been able to sit down yet ,and I'm already hearing about you!" Nakia said.

"What you hear about me?"

"I heard that Ina slammed the door in your face. What was that all about?"

"Nah, she didn't slam it in my face. I was already out of her office by the time she made all that racket."

"But you were in there, and you two had an argument or something?"

"We had some heated words, but mostly I was just trying to clear the air so we could reach some kind of common ground."

"Yeah, right…"

"It's true, Nakia. Ina is still angry with me about whatever, you know how it is."

"Maybe you should just keep your distance from her."

"Yeah, I probably will from now on."

"Why did you even go in there?"

"I thought we were still cool enough to say good morning to each other, and then I'll admit that once I saw Delores standing in there, I got a little too happy."

"Delores?"

"Yeah, you know her?"

"A little bit. She's nice."

"She's more than nice!"

"Yeah, whatever…"

"You jealous?"

Nakia laughed. "Of what?"

"Nothing, just teasing…"

"Uh-huh, you interested in Delores now?"

"To be honest, hell, yes..."

"Then ask her out, silly!"

"I sent her an email just now."

"An email. What are you, shy now?"

"No, Nakia." I chuckled slightly. "I just want to take a different approach. I don't want to go over there, start flirting and add more to all the gossip already being spread."

"Yeah, they definitely talking about you today, boy."

"Yeah, this office is a trip the way shit be getting spread all over the place. I'm surprised you don't mind when they talk about us."

"They not talking about us, and if they are, let me find out who it is, so I can nip that in the bud, immediately."

"It's funny how you move your head around when your attitude is on the rise. You still got a little hood left in you, huh, Nakia?"

"Yeah, whatever!"

Nakia was smiling but she couldn't deny her personality traits. Her being so real and sincere is what I've always found so attractive. She's the type of woman that you can have conversations with for hours and never get bored. You just want to sit back and listen until it's your turn to say something that hopefully sparks her interest to keep on talking.

"Well, I need to go, Avonté. I was just checking on you. We still going to lunch or are you trying to hook up with your latest pursuit?"

"That's funny but yes, we definitely still on for lunch."

"Okay, see you then."

"Okay."

As Nakia walked out of my office, my attention was captured by her bottom half. That was quickly followed by a smile, my own smile, of course. Nakia got the right amount of thickness on her. If I had my choice I might be feeding her some soul food so she can gain even more weight down there. She had my imagination jumping off the meter. I wonder if I'll ever get to enjoy a passionate moment with her. Right now, I'd give anything just to see her without any clothes on. *Let me stop!*

It was time to do some work. I needed to make a few phone calls back East to one of our affiliated offices. I love talking to folks with different accents and opinions. I hope to make a trip out that way soon and talk to this secretary named Valerie Willis. She's usually the one that answers whenever I call. That lady makes me swivel around in my chair, forgetting that my call is about business. That's usually a highlight for me whenever I get a chance to talk with her.

As I was dialing the number back East, I noticed that I had an email response from Delores. Immediately, I put the phone down and opened up the email. As one might notice, I have my priorities in order. If I didn't have my own office, I wouldn't be able to get away with half the shit I do on company time. *I guess I got it like that!*

Delores didn't waste time getting to the point in her email. She didn't even have to worry about any typos 'cause she was very brief, which is a good thing I suppose.

"Let's get together after work," she wrote in her response.

Damn! I thought to myself. I couldn't believe hooking up with her could be that easy. Maybe I needed to start going online and be some kind of Cyberspace Romeo. That might just turn up the heat on my sex life, but first things first.

"Cool, I get off at 2:30 today since I came to work early. Is that good for you? I can wait, if necessary," I wrote back to Delores and then took care of my phone calls.

This day was turning out to be pretty cool. I made my phone calls back East, Delores agreed to hooking up after work, and I was about ten minutes away from having lunch with Nakia. I kept my door open as I sat behind my desk. I gazed out into the area with all the cubicles and folks walking by. Delores passed by a couple of times, acting nonchalant and trying to play off the obvious looks of admiration that I gave her. She had on one of those animal-print dresses underneath a black coat, which seemed to be bringing something out in her today.

She walks with a quiet confidence and a shy sensuality. When she smiles, her Asian eyes close slightly. She loves to run her fingers through her long black silky hair, I can tell. I hope she'll let me run my fingers through her hair. I can already envision myself doing a lot of things to her with my fingers.

Well, seconds were ticking by and I knew that at any moment now, Nakia would be telling me she's ready to go. She's never late for lunch, especially when I'm buying. This has become a ritual recently that is cutting into my expense account in a big way. I think she should start paying for a good portion of the lunches we have, but she's pretty good at manipulating the situation in her favor. Whenever we both take that last bite of food, I sit back to look at the expression on her face. That's usually when she smiles and asks me in a seductive tone, "So, how did you like your food?" That shit works all the time, too, because soon after, the waiter approaches and there I go, reaching for my wallet.

"I'm ready to go!" Nakia announced, interrupting my thoughts.

"Uh-huh..."

"Okay, why you got an attitude now, Avonté?"

"No reason, let's go."

I'm thinking, *I need to put myself on a no money diet!*

As we walked out of my office, Nakia continued to question me. She almost bumped into a few people because she had her attention so fixed on me.

"You better watch where you going."

"And you better tell me what's wrong. Avonté..."

"Nothing is wrong. Come on, here's the elevator."

We stepped inside. Nakia kept looking at me and trying to detect what I was thinking. I was secretly enjoying her frustrated attempts to read my mind. She leaned against the wall and folded her arms.

"I'm not gonna rest until you tell me what's wrong with you."

"Nakia..."

"Don't 'Nakia' me 'cause I know you, Avonté. I know when something is on your mind."

The elevator doors opened on the street level and we got out. Nakia was very convincing in her efforts to explain how much she knew me. She read me the "Riot Act" all the way down the street as we walked to the Bistro Café on the corner. It was only a block away from the office, which was a good thing, considering the whole point of the one-sided discussion was lost completely.

"Nakia, listen," I said before opening the door for her to go inside the café. "I was only thinking about how I always seem to pay for lunch, and you walked in when I was reminiscing about some of our lunch dates. Nothing's wrong, trust me."

Nakia paused for a moment. "You sure nothing's wrong?"

"Nothing at all."

"You want me to pay for lunch today?"

"It's nice of you to offer, but I can already see that you forgot your purse, and that dress you wearing doesn't have pockets."

"We can go back, if you want?"

"No, Nakia, it's cool. I'll pay for lunch—again."

"You're so sweet."

"Uh-huh."

Once lunch was over and I returned to the office, I had to make a mental note. *Make sure to stop by the ATM machine.*

I love hanging with Nakia but that eight-point-whatever percent sales tax just eats up all my spare change. I felt like asking that homeless person on the corner if he could pay me back the money I gave him last week and the week before that. I'm making decent money now, but my expenses have increased with the apartment and trying to wine and dine. Oh, well, despite all my complaints about financial issues, I'm enjoying every chance I get to spend with Nakia, and my days ahead of me as a single man look mighty bright, *thank you very much!*

Another thing that keeps me smiling is the fact that after lunch is over, the rest of the day just flies by. I know it seems like I just sit around on my hands waiting for my next opportunity to see Nakia, flirt with Delores and fuck with Ina, but I do manage to take care of my responsibilities at this agency. I've scored a little longevity by bringing in a new client with no help from management. Other agencies were trying to grab this client but I'm the one who came through. The client is a brand-new magazine called Essential. I showed them that we mirrored exactly what they wished to portray to their readers, so it was just a matter of reeling them in—slowly. I even convinced Sharon McNair, our VP who supervised Ina and me, to let me borrow her Mercedes S500. She has a silver one with chrome wheels parked near the elevator in the garage below. I like to walk by and look at it every time I come to work.

I got to get one of my own someday! That's what I usually say to myself as I salivate and dream about owning that car.

I felt on top of the world when she allowed me to borrow it. I let her know that by me driving her car to meet the executives over at Essential would pretty much guarantee them as our client. She bought that reasoning—hook, line and sinker—but the cool thing was that my strategy actually worked. There I was pulling up in the driveway of some remodeled office building with none other than Nakia by my side just excited as I was. She looked so beautiful yet professional, dressed in a yellow business suit with a short skirt. I was in black with a gray shirt and platinum tie.

"You don't have nothing else you could wear?" Nakia joked, although she had me worried for a second.

"You don't think this is cool?" I asked her, almost in a state of panic.

I'd forced my own hand with all the promises made about bringing in this client. Then I noticed Nakia laughing as we approached the front door to the office building.

"Oh, wait, you just messing with me, huh?" I asked her.

"Yep..."

"Probably 'cause you like what you see."

"Whatever, Avonté..."

We strutted out of that office an hour later with the contract in hand and a reason to celebrate. Nakia and I took an hour to get back to work even though it was really only a thirty-minute drive between the offices of Essential magazine and Montaqua Publications. I wasn't prepared to part with the keys to Ms. McNair's Mercedes so quickly. Nakia enjoyed that little outing, too. She'd be lying if she said anything different.

All this reminiscing has killed enough time for me to start thinking about Delores. Keeping up with all my intentions from one woman to the next is gonna take some serious mental gymnastics. I guess that as long as I don't make any promises I can't keep, I'll be okay. I got an hour to spare and the only place I can think about taking her right now is Popeye's chicken. Maybe I'll hook her up with one of those popcorn shrimp baskets. If she loves it, then she's sincere and if not then I don't need to be bothered.

Well, moments ago I just got the best news that any man waiting on a lady could hear. Delores called me on the phone. She was sitting at her desk and tried to keep our conversation hush-hush. I asked her why she was speaking so softly and she responded in a very sexy tone, "You know why."

"No, I don't," I said, trying to play the naïve role.

"I think you do know Avonté but let me just get to why I called."

"Okay."

"I know we're supposed to go somewhere after work, but I'm thinking it would be better if I just go home, change into something casual and then come over to your place."

"Damn, okay."

"What's wrong?"

"Nothing, just surprised but I do like your plan."

"Oh, you do, huh?"

"Yes, can you see me smiling?"

Delores turned her chair around and looked in the direction of my office. "Yeah, you're silly, Avonté. You gonna get me in trouble."

"I think it's the other way around, Delores. You gonna get me in trouble because I'm always leaving my door open just so I can check you out."

"I imagine you check every lady out, Avonté."

She had me tongue-tied for a moment, so I had to change the subject slightly. Truth be known, I do check out every lady that passes by.

"What time you coming over?" I asked.

"How's seven-thirty sound?"

"Sounds good to me."

"Okay, then I'll see you tonight."

"Looking forward to it."

"Hmm, me too Avonté."

While driving home from work I saw a bunch of images that reminded me of the time of year. I need to get my shit in gear and figure out what I'm gonna get Delores for Christmas. I asked Nakia earlier if she had any suggestions, and she just looked at me strange before uttering some craziness.

"Oh, please! I'm not about to help you with something you can use to get between that girl's legs," she told me.

"It's not about that! You know I pulled her name so I have to get her something."

"Yeah, but you didn't care before, Avonté, so why start now?"

I responded with a shrug as I brushed off Nakia's comments.

She hates it when I wave my hand at her like she doesn't know what she's saying. Then again, I hate when she's able to read me so easily, but I guess anybody with 20/20 eyesight can figure out what I'm up to.

Now that I got my own place, I'm trying to put in some serious effort to entice and motivate any ladies that I'm interested in. Lord knows how patient I've been with Nakia, but right now she don't really count since we just friends. Well, she does count, but since I can only look and not touch, my pleasures don't need much effort where she's concerned.

Now Ms. Delores, on the other hand, I have a feeling she might be high maintenance. That long gorgeous shiny black hair got to cost a pretty penny just to maintain, let alone the rest of her beautiful body. Yeah, I've got to put in some overtime here and actually care about what I'm gonna get this woman. My decision may make or break my potential in her life. Meaning that if I get her something good, then she gonna give me what I want. Is it a secret what I really want? *I don't think so!*

What a game we weave around ourselves. Speaking for the Gents and the Brothas, I know we spend way too much time trying to get a woman in bed. Hell, we don't even care if we get them in bed just as long as we get to see them naked and know that we had some kind of sex with them. I can't speak for the Playas yet, but if I keep at it, maybe one day I'll be able to. Not that it's a goal of mine to be a Playa, but I would love to experience that feeling at least once. I guess if I ever get with Nakia, then that might elevate my status because she ain't an easy catch for any man.

That dude Orlando had it good but he messed up. Right now, he's trying to fix his mistake by sweet-talking her every other night. Nakia told me he's been calling her a lot and my usual response is "Why?" My question is only motivated by jealousy, though. Yeah, I'm guilty of that shit.

I'm not the only one who's jealous around here. I noticed recently Ms. Ina lurking around corners looking and lingering at any male/female combination in her sight. I don't know what's going through her mind these days since we don't talk, but I do recognize a little bitterness in her. She's kind of quiet. I'm sure she talks to Nakia about things. I often wonder if they talk about me. Nakia won't tell me. I've tried sneaking that question in practically every conversation we've had, especially when we talk about work. I always end up with the same response, reminiscent of a huge red stop sign.

"Don't start!" she'd tell me.

"Aight..."

Nakia loves to burst my bubble whenever I see some signs of hope going on. She's a beautiful friend to have and despite my sarcasm for the moment, I actually mean that. I figured out a way to touch her heart this holiday season. I know I'm probably wrong for trying to manipulate things in my direction but that's a part of my competitive nature. I figure shit out in both my personal as well as my professional life to get what I want and desire. I'd like to hook up with Nakia as more than just friends, and I figure I can accomplish this by doing something nice for her daughter as well as her little cousin that she told me about recently. That little man doesn't have a father figure in his life, so I might take him to the park or something.

Then for her daughter I can buy her a doll for Christmas. I better do some overtime so I can afford all these gifts I'm buying this year. First and foremost comes my mother, of course. Yeah, I'm still a good son.

Now that my plans are in motion with respect to Nakia, I can return to concentrating on Delores. I'll be honest and say that my intentions with her are pretty selfish. I'd like some sort of no strings attached situation, and I'm hoping the girl is advanced enough to deal with that. I don't want to hear no "you-got-some-nerve" drama going down after I've been honest enough to express what I want from her. She can either take it or leave it. I ain't gonna lie, I'm probably gonna kick my own ass if she says "no" to my so-called honest approach. I've had female friends in the past advise me to be open and honest about what I want from a woman. Well, that's what I'm doing, and we shall see where it gets me.

Excitement and disappointment seem to go hand in hand for me these days. I have expectations of promptness when a woman makes a date. She'll never find me showing up late unless something major happens or I got a better offer. Right now I'm sitting in my living room waiting on Delores to show up. Maybe the girl got cold feet or couldn't figure out the directions to my apartment. I wrote it out pretty clearly and I used a black felt-tip marker so there's no excuse for her not to be able to read the shit. *Listen to me, just going on and on.* Sometimes I wonder if my complaints are legitimate or if I'm just one frustrated individual... If I had an alter ego sitting on my shoulder, he'd probably be whispering to me, "Issues, my brother. You got issues." I must be losing it, with all these thoughts running through my mind.

Ah, well, if Delores ain't gonna show up, then let me see who else I can call. *Who am I fooling?!* My black book is tiny because I only have about four phone numbers in it. The number that I dial the most these days belongs to Nakia, although you could probably say she's a close second to my mother. I don't dare call Ina so I'm just gonna have to recognize the power of prayer and wishful thinking as I sit back on my *new couch* and surf through all the cable channels, waiting on Delores.

My newfound independence is not working out like I imagined it would. I thought I'd have so much sex by now that I'd be leaning toward celibacy by choice. I'm getting pretty good at keeping my one-bedroom apartment clean and odor-free. I was hoping to impress Delores tonight with the tropical aroma floating around. Plus, my selection of soul classics and current slow jams is bound to inspire her panties to drop. When I got paid last Thursday, I bought a couple of greatest hits packages by the Ohio Players and the Dramatics. I've been grooving to them all week. Now I see why my mother always smiles when she hears them old songs. I guess the drawback of being so young is that I'm not very aware of the music from the seventies. My mother laughed when I tried to convince her how great K-Ci and JoJo are.

"They really are great singers!" I told her.

She just laughed.

"Hey, we should be allowed some musical memories, too, you know!"

My arguments usually fell on deaf ears, where my mother was concerned.

An encouraging sound just interrupted the thoughts I was having about my mother and our old-school music debates. I had begun to wonder if my phone would ever ring tonight.

"Hello," I answered.

"I had such a time trying to find your place!"

"Delores?"

"Yes, you forgot about me already?"

"No, I thought you weren't coming over."

"You don't have much patience, Avonté."

"True, I'm guilty of that. Where are you now?"

"Outside waiting for you to buzz me in."

"Oh, why didn't you say so!"

"I just did."

"Okay, I'm gonna buzz you in. Just come up to the second level, make a right and walk around the corridor. I'll meet you halfway."

"You better 'cause I'm not about to get lost again tonight."

"You're funny, Delores. Hold on."

I proceeded to buzz Delores into the building. I gave her a couple of seconds before I walked out into the corridor to see if she was coming around the corner. I could hear her footsteps in the distance.

"Delores?" I yelled out.

"Avonté, where are you?"

"Over this way..."

The recognition that comes along with a smile does something to me, especially when that expression comes from a woman. Delores gave me one of those look-at-that-brotha smiles and walked a little faster so that she could greet me with a special hug.

"Hey," she said softly in my ear.

"I'm glad you're here.".

"Thank you. So, you're not mad that I'm an hour late?"

"Nah, it's cool."

"You sure? 'Cause I can leave if you don't want me to come in!"

Delores turned slightly to the side, and I couldn't help but notice the shape of her booty. I'm pretty sure she did that on purpose. Teasing me with what I'd be missing if I allowed her to leave.

"Wouldn't make sense for you to leave now, Delores."

"You're very sweet, Avonté."

"I hope you'll say the same thing later."

Delores had me in the palm of her hand, and she knew it. There I stood in the corridor, in front of my door, just nibbling on every little bit of flirtatious innuendo that she set up for me. I stepped to the side and gestured for her to walk inside my apartment. I smiled with delight as I admired her body from her head to her feet. Delores had on some tight black leggings and a big denim shirt, which seemed to move out of the way whenever she wished to show me what she was working with. I don't think this is a new experience for her, showing up at a man's place with something sexy on her mind. I wasn't mad at her though. I looked forward to exploring her mind as well as other places down south, so to speak.

As Delores walked inside my living room, I got a sense that she was pleasantly surprised. She nodded her head in approval of my clean and odor free bachelor pad.

"I love that scent you have in here! Is that coming from those candles?" she asked.

"Yeah, it's sort of a tropical scent. I'm really into aromatherapy these days, and I also like to use those body lotions and bath oils."

"I'm impressed!"

"Yeah, I love it when I get that smell floating through the air after I've taken a shower. That's why I always leave the bathroom door open when I'm in there."

"I hope you don't leave it open all the time!"

"Oh, you got jokes, huh?"

"Nice to see a man with a sense of humor…"

"Well, it's a treat for me to have a conversation with a lovely woman in my living room. Excuse me for not having asked you to sit down."

"I did wonder if we were gonna just stand here and talk all night."

"I know, huh? Sorry about that Delores."

"That's okay. May I?"

"Please. Would you like something to drink?"

"What do you have?"

"Hmm, I have some Chardonnay, some Kool-Aid, half a bottle of grape soda and some sparkling cider."

"Okay, you have quite a selection, huh?"

Delores was trying to play like she was a comedienne with all her sarcasm dripping from her sexy ass lips.

"I try to be prepared. I didn't used to keep any wine, but a friend of mine hipped me to the Chardonnay when we went to see Erykah Badu in concert about a month ago."

"Oh, really, how was it?"

"The concert?"

"Umm, yeah, unless you want to tell me about the lady."

"Oh, uh, the concert was great! Erykah was beautiful. Her whole vibe was about being free. She had me wanting to sign up for any and all women's rights organizations!"

"You're funny. Did it inspire the lady you were with?"

"Who, Ina?"

The mention of Ina's name inspired Delores to pay closer attention to what I was saying. I was in the kitchen waiting on her decision as to what she wanted to drink, and there she was on my couch, fishing for something.

"Did you say you wanted some Chardonnay?" I asked.

"Yes, that would be fine."

"Cool."

"You trying to avoid my question, Avonté?"

"What question?"

"Was Ina inspired by the concert?"

"Hmm, I guess in a way she was. I mean she was definitely trying to sing along with Erykah, but she kept messing up all the words. I don't think she minded as much I did though."

"I can't imagine Ms. Ina letting her hair down like that and enjoying herself at a concert."

"Don't be fooled by her no-nonsense, all-about-business persona at work. Ina has her fun and even gets her freak on."

"Oh, really? Do tell..."

"What you trying to get me to say, Delores?"

"Nothing in particular. I'm just curious."

"Well, I have to admit that thinking about that concert brings back cool memories for me."

"How so?"

"'Cause Ina kept talking about how the whole vibe of the concert made her appreciate her friendship with Nakia. She thanked me a lot that night because up until then, she was feeling guilty about something that could cause some tension between her and Nakia."

"Oh, really? Come over here and tell me."

"Okay, hold on."

I have to admit that I loved the spotlight of attention from Delores. Talking to her was quickly becoming addictive. I was probably falling for her beautiful smile, not to mention those delicious thighs that looked so lovely on my couch. She was touching all the right buttons and making me feel at ease, spreading gossip about Ina and Nakia.

After I grabbed the bottle of Chardonnay, a couple of glasses and some Ritz crackers, I joined Delores on the couch. The sound of the wine being poured was really nice, especially when followed by looking into some gorgeous brown eyes. Delores has what it takes to make me lose my mind, for real.

"Okay, now that we've had a sip of wine, Avonté, tell me what Ina was feeling guilty about," Delores said.

"Well, I don't know if you ever seen or met that dude that Nakia used to go with."

"I've heard about him. Some of the girls at work say he's fine, and he used to send her flowers all the time."

"Yeah, he carries himself well," I replied with a hint of jealousy on my breath.

"So, what about him?"

"Well, one time he came up to the office, and things didn't go too well with him and Nakia. They had an argument or something."

"Oh?"

"Yeah, and then on the way out of the office, he ran into Ina. She didn't give me details, but those two ended up in the Marriott hotel down the street."

"You're lying, Avonté!"

"Nope, it's true."

"Wow, I didn't think Ina had it in her…Go 'head, Girl, with your bad self!"

"Well, she doesn't feel too proud about it, and going to that concert with me somehow hit home with her. Even though she hates me now, I still have respect for her and remember some good times."

"I'm sure you do."

"Yeah, so, you think we can change the subject?"

"What you want to talk about?"

"Well, if we have to talk, I'd rather it be about us and where this night is gonna lead."

"Where would you like it to lead?"

"Well, I've got these Ritz crackers here and some pizza rolls waiting to go into the oven, so I figure we can make a night of this and have some fun!"

"Aren't you Mr. Romance?"

"Can't you see my reflection?"

"I see you trying too hard when all you have to say is you want to have sex with me."

"Damn, and being that open would work with you?"

"Yep…"

"I'm speechless."

"You better get used to us ladies these days. Time is too valuable to be shy and waiting."

"At work, you seem shy!"

"Honey, I can't let everyone know my business."

All I could do was just sit back and check out Delores. She definitely surprised me with her openmindedness. I wasn't expecting her to be so ready and willing for a night of intimate contact. I thought I'd have to put in some serious work before I'd be allowed to touch the booty. She was already sitting close, brushing against me and causing my "little man" to rise to attention. One glance at her cleavage, and the scent of her smell had me both excited and nervous at the same time. If there's such thing as being able to smell lust in the air, my nose was wide open because something powerful was lingering in our presence. I watched as Delores moved her hands back and forth. up and down my legs. She smiled at me whenever I glanced down at what she was doing. It was like she had something sexy on her mind and either I needed to say, *Get to it, Girl,* really quick or she was about to take matters into her own hands. She had the eye of the tiger, the eye of the storm; hell, she had everything brewing inside her soul. I was afraid I couldn't hang but that didn't mean I wouldn't have fun trying.

"You're enjoying this, aren't you?" Delores asked.

I just smiled and nodded my head. If we didn't hurry up and get to the good part, I could see myself with a big giant wet spot on the front of my pants—real soon.

CONFESSION TIME

I wish I could say that I tossed and turned because of what I'd done. Sleeping with my girlfriend's man. Hell, I might as well not sugar-coat it with careful words. I fucked him. I had sex with Orlando in broad daylight after he'd come out of the office. He'd come to Montaqua to make amends with Nakia, but I guess she didn't accept his apology. I really didn't get any details at the time. When I bumped into Orlando outside, all I could see was his fine self, looking dazed and confused. I really didn't care about the confusion 'cause I was more interested in seeing how far I could get with each sexual innuendo that I threw at him. I never imagined it would get me what I actually wanted.

Fantasies can come true if you think about them hard enough. As I mentioned, Orlando was confused after speaking with Nakia in her office that day. I asked him what was wrong and if I could help him in any way.

"You want me to talk to her?" I asked, hoping he would answer back with 'no'.

"No, at this point, I don't think that would do any good."

I quietly celebrated inside, but on the outside I was sympathetic and played the role of being on his side. I touched his arm and he didn't seem to mind. Then I moved closer and hugged him slightly. He didn't back away. I placed his arm around my waist. His hand seemed to find a resting spot in the small of my back, and it felt as though he'd discovered the softness of my ass because I felt his hand move down slowly. That was my cue to move in even closer, yet still show him sympathy for what he'd gone through with Nakia. The sympathy wasn't real, but me getting aroused was as real as a heart attack.

"So, what are you gonna do now?" I asked.

He didn't respond right away. That gave me more reason to smile.

"I'm sorry, what did you say?" he finally said.

He was past late and besides, something else was on his mind at that point. He may have looked vulnerable, but the rise in his pants showed me that his libido was still intact. Men are so easy to figure out if you make sure to stand really close to them.

Orlando tried to explain what happened in the office, and I only halfway listened to him.

"I brought her flowers and tried to be completely honest with her," he told me.

"She didn't want to listen?"

He shook his head "no," and I did my best to comfort him while keeping in mind that we were out in public—still. I had to brainstorm for a moment as I realized there was a Marriott not too far from Montaqua. We often use it to hold meetings or have out-of-town guests stay there. I asked Orlando if he'd mind walking with me to the hotel. "I have to check on a room for a client that's coming in tomorrow. We can talk along the way," I explained. "Do you mind?"

"No. Might do me some good to walk."

At that point I couldn't tell if he was on to me. I had ulterior motives coming out of my ears, but I guess he was too busy stepping in all that self-pity to recognize he had a Sistah trying to lead him to temptation. Unknowingly or perhaps not admitting, he followed without hesitation.

Well, I didn't want him to figure out my motives too soon, so I remained sympathetic to his Nakia worries. I continued to ask him if he'd given up on her and whether or not he understood why she was mad at him.

"I realize I did wrong by not calling, and I'm not sure I can explain myself. I wasn't out there messing around. I was just to myself and not used to having someone waiting for my call."

"Maybe she'll wake up tomorrow and accept your apology. Nakia isn't that hard. She was just hurt behind not hearing from you..."

"She was pretty angry, so I don't know."

I excitedly changed the subject once I saw the entrance to the hotel.

"Listen, I need to make sure the room is to our satisfaction for an important client. Do you want to wait here or you wanna come up and see it with me?"

"I don't mind going up with you. It'll take my mind off of Nakia."

I smiled and thought to myself, *I'm about to blow your mind, sweetie!*

When Orlando and I walked inside the suite, I saw a hint of a smile come across his face. His eyes instantly looked in the direction of the bedroom. I got the feeling that being in a hotel room was the equivalent to being on his home court. He seemed to light up. He looked in the fridge. He checked to see if the room came equipped with drinks. It did and I just stood back while watching this man come alive.

"Is it too early for you to drink, Ina?" Orlando asked in a coy manner.

I shook my head "no" before asking, "What are you up to?"

"Nothing, just need to get my mind off of things..."

"I know other remedies for doing that," I said seductively.

My hint was heard loud and clear.

"You've got me wondering what *you're* up to, Ina."

"I think you already know, Orlando."

"I believe so..."

Orlando took a sip, which looked more like a let-me-prepare-myself swallow. I moved closer and kissed him softly. I raised my level of seduction like never before. I could feel his dick rising again, and this time there was no turning back. Knowing that I was doing something that wasn't right made the moment even more exciting. I knew at the time I was wrong, but I'd been wanting to get with Orlando for the longest. He didn't resist. He didn't pull away. He didn't stop me from unzipping his pants, and he didn't seem to mind me going down on him. I could feel his legs getting weak. Maybe he was surprised by what I was doing or maybe I was just that good. Shit, I surprised myself. I had all this pent-up sexual risk-taking in my blood, and that had me on fire. The harder I sucked, the more Orlando's knees began to buckle. I brought him down to the floor. I was all over him then. I may have given him good head, but what I did when I climbed on top of him would make all those erotica writers take notes.

I was already wet with anticipation so there was no need for me to take it slow when I sat on his dick. I slid down like a first-class fire woman. Then I rode him hard and wild. I gripped his chest. He had a few hairs, but when I was done, he was bare.

He moaned, "Damn, Ina!"

I know I was hurting his back. I probably gave him carpet burns, but I was getting mine. Yeah, I fucked him hard. I was the aggressor, and he never knew what hit him. He was never able to take over 'cause I wouldn't let him up until I was done. I'll give him one thing though. He stays hard for a long time.

And after that was all over? I wish I could say that I never looked back. I look back all the time, but what I did has to remain a secret. I'd never realized that I had such a sexual appetite, and maybe that's why I battle back and forth with being alone, keeping to myself and never dealing with men ever again. Then I think to myself, *I need a man's touch.* I need that warmth and companionship. My dildos and vibrators give me intense orgasms, but they do nothing for me as far as conversation. I need that or should I say, I'd like to have that.

Orlando didn't give me much conversation after that moment. After he came and realized what he'd done, he got so quiet that he pissed me off.

"What? One sip of wine and you lost control? You couldn't say no?" I asked him sarcastically.

He just looked at me. I got up and left his ass right there on the floor. I freshened up in the bathroom and walked back to work. I'd wait a while before I looked Nakia in the face. A couple days were enough for me to bury my guilt underneath a blanket of secrecy. I knew Orlando would never confess. That's my confession. The secret that I hope to take to my grave...

Take Charge Of My Issues

I never thought I'd see the day when I would no longer be excited about going to work. I feel myself showing signs of laziness and trying to think of excuses not to even get up in the morning. I'm a mother so it's pretty easy to find the motivation though. But lately, things at work have started to tick me off. Some of those girls act like they don't have anything better to do but gossip. Yes, I did say girls, or should I say *chicken heads!*

I want to call them something else, but I'm trying to be a lady. I mean, even today I started to lose my mind 'cause when I walked past the lunch room I could hear these three girls debating over who was more "fly": Christina or Britney. Ain't nobody at this company with those two names, so I know they were talking about those two pop stars we hear way too much about. That put me in a bad mood for the rest of the day. I had to take full advantage of my breaks when I had a chance 'cause if I didn't, it wouldn't have been a pretty sight. I might've called everybody that crossed my path something terrible. That would go against all the hard work I've put in to change my life around the way I have.

I mean, I have really changed since I first started working at Montaqua. I've matured, although I do have my moments when the ghetto in me slips out. Still, I'm very proud of myself these days despite not being excited about the workplace or should I say the people in this workplace.

One thing that I can say keeps my days interesting is when I visit Avonté or Ina. They still not too crazy about each other, and I think they both need to just chill. Avonté is so proud of his new bachelor pad. He comes to work with a smile on his face all the time. I keep warning him to be careful 'cause I know he's messing around with several ladies at the office, and they probably know it too. Once them silly girls get over their fascination for Christina and Britney, they gonna focus on Avonté's ass and start spreading things that he may not want folks to know, especially Ina. She's probably waiting for some delicious dirt about him. Ina gets one of those sick-to-her stomach looks when she sees Avonté from a distance. It's really strange to see how different she's become.

This office is so full of people with issues, and damn if I ain't one of them. Hopefully mine will become a thing of the past because when I look at Ina, I'm basically looking at myself. She's going through bitter times and being fed up with men. I'd been going through that stuff myself, but I never noticed how ugly my attitude was—until now. Watching Ina makes me constantly wonder, *Was I like that?* Then I think about what kind of friend I truly am because it wasn't too long ago when Ina had such a positive outlook on everything. She'd say something sweet about a man, and I'd respond with a negative statement that would make her feel like she walked into a brick wall. Now I see her doing the same thing that I did. If I tell her something nice about a man, she don't want to hear it, at all. She's given up on men, and sometimes I don't blame her. Back-to-back disappointments can do that, you know.

First it was Avonté, though I knew he wouldn't be the one for her. Then it was Sebastian who, by outer appearances, looked like the perfect knight in shining armor for my girl. Then he turned out to be Mr. Wonderful with a wedding ring, wanting to have his cake and pecan pie on the side. Ina was so happy during those first moments when Sebastian seemed like he was potentially...the one. I didn't really pay much attention to her happiness because I was wallowing in my little world of anger and bitterness. Now Ina occupies that world, and I'm finally realizing that it doesn't have to be that way for me.

Ina and I kind of go back and forth about men and relationships each time we get together. Her outlook is that a man can't do nothing for her except to occasionally scratch her itch and lift something heavy. My outlook is a lot more positive, to say the least. I need a man's touch, and I especially love it when I'm in the company of a man who truly knows how to express himself. I know that's a lot different from the way that I felt a month ago, but things change and I've changed, thank God. Being angry all the time can really wear you down—mentally, physically and spiritually. When I was all bitter and thinking about my own disappointments and problems, I couldn't see all the other positive things going on around me.

How can you be a friend, if you're so wrapped up in your own issues? I want some positive energy to rub off on me, but it can't happen if I've got this shield of resistance creating a wall between myself and anything good happening for others. Ina is doing that right now, but if you ask her about it, she'll just say she don't care. I know that feeling because I'd say the same thing—until now.

Well, even though work has become somewhat routine and folks get on my last nerves, everything else has been going pretty good. Tanisha brought home a nice report card, along with a bruised knee from climbing trees. She also brought home a jar of ants that she somehow left opened. Oh, you should've seen me trying to maintain my composure that day. I didn't want to be screaming at her on the same day that she'd made me so proud with her report card. She keeps my life interesting in the most important way. She's my reality, especially when I allow all the other nonsense to take me away from where my attention should be.

I had a wake-up call when I noticed that my anger toward men was rubbing off on her. She'd hear me on the phone shouting at her father. And a couple times when Orlando came over to apologize, she'd see me with a cold exterior turn my back on him as he tried to reach out and say he was sorry. I witnessed her "trying to be like Mommy" when I overheard her shouting at Trent and telling him to stay out of her life. I couldn't believe my ears, but then I looked in the mirror and instantly realized whom Tanisha was imitating. I felt ashamed and it broke my heart. That's when I began picking up the pieces. I promised myself I would listen more and make stronger attempts to be patient. That doesn't always come so easy, but I'm trying to practice every day. I've got to stop allowing people to tick me off, but that's definitely easier said than done, believe me.

I want to be a positive influence on my baby and hopefully I won't ever allow one single man to turn me against the entire world—again. I'm tired of feeling that way, though I know we have our ups and downs.

Well, I'm glad that I made such a positive change of attitude, so close to Christmas. I'm really looking forward to it this year because I have my own money to spend on gifts. In previous years, I've always relied on my ex-boyfriend Terence to pay for everything, even though I was the one picking out all the gifts. That didn't give me much satisfaction, but this year, I'm gonna be like Mrs. Santa Claus! I'm gonna really outdo past years with the stuff that I get. Of course, I have to buy something special for my immediate family. Tanisha is gonna be buried in toys and clothes, for sure. But also, I want to get something really nice for Ina, so I can thank her for being a friend this year and for teaching me so much at work. She's been a big reason for my growth and maturity.

Then I want to get something for Avonté. I'd like to find a nice painting that he can put on his wall. Something to really complement his apartment and also reflect the kind of person he is. First thing that comes to mind is one of those velvet portraits of naked black people like what my relatives used to have on their bathroom wall. Avonté is such a playboy now. I'm only teasing but I am gonna find him something nice. Hopefully it'll be something that inspires him to do right in his life. I'm learning that we should surround ourselves with constant reminders as to why we should remain focused in a positive direction. Tanisha reminds me every day.

Well, speaking of positive direction, another reason why my bitterness has subsided is because I'm talking once again with Orlando. Though I kept telling him "no," he never went away. He never stopped trying, and that made it hard to keep up my cold exterior when deep inside, I just wanted to be held by him. He's such a cutie pie to me and not to mention, fine as hell, too. Okay, so I miss the way he used to touch me. Okay, it's been a while, too. Orlando is definitely what one would call an experienced lover. I miss that, although it's not like I can compare him to others.

Orlando makes me purr sometimes. It's as if I get "caught up in his rapture." He still got that smooth charm about him and that sexy-ass voice. All his attempts at apologizing seemed so sincere to me. It became quite hard to resist. During his first two tries, I was still very bitter, and my disappointment was about as fresh as new paint on the wall. He failed to pay attention to all the warning signs. He'd get his feelings hurt 'cause I definitely wasn't having it as far as his apologies were concerned. I'd refused at least five dozen roses, three exotic flower arrangements and a couple of diamond heart pendants. Orlando was trying his ass off. I'd finally come around when he brought me a card that he made. I thought it was so sweet and sincere 'cause here was this grown man, reduced to the efforts of a little boy, trying to win my heart back. I couldn't believe how badly he wanted a second chance at pursuing me. A brotha with his kind of money and good looks can basically have anyone, but he keeps chasing me.

The interesting thing about that is I'm no longer impressed like I once was. I mean, I doubted myself so much before because I'd never had a man like him pursuing me. I worried about having things in common and understanding his life. Now, I'm inspired by his perseverance to get where he is. He's achieved a lot and I respect that, but I don't trip like I used to, thank God. I'm not gonna put myself down anymore just 'cause this man's seen more than I have.

I've definitely grown from all the heartache I've been through. I haven't yelled at a man in over three weeks. Orlando seems to love the change in me, but at the same time he seems a little timid about asking me something or sharing what's on his mind. I like having a man always worried about what I'm thinking, but at the same time, I don't want to see Orlando become a wimp or a brotha that I can wrap around my finger. I enjoy a little sense of power. Still, I want a man in my life that can make some decisions, especially when I have no clue what to do next. So far, Orlando is still that man, despite being so apologetic all the time.

One night, I tossed and I turned though I wasn't asleep. I wasn't even in bed yet. I was sitting on the couch, reading Vibe magazine while hearing Conan O'Brien on television. The house was pretty quiet. Mommy was in her room sleep and so were Trent and Tanisha. I was so happy to have the rest of the house to myself. Nobody was around and I felt like I could just relax and be myself. I could be Nakia and not have to worry if young eyes were watching, taking notes and imitating me touching myself. Yep, that's what I was doing.

I put down the magazine and turned the channel. Mommy didn't know that I'd ordered the Spice Channel for our cable system, which usually begins playing those dirty movies long after she's gone to sleep. I'd kept my hand on the remote just in case I did hear a noise. I'd be so embarrassed if my mother walked in on me.

As I sat on the couch keeping one eye in the direction of the hallway and the other eye on a black couple seriously getting their freak on, I almost jumped clean out of my skin because the phone rang. It was Orlando who had me believe that he had some kind of ESP. He seems to always know when I crave the sound of a male voice or better yet, when I'm feeling hot and bothered.

"Hey, Nakia, you busy?"

"No, just up reading. Nice to have a little time to myself, you know."

"Hmm, so true. What you reading?"

"Vibe magazine."

Orlando laughed. "That's not reading! I thought you were talking about some serious reading like some Alice Walker-type stuff!"

"Oh, well, I like to read books sometimes, but it's hard for me to really get into a good story. My quiet time is very brief with work and being a mother."

"Uh-huh, you know you got time to do anything you set your mind to."

"Maybe so, Orlando. So, what are you up to tonight?"

"Hmm, what would any man be up to, calling you so late at night?"

"I don't know, you'll have to tell me."

Orlando waited for a moment. I could hear him chuckle slightly before being daring enough to say what was on his mind.

"I want to come over or you come over here. Either way Nakia, I think we should be together tonight."

"Oh, you do, huh?"

"Yeah, I sure do."

"And why is that?"

Orlando chuckled again with a hint of bashfulness coloring the sound of his voice.

"I just think we should, Nakia," he told me. "Besides, I hear some moaning and groaning over there, so I know you ain't up watching Leno. I got the Spice Channel over here, too, you know!"

Orlando had me feeling so embarrassed as I instantly wondered if anyone else could hear the sound of my TV. I snatched the remote and hit the mute button. Better yet, I changed the channel to some cartoons so I could get my mind off of sex, which was close to impossible to do.

"That's a good idea, turning the sound down," Orlando teased.

I panicked. "You could really hear it?"

"Nah, not that much, just a little bit."

"You just trying to get me in trouble."

"I could do that better if you came over. How about I send a car over to you?"

"Oh, you really desperate now, huh? You gonna send a limo over here?"

"No, I'm gonna drive over there and get you!" Orlando laughed.

"Funny. You seem to be in a good mood tonight."

"I feel good to be talking with you, Nakia. It's like life feels good again. I've been going into work every morning with an extra pep in my step. I did real good with a client yesterday, so I'm feeling the positive effects of having such an incredible lady in my life."

"Wow, I do all that for you, huh?"

"Yeah, you do."

"Thanks, I'm flattered."

"Then how about I send that car for you?"

"No, sorry, but I have an early day tomorrow. I promised a friend that I'd go shopping for a Christmas tree with him."

"Him?"

"Yeah, Avonté."

"You guys just friends, right?"

"Is Orlando getting jealous over there?"

"Nah, just seeing what I'm up against."

"Don't go there, sweetheart. Avonté is just a friend and besides doing that for him, I also need to do some shopping for my family. I want to avoid the mad rush this year."

"It's cool, I understand. I hope I'm on your shopping list?"

"Could be."

"Thanks. I guess I'll call you tomorrow night and see what you're up to."

"Okay, goodnight."

When Orlando hung up, I felt a little satisfaction knowing that he had gotten so jealous over me hanging out with Avonté. There's nothing for him to worry about, but at the same time, it's not like Orlando and I have reunited with a commitment that we were now an item. I mean, first things first. We've got to build that trust factor back up and even though he stirs something inside of me, I'm very cautious about falling for his charm and fantasizing about us being involved with each other, seriously.

Shit, I'm tired of getting my hopes up and then being let down 'cause some man done changed his mind and can't be faithful to what he started. I've let these men cloud my judgement for way too long. I haven't even spent much time with my girl, Ina. It seems like our friendship sort of cools down when we're both dealing with issues concerning men. She's probably been listening to the same gossip that I hear every day at work. Since things didn't work out between her and Sebastian, she walks around with an attitude, especially when she knows he's in the building. The worst part of it all is that there might be a merger between Sebastian's company and Montaqua. That would be like putting a stake in Ina's heart because people can be ruthless around the office with all that *he said-she said* gossip.

I've wanted to slap a few of those chicks who spread rumors, but I'm trying to stay on my path of really growing and becoming a better person. Still, they test my nerves constantly at work and come to find out, Avonté's friend Delores has got the biggest mouth out of all of them. I haven't talked to him or should I say expressed my opinion about her, but I may have to one of these days. I'll see Avonté tomorrow so maybe I'll bring it up then. Though at the same time, I'd hate to ruin the day thinking about that *heffa*.

Morning came pretty fast. My mother made the greatest breakfast and I couldn't help but feel spoiled and guilty. Here I am a grown woman with a child, still letting my mother do so much for me. Actually, I don't have a choice because one thing I can never do is say "no" when she tells me it's time to eat. She'll look at me as if I said something in another language and will stand there until I've corrected myself. I experienced that this morning as I tried to get in an extra twenty minutes sleep. I'm glad that I got up because not only was the table surrounded by love, but also the aroma of the food was so heavenly.

I remember how much I used to enjoy breakfast when I was a young girl, growing up in this very same house. Now to see my daughter smiling away each time she bites into that delicious toast with butter and grape jelly truly warms my heart. Then there's little Trent who won't be little for very long if he keeps eating pancakes the way he does. I tried to get away with toast and coffee, but my mother wouldn't stand for that.

"You get you some eggs and grits, Nakia. You see the way these women look on television now? Men don't want no skinny girl anymore."

"I'm through trying to figure out what men want, Mommy."

After stuffing myself and making sure Tanisha was cleaned up and ready for her day, I took a shower and concentrated on me. Moments to myself have become very important because I know that once I step out of the house, anything can happen.

Hanging with Avonté is sure to be interesting. I enjoy his company until he starts going overboard with talking about himself. I'm just glad he's not some pretty boy, always walking around with a mirror in his pocket. I guess in a way, he's just as bad, but he makes me laugh. I see him looking at me with flirtatious eyes, but I'm glad he respects the boundaries of our friendship.

Showers feel so good to me in the morning. Mommy keeps the bathrooms so sparkling clean that I always have to spend an extra ten minutes cleaning up behind the mess I make. As I went back and forth trying to figure out which color jeans I wanted to wear, I could hear someone knocking on the screen door, followed by Tanisha screaming out to me.

"Mommy!"

"Tanisha, stop yelling in the house!" I replied.

Moments later, I could hear the voices of my mother and what sounded like Orlando. My heart started to beat rapidly, not because I was excited but because I was about to get angry. I remembered telling Orlando last night that I had things to do today with Avonté. Now here he is showing up at my door, unannounced. I rushed to put on the rest of my clothes, so he wouldn't catch me even more off guard. My attitude was on the rise as I listened to the voices in the distance. It was definitely Orlando and he was sweet-talking my mother. Within moments, Tanisha walked into my room with a stuffed teddy bear in her arms.

"Look what I got, Mommy," she said.

I tried my best to smile, but my teeth gritting so hard almost made that impossible. "Who gave that to you?" I asked her.

Tanisha bashfully swayed back and forth. "Orlando," she replied as though she'd discovered love for the first time.

"Is that who was at the front door?"

"Uh-huh. He's talking to Grandma right now."

I couldn't believe that Orlando would take it upon himself to come over like this. When a man crosses a certain line, I feel really uncomfortable. Maybe I should've seen this coming when I picked up on the jealousy during last night's conversation. Still, the possibility of Orlando acting this way never crossed my mind. I guess it doesn't matter if someone seems like they got it together. Nobody is immune from doing something to piss the other person off. Right now, I'm pissed. Maybe he's one of those people who once in every blue moon does something stupid. Now that doesn't make no kind of sense, 'cause the sun is out.

As much as I hate to display my attitude in front of my daughter, I hope there'll come a time when she understands why her mommy had to do the things she did. Listen at me sounding all old and shit. I just need to set the brotha straight, if we intend to keep seeing one another.

After I collected myself and took about five deep breaths, I walked into the living room. There was Orlando, with flowers in his hand and a huge smile. I wanted to curse him out even more because he looked so good standing there. How was I gonna tell this man off when deep down, he was turning a Sistah on with his Steve Harvey-style, navy-blue suit? The colors looked gorgeous against his brown complexion. *Stay focused*, I kept telling myself as I inched my way closer to where he stood. He smiled with more confidence as I greeted him.

"Hello," I said calmly. "What are you doing here?"

"Just wanted to surprise you. I threw on a little something and stopped by the flower shop..."

"I see. Maybe you should call first when you feel this need to interrupt plans that I've already made."

"Do I detect a little disappointment, Nakia?"

"Orlando, I appreciate the flowers and I appreciate you for doing this, but we talked last night and it seems as though you have little regard for the fact that I made plans with Avonté today. You do remember I said I would be going shopping with him, don't you?"

"Yes, I remember."

"And?"

Orlando smiled, wiped his shoulder as if he had some lint on his suit and then returned to acting as if he'd done nothing wrong. He just stood there waiting for my next comment as though what I'd already said made no sense to him.

"Am I getting through to you, Orlando?"

"I know about your date with Avonté, yes."

"It's not a date. I'm just helping him shop."

"He couldn't find someone else, huh?" Orlando asked sarcastically.

"Oh, no, you are not jealous, are you?"

"Nah, but I am curious to meet this guy."

"I'm trying to be calm here, Orlando, because my daughter is nearby and my mother is in the other room..."

"Yeah, your mother is very nice," Orlando interrupted.

I paused before taking yet another deep breath. I couldn't believe Orlando's display of jealousy. I felt as though I were standing next to a desperate man trying to force the situation in his favor. I couldn't understand his actions, and I wasn't about to make an attempt at figuring this thing out, at least not today.

"Orlando, I'm sorry but I have to ask you to leave," I told him.

"Leave?" he questioned as if he'd never heard that word. I imagine he probably hasn't ever been told to leave.

"Please? Don't make this ugly or anything. Maybe we can talk tonight and come to some kind of understanding about all of this."

Orlando simply nodded his head and placed the flower arrangement on the nearby coffee table.

"Thank you," I said while noticing his wounded look.

"You're welcome."

Orlando turned and walked toward the front door without so much as a hint that he would hug me goodbye. He opened the screen door and let it slam shut behind him. I watched as he reached the front gate and noticed that he never looked back. Then to add insult to an already screwed-up moment, Avonté was right there to greet Orlando. I couldn't hear any verbal exchanges between the two, but it was pretty easy to recognize the ego-induced posturing and the quick up-and-down glances that they gave one another. I'm thankful that neither one tried to start anything. I already had the screen door open so that Avonté wouldn't feel so inclined to question the looks that Orlando gave him. It would be so not cool to have two men fighting in my mother's front yard.

Avonté walked inside with a little smirk on his face. I think he was enjoying himself, probably thinking that he was the *chosen one* and Orlando was the one that got turned away. Little did he know, but it hurt my heart to see Orlando walk away so angrily. I don't understand why he came over like he did. Maybe I'm to blame. I don't know. Maybe he's just trying too hard to win me back and it's causing him to seek out desperate measures. I'm probably trying way too hard to understand men, and this one pacing back and forth in my mother's living room did very little to clarify any kind of confusion.

"Hey, Nakia, what's up with your boy?" Avonté asked.

"Don't you start with me, Avonte."

"Why you say it like that? Did you two have an argument?"

"No, we just got our signals crossed and had a little misunderstanding."

"Oh, is that what you want to call it. I think something happened, but by the look on your face I guess I better not push too much, huh?"

"You got that right!"

Avonté smiled and retreated toward the couch. I can give a look that'll let any man know they're venturing into dangerous territory. Avonté knows me well enough to figure out which buttons not to push.

"Let me get my stuff so we can go," I told him.

"Okay, cool. This is gonna be fun, but don't try to have me spend all kinds of money today!" Avonté said as I walked toward my bedroom.

"Uh-huh," I mumbled.

"I'm serious, Nakia, you know my budget is tight!"

"Okay, Avonté."

The weather was absolutely gorgeous outside—not a cloud in the sky and not too much smog floating around. Avonté had some really nice music playing—mostly from artists that I didn't recognize, but the vibe was really cool. I looked over at Avonté and wondered about him—a little. I can't believe that he and I have become good friends but it's been interesting, to say the least. I just watch in amazement sometimes when I witness how he acts. He's got the good looks, the education and a career, but he easily falls prey to his girl-chasing habits. That's definitely his downfall and one of the reasons why I've never allowed myself to become attracted to him as more than just a friend.

I guess we both have things on our mind because neither of us has said a word since we left the house. Maybe Avonté senses that he got on my nerves for a moment there and was waiting for the green light to speak. For me, I was just lost in thought. Avonté was just being himself earlier, and I can't fault him for that. Orlando wasn't himself, and that has me feeling kind of strange.

As the music faded, it brought more attention to the silence in the car. I didn't like the uneasy feeling, especially 'cause today is supposed to be fun. How can two people go shopping for a Christmas tree if they're all wrapped up in their own personal issues? Me and my man trouble, and Avonté and his, well, everything with Avonté is an issue. I decided to break through the wall that seemed to separate us from conversing.

"Hey, what you been up to lately, Avonté?"

Avonté smiled instantly. He looked over at me as if he wanted to thank me for finally speaking to him.

"Whew, Nakia, I've been having a great time being able to come home to my own place. It's like a freedom that this brotha never knew before!" he said, while keeping his eyes on the traffic ahead.

"You don't miss your mother? Although, she's probably enjoying her freedom, too, huh?"

Avonte scowled. "I'll pretend I didn't hear you say that!"

"What? I'm not trying to be funny."

"I know, I'm just playing. Yeah, my mother is enjoying the freedom 'cause she already got my room turned into a special reading room. You should see how she got it all fixed up. Plus, she took down my Halle Berry, Nia Long, and Sanaa Lathan pictures that I had on the wall!"

"You're silly..."

"Hey, I'm serious, shoot. I even demanded to know where she put them, too."

"And what did she say?"

"She looked outside and pointed to the sanitation truck, picking up the trash. I stood there looking like my dog ran away and the house burned down."

"Come on now, Avonté."

"What?"

"Can't you just find some more pictures of those ladies or just watch their movies?"

"Yeah, I guess that's some extreme shit, huh?"

"You need help, boy!"

"Shoot, I'm about to put that model Shakara up on my wall when I get back to the crib!"

"Who?"

"Never mind—only the fellas would know who I'm talking about."

I had no clue, so I turned my attention toward life on the streets. There's never a dull moment on Crenshaw Boulevard. Someone is always causing a scene. Ladies dress in everything imaginable, from respectful to hoochie. There's just way too many wig stores and barbershops. For the life of me, I could never figure out how they survive, but they do. They've been here for years and probably always will.

I've seen a lot of Starbucks popping up everywhere, so it kind of makes me wonder why they can't put one on this street, especially with it being so much traffic all the time. I guess they don't want one this close to the hood, giving black folks reason to loiter and actually talk to one another.

"What you thinking about?" Avonté asked.

"Just amusing myself with thoughts about the hood."

"What hood?"

"This one we're driving in!"

"This is not the hood, Nakia. You live in the hood, lady."

"Just drive!"

I told Avonté about this place in Leimert Park that sold Christmas trees and all the proceeds go to a foundation for African-American children. I'm trying to really get into the spirit of giving this year more so than the spirit of impressing somebody with what, how and where I bought their gift. I don't mind so much the "commercialism" of the holiday season, but I do mind if someone is not truly giving from the heart. I think Avonté probably gives to impress, but I can't fault him too much on that because it seems to go hand in hand with the lifestyle that he's trying to be a part of. That *hey-baby-I'm-what-you-need* mentality be on full display—constantly.

"Hey, have you bought that gift for Delores yet?" I inquired as Avonté glanced over at the action outside of Krispy Kreme Doughnuts. The place hasn't been there that long, so folks are jam-packed inside like they never had a donut before.

"Nah, not yet. I was hoping you'd give me some suggestions."

"Okay. What is she into? You two been hanging out a lot, right?"

"Hmm, I wouldn't say a lot..."

"What do you think she'd like?"

"I don't know, but I want to get her something that has her thinking she can't do without a brotha! Have her wanting to say, *Baby, I'm what you need!*"

Oh, here we go, I thought to myself.

"Why you laughing, Nakia?"

"I'm sorry, just a thought that I had earlier that you kind of reminded me of just now."

"Oh, well, maybe you can suggest something that ain't out of my price range, you know?"

"I'll do my best. They have some little shops in Leimert Park, so maybe you can get her something unique and really cute. I've spoken to Delores a few times, but I didn't get a sense of who she is. Buying a gift for someone is to me like showing that you've been paying attention to who they are."

"Now you putting pressure on a brotha."

"Oh, please, what pressure?"

"Making me feel like I haven't been paying attention to what the girl likes."

"Oh, well, I haven't accused you...yet."

"But, you're on the verge of it..."

"No, not really. It's like, I know exactly what to get Ina cause all you have to do is listen to her talk about what store she went to over the weekend. Nine times out of ten, she didn't buy whatever caught her eye, so that makes it easy to know what would make her happy. See what I mean? You have to pay attention."

"No comment," Avonté replied while turning left off of Crenshaw and onto Stocker Street.

"You haven't told me how things are going between you and Delores. Is that a love connection or are you two just friends?"

"Hmm, a love connection? Nah, we just hang out together, get our freak on and chill at my place."

"Is that all you want from her?"

Avonté paused as he searched for a place to park.

I waited for his response. "Well?" I asked.

"Hmm, it's hard to say, Nakia. I think that any hint of commitment for me right now is a scary proposition unless I instantly feel something. With Delores, I'm attracted to her and I like her, but I'll admit it's about 90 percent physical. I don't get those urges to call her up just to talk. Know what I mean?"

"Yeah, I do."

"You probably don't think that's cool, huh?"

"I can't judge and tell you how to live your life, Avonté."

"But?"

"No 'but' to it. I don't really know what to say."

"You're just being kind right now, Nakia."

"Yeah, well, since I don't really know Delores, I don't feel like I have to protect her from you."

Avonté laughed. "See, that's what I'm talking about!"

"Just park the car."

"Uh-huh, okay, Nakia."

"I wish I could say more, but I'm not about to imagine myself in her place and tell you what I'd feel. We'd be fighting right now 'cause if you only ten percent into who I am and ninety percent into my body, I would kick you to the curb!"

Avonté laughed nervously. "Okay, didn't mean to push that button."

We walked down the street, noticing the changes that had been made to the area. I was pleased to see that there were no new wig stores. One is enough, I think. There's some really nice Afrocentric shops and even a gallery with beautiful artwork in the area. I remembered that I wanted to get Avonté a painting, but I didn't want to buy one and have him not be surprised when he opened the package. Then I started to laugh to myself because I figured if I only wanted to spend a few dollars I could buy him a magazine with one of his favorite ladies in it and a cheap frame to put the picture in after I've ripped it out. Avonté is silly enough to actually be happy with that. Maybe I'll just get him some cologne because his appreciation for the arts just ain't what it should be for a college person. I know more than his ass does.

"Damn, Nakia, you always drifting off, thinking about something."

Avonte interrupted my thoughts before I could realize that I was daydreaming.

"I'm just looking at that art in the window," I told him.

I pointed to a gorgeous painting of a black woman and her child. Avonte kept walking, so I wasn't able to go inside to get a closer look.

"Wait!" I shouted, still making an attempt to go inside the gallery.

"Sorry about that, but come check this out!" Avonté waved his arm in a *hurry-come-quick* fashion.

I was about to unleash my attitude on him, but then he showed me the cutest little trinkets and earrings.

"Wow, this would look cute on Tanisha."

"Do you think Delores would be into something like this?" Avonté asked.

"Hard for me to say. Does she appreciate handmade jewelry?"

"Seems like she should, if I buy it for her."

"You still want to see her, right?"

"What you trying to say, Nakia?"

"I'm tempted to say that maybe you should go to Macy's and get her something expensive."

Avonté looked disappointed that he couldn't figure out what to buy Delores. I almost felt sorry for him, but I knew that somehow he'd come through whether he bought something today or not. I don't know why he's so serious about buying her something since it doesn't appear he's interested in a relationship with the girl.

I was actually having fun, hanging out with Avonté. It was cool not to feel any pressure between us. He wasn't trying to bump into me or put his arm around me like those first times we'd hung out. It's funny to me now, but I do recall him bending over in pain because I elbowed him in the ribs one time. I guess the thought of pain is always a good reminder not to repeat your mistakes.

"You ever been inside that place?" Avonté asked while pointing to a storefront that looked like it was once a nightclub or a movie theater.

"Maybe once. This whole area used to be a sort of a mecca for black culture. I'm really glad they're rebuilding."

"Yeah, it looks good, I'll have to admit."

"Where do you usually hang out?"

"Century City. I try to do the upscale thang, nightclubs, all that stuff. You know I'm always trying to network and move up the ladder."

"Is that what you do, even at nightclubs?"

"There you go again, Nakia, trying to be funny."

"No, Avonté. I'm just asking a simple question."

"Yeah, right. Anyway, is this the place you're talking about with the Christmas trees?"

"Yes, that's the place."

"Oh, okay. The trees look pretty nice. I should've parked a little closer."

"Well, let's see if we can pick out a tree and then you can go get the car."

"Okay, cool."

"I can't imagine you'll be like Charlie Brown and pick the smallest, ugliest tree!"

Avonté laughed. "I was just thinking about that cartoon. Nah, I'll probably do the opposite and try to get the biggest."

"You have to remember how big your apartment is. Don't get something that you can't fit into your living room."

"I know. You don't have to tell me that, Nakia."

I gave Avonté a big smile. "Just making sure..."

One of the worst moments I hate to experience is when a familiar face walks into my life unexpectedly. It's like those uncomfortable cases when you're laughing with your mouth wide open and all of a sudden, an ex-somebody walks into the room. You just sit there trying to figure out how to brush off your embarrassment as quickly as possible before that person approaches you with the typical *hey-stranger-how-long-has-it-been* greeting. And God forbid if they should look twice as good as they used to. Well, that kind of moment just happened. Avonté picked up on my body language and how quiet I'd become. First, he looked at me and then in the direction of where I was staring.

"Hey, isn't that...?" he attempted to ask.

"Yes, and don't look or say anything! Maybe he won't notice we're here."

"What, you don't want to talk to him?"

"No. His phone calls are enough for me. I'm not sure if I can handle talking to him in person. I can't believe he's here. Why of all days did he have to be here, today?"

"Why you acting like that, Nakia? Plus, this man is the father of your daughter, right?"

"Yes. I guess I'm tripping but seeing him after such a long time feels strange."

"Don't you see him when he comes over to get Tanisha?"

"He doesn't come that often, but when he does, I'm either not home or I'll just stay in another room."

"Oh. Well, Nakia, we can do this another time or maybe come back later."

"No, I'm not gonna start hiding just 'cause my ex is close by."

"Yeah, but it doesn't seem like you trying hard not to let him see you either. You're looking at him like you miss seeing him."

"Huh, you need glasses!"

"Well, I've seen that look before, Nakia. Of course, I've never seen that look directed at me, but that's another story, for another day." Avonté laughed.

I giggled nervously and tried my best to smile. I really felt anxious seeing Terence. The worse part about it was that seeing him felt really good, too. I guess in a way, I discovered that maybe I did miss him a little.

As I was walking with Avonté, I felt like the biggest hypocrite. There I was telling him how I wasn't trying to hide from my ex but truthfully, that's exactly what I was doing. I had Avonté walk as far in the opposite direction of Terence as possible. I was pointing to the ugliest Christmas trees. Avonté was looking at me like I was crazy and had lost my mind. I think he could sense that I was just stalling for time and trying to avoid potential embarrassment.

He asked, "You expect me to buy something like that?"

"No, I'm just pointing out different types of trees to you!"

"No, you trying not to be seen."

"Whatever!"

"Uh-huh. Maybe you should stand in front of me and let my body shield you from being detected."

"You like seeing me embarrassed and uncomfortable, huh?"

"No, Nakia. I do think it's funny though, but I told you, if you want to leave, we can."

"No, I'm fine."

"Uh-huh."

No, I wasn't fine at all. I felt nervous. I don't know. Part of me wanted to just get it over with and say hello, and the other part, well, basically, I just wanted to run and hide. I don't know what had me tripping like that. No, actually I did. I found myself in that quick instance feeling very attracted to Terence. I guess because it'd been a while since I'd seen him and also because we share so many memories. I don't know. One thing for sure though, Terence has been keeping himself in great shape. I was probably sounding so mixed-up right then, and Avonté was doing absolutely nothing to help me get over my self-inflicted anxiety.

I decided to let Avonté walk ahead and do his thang. I figured it might be best for me to just stay right where I was, behind a huge Christmas tree. Avonté kept looking back at me with this ha-ha expression. He was enjoying himself, and I was steadily trying to keep track of the whereabouts of my ex. Avonté kept distracting me with his wild arm movements. He found a couple of trees that he liked, but I wouldn't budge from my very safe spot. Or, so I thought it was safe.

"Nakia, that is you, huh?" a male voice said from behind.

It didn't take much for me to figure out the voice.

"Terence, hi, what are you doing here?" I responded somewhat nervously.

"Just trying to find me a small tree. It seems like nobody sells those little ones that us bachelors like to buy."

I had to contain myself from making a remark about his state of bachelorhood. If he had played his cards right and not allowed our relationship to end, then he wouldn'tve been having his current problem.

"So, how have you been?" Terence asked.

"I've been okay. Your daughter is fine, too, just in case you wondered."

"Ah, that's cold, thinking I wasn't gonna ask about her. Plus, you know I talked to her the other day."

"Yes, you did."

"Do I hear an apology floating in the air somewhere?"

"Not really."

Terence stepped back. He couldn't believe the coldness of my emotions. To be honest, I wasn't sure why I was being so cruel either. Yes, it hurt that we broke up, but truth be known, he has continued to see and provide for his daughter.

"Well, let me try this again, Nakia." Terence smiled.

He looked pretty good, but I didn't want him to know that I noticed. I kept my shield up and glanced away if I felt myself wanting to smile or look even a little bit interested. I waited for his next attempt at having a conversation.

"Listen, I was thinking." Terence had a gleam in his eye as if he were about to ask me on a date or something.

I was not looking forward to telling him "no," so I started to visually search for Avonté. He was somewhere, still trying to find the perfect tree, I was sure.

"Well, I don't want to hold you up, Nakia," Terence said, noticing that I wasn't giving him my full attention.

"Yes, I came here with a friend, and it seems disrespectful not to be with him right now."

"Him?"

"Yes. He's just a friend and also works at the agency."

"Oh, okay."

"You say that like I need your approval, Terence."

"Nah, I'm not trying to start any drama with you, Nakia. I'd like to be able to call you sometime."

"We've spoken on the phone."

"Yes, but I want to actually talk with you. Seems like our conversations are about one thing, and that's either money for Tanisha or when I can come over and get her."

"We're not together anymore, Terence."

"I know this."

"So, you can't expect me to drop everything when you call or come by."

"No, I don't expect you to, Nakia. I'm just saying that I'd like to talk with you. I mean, it seems like we can still be friends. I'm making all kinds of changes in my life. Positive changes, you know."

"I'm glad but I'm making changes, too, and I want to be able to really give my daughter a good life."

"I want the same."

A hush had come between us as if the curtain had closed on our attempted conversation. I began to feel as though maybe something was wrong or perhaps all the bitterness had finally caught up to me. After the chitchat was over, Terence picked up on his cue to finally give up and go on about his business. I watched him walk away, noticing that he never turned to look at me again. I felt a little bad because his initial enthusiasm for seeing me had all but disappeared. He'd become the second man that I'd turned away today. My conscience kicked in. Maybe I should talk to Terence. Maybe I should also be more forgiving of Orlando and give him a chance to redeem himself. I never expected to have all these choices in men. However, Avonté was no choice at all for me, and he confirmed my decision by making a total fool of himself with this overpriced, way-too-big Christmas tree that he was dragging behind him.

"No, you didn't just buy that!"

"Why, what's wrong with this one?"

"That's too big for your apartment!"

"Nah, it'll fit."

"How you figure that?"

"I'll force it to fit."

"You might have to cut it in half."

"That'll work!" Avonté said as he continued to drag the tree in the direction of his car. I followed right behind, but I wasn't about to help him tie it down to the top of his car. I just came to help him choose a tree, not to do hard labor.

"I'm not gonna ask for your help. I see you trying to walk behind me like you don't know me...," Avonte said.

I guess the look on my face gave away exactly what I was thinking. In this case, I was glad that my mind was so easy to read.

Well, after finishing up my day with Avonté, I was really happy to be back at home. I received a very warm welcome from Tanisha and Trent. My mother had dinner waiting for me at the table. I feel so guilty with her always cooking for me, but I guess being a mother is a lifetime thing. You never stop doing stuff for your child. My mother made some of her famous gumbo and it was so delicious. She put all kinds of seafood in it, plus she added some vegetables and sausages. You name it; she had everything in there. My mother can throw down in the kitchen. She made the gumbo a little bit on the spicy side 'cause fire was coming out of my ears. Still, it was good and even Tanisha liked it a lot, so that was a good thing.

I was tickled to death seeing Tanisha mop the kitchen floor while I was eating. I don't know what gave her the idea, but I guess she had seen me doing it a few days earlier. I didn't want to discourage her by making her stop. She was creating a mess, but she looked so cute. Maybe I'll give her a bigger allowance since she did that on her own.

I found a note on the kitchen table when I sat down, telling me that Orlando had called while I was out. This seemed like the perfect opportunity for me to show that I wasn't as mean as I sounded earlier. I wanted to at least end my day on a positive note and maybe I could do that with Orlando. I realize now that I've done wrong by building him up to be the "perfect man," because it's become so hard to forgive him for being anything less. Maybe it's time to appreciate who he truly is.

Well, considering that I was feeling lazy and didn't want to get up from the kitchen table, it was time to exercise my rights as a mother.

"Tanisha, go get Mommy the phone, okay!"

"Okay," she replied before dropping the mop and running out of the kitchen excitedly.

Two seconds later she had the phone and a smile that melted my heart.

"Why don't you go play, sweetheart, okay?"

Tanisha grinned and left me alone to make my phone call. I focused on each number as I pushed the buttons on the touch-tone phone. I hesitated in between each number, thinking about what I might say. The conversation would surely start with a little bit of tension, but knowing that Orlando made an attempt to call me earlier put me slightly at ease.

I took a deep breath after every ring. *Where is this man?* I wondered. I didn't remember if he told me he had caller ID or not. Maybe he saw it was me and wasn't gonna answer the phone. I heard five rings and still no answer. I was always told that you should let the phone ring ten times before hanging up, but all I could stand to listen to was six. I just couldn't wait four more. I decided to hang up. *Click!* I thought to myself as I tried to justify my quick action. Who was I fooling? I really wanted to hear Orlando's voice tonight, so giving up wasn't an option for me. I dialed his number again, but this time there was no hesitation.

Orlando answered. "Hello?"

"Hey," I replied, knowing that he'd recognize my voice right away.

"Nakia, glad you called."

Orlando never did disappoint me in sounding so good. The man could melt butter with his smooth-as-silk voice.

"Was that you that just called moments ago?" he asked.

"Yeah, but the phone just rang."

"Sorry about that. I was on the other line with a business call and didn't want to chance putting my client on hold. Hope you forgive me for that as well as what I did earlier today."

This was the Orlando that I knew, cared for and was afraid of, I thought to myself. I just started smiling uncontrollably and almost knocked over my half-empty bowl of gumbo sitting in front of me.

"What you doing, Nakia?" he asked in a genuinely curious tone.

"Nothing. Well, thinking and just feeling much better now that I'm talking to you."

"Glad to hear that. I thought you might still be mad at me. I can only imagine that I disappointed you with my strange behavior, but I was tripping and I was desperately trying to hold on to you."

"You were?"

"Yeah, but after some serious soul searching and kicking my own behind, I realized that I just needed to be myself and maybe do a little praying, too. I have to be confident that you'll see me for who I really am and things will work out."

Listening to Orlando talk this way was both interesting and arousing. It felt as though we'd returned to those nights when we sat up talking for hours. I'd listen to stories about his life, and he'd listen to me dream out loud about what I wanted to accomplish so that I could give Tanisha a good life. I've missed those conversations...a lot. There's just so much I can talk about with Avonté or Ina. But with Orlando, every-thing is open for discussion, and I usually end up coming away with a better understanding about myself as well as wanting to get with this man 'cause he has me feeling so turned on.

"Hey, what you thinking right now, Nakia?" Orlando asked in a sexy I-wonder-what-she's-wearing kind of voice.

I decided to beat him to the punch. "What are you wearing?" I asked.

Orlando was speechless at first. I could hear him laugh quietly. He was surprised by my question.

"Hmm, where you trying to go with your question?"

"Where would you like me to go?"

"Okay, well, you caught me off guard." Orlando laughed.

It was funny to actually catch him struggling with what he wanted to say. I could tell he was just being cautious and at the same time, unsure about how far he could take a conversation with me. I'm to blame for his hesitation, but my guards were down and I was ready for anything he'd say to me.

Eventually, I let Orlando off the hook. It was really sweet that he didn't want to go "there" with me—"there" meaning he was a gentleman and didn't try to talk about sex. Actually, I wouldn't have minded. I've spent many nights recently, tossing, turning and fantasizing since the last time Orlando and I were intimate. It's kinda funny that he and I haven't been intimate very much, but I guess that's due to the fallout behind that trip he took. Now, I just want to start over and see what happens.

"I'm really grateful that we're talking again, Nakia," Orlando said.

I blushed for a moment, and I think he picked up on the fact that I was fidgeting. In a minute I was about to put some deep scratches in my mother's china if I didn't stop. I was using the spoon to write out Orlando's initials, "O D." I hope that's not something that's gonna happen to me because already I was beginning to feel light-headed. The sound of his voice still made my heart beat through my chest. I began to wonder just how far things would lead if I were really willing to give Orlando a second chance.

I sighed. "I'm glad we're talking again, too," I reassured Orlando.

He spoke softly. "Thanks, I needed to hear that."

"You're welcome, sweetheart."

"Sweetheart? I must really be living right, huh?"

I laughed and found myself responding to his comments with silence. Everything he said made me happy, but my natural reaction was to take it all in and think about how I'd respond. I know it was driving him crazy. I needed some time before I could share all of my thoughts. I believe that when trust is broken, you can't just order it up like a slice of pizza, thinking that it's "all good." I could sense in Orlando's voice that he wanted to feel like all was forgiven, but for me, it was more like I'd become comfortable once again talking to him. I was willing to continue to talk with him just as long as he was open and didn't play games.

I'm shaking my head right now. Not because I'm enjoying this conversation with Orlando but because I've heard those words over a million times since I turned 20. That tired-ass *let's-be-open-and-not-play-games* speech.

"Hello, you there, Nakia?"

Orlando snapped me out of the attitude that I was about to let take over my soul. Thinking too much can cause a sistah to want to hang up on a man, even if he's fine and got the sexiest voice in America.

"Uh-oh, am I still in trouble?" Orlando asked.

"Huh?" I replied, confused by his statement.

"You seem to be lost in though,t or something has grabbed your attention over there."

"No, I'm sorry. My mind did wander for a second, but I'm still here."

"Okay, I'm glad."

I smiled and thought for a second. This time my thoughts were good. The conversation flashed through my mind. I felt as though we'd made a real connection. Maybe we'd even repaired some of the damage, but I didn't want to let Orlando know just yet. He might start celebrating or thinking he could come over unannounced in the morning to take me to work. Actually, it's gonna be nice not to have to deal with Avonté's *when-you-gonna-buy-you-a-car* attitude or have to endure those overcrowded buses in the morning. Last week I fell in some old man's lap and I could've sworn he smiled 'cause he got him a quick feel. That pissed me off. But before I fall prey once again to my attitude, I needed to put Orlando at ease. Already another five minutes had gone by. He listened patiently to my silence, and there I was listening to my inner voice bitch about stuff that was too early to be concerned about.

"Orlando?" I said his name with a sweet innocent tone.

"Yeah, I'm here."

"Sorry about that. I keep drifting. I guess I'm tired. It's been a long day. I've been on my feet shopping and helping my friend pick out a Christmas tree. Then on top of that, I had a run-in with my ex. Seems like a lot happened to me today."

"Nakia, you don't have to explain. I'm just glad we got a chance to talk. I learned quickly that I need to be patient and keep trying to convince you that I'm here for you."

"Aww, that's sweet, thanks."

"No problem."

"Listen, can you give me a ride in the morning? Say, around seven?"

"I'll be there."

"Thank you, Orlando."

"Goodnight, Nakia."

"Night."

I lingered for a while before I hung up the phone. Then I tasted some more of my gumbo. It was cold and surely a sign that I needed to take my butt to bed.

Underneath It All

Monday morning arrived and the possibilities for a good week were endless. Honey, I was feeling great. I got a little raise and a brand new job title. My boss heard that I was preparing my resume and thinking about testing the waters to see who might be interested in a thirty-something Sistah with a lot of knowledge about the advertising world. I guess it helped that I left my computer on with my resume in full view for everyone to accidentally see. I've always had a knack for letting folks discover something about me, on purpose. I've wanted this new job title more than I've wanted a new man. I had a devious *Erica-Kane-soap-opera* grin on my face when my boss, Sharon McNair, came in and uttered her first words of congratulations to me.

"How does it feel to be a part of management, Ina?" she asked, thinking I'd be overjoyed and elated, or is that the same thing?

Well, I did play it off with a little humility and thanked her as though I was anxious to get started with my new responsibilities. I'm not sure she bought into it. I think she was happy that I accepted the position, so she could go back to the people she reports to. You know, give them the good news. I'm not trying to brag, but I could tell they didn't want to lose me. I always go the extra mile, so they better had come off of some money and show some appreciation for all my efforts.

Well, "testing the waters" is something that I've been doing in other aspects of my life, too. I've been going out a lot recently to some of those new intimate nightclubs with the whole laid-back, ultra-cool environment. A place where one gets the impression that people with intelligence come to exchange numbers so they too can have the hook-up on some future booty calls. I know I'm tripping. I'm thinking of becoming a travel agent for the sexually liberated. I guess my recent past has revealed that I'm not shy about sex—at all. Still, I haven't been looking for anything or anyone in particular. I've met some new friends but nothing has happened to portray any kind of seriousness. A Sistah just wants to enjoy herself a little.

I'd like to discover that there are some good men out there that can truly hold a decent conversation. I can't stand always having to ask, "What are you thinking?" or "What's on your mind when you look at me like that?" All these damn guessing games just drive me up the wall. Got me feeling like Patti LaBelle when I saw her screaming at some-one not saying a word. "Talk!" she'd shout.

I've been frequenting this one club in the Valley lately, a little place called Stevie's. Sometimes they have open microphone nights for poetry readings, and other nights they have live entertainment. A little jazz rather than that stuff you hear on the radio today. It's really nice to just vibe off of people enjoying some real music for a change instead of hearing music like what I heard the other day, talking about "lick my pussy just like that!" At least at Stevie's, you can see folks just smiling and looking at each other with good positive energy. Then sometimes you can tell when a connection is made between two people because you can visualize one of them reeling in his or her catch for the day on some giant-ass fishing pole. I'm tripping again.

One thing that I've noticed is that men of all complexions and financial status seem to think way too much of themselves. Yeah, here I go again, thinking negatively, but it amazes me what a Sistah has to go through just to get a compliment. I'm starting to believe that I need to go back to the Stone Age just to find a man that's genuine. I don't know. I guess I hear so much about those *too-good-to-be-true* men that it gets frustrating when I find myself not having one of my very own. I can list two men in my recent past who appeared to be "too good to be true," but I quickly found out that was a lie too. I don't have to say their names 'cause anyone would know who I'm talking about. Okay, Orlando and Sebastian. There, I said it.

Another sign of me tripping is that I've even considered going to the country to find myself a man. That idea quickly disappeared because I can't have somebody in my life, lagging behind and not understanding my needs. How can some Brotha, fresh out of the country understand why I need to do five things at once while driving to work every morning? I have to have my morning coffee. I've burned up three Mr. Coffeemakers in the last two years. I got to listen to the Steve Harvey morning show 'cause Lord knows, he makes me laugh with his silly self. I'm always calling up my voicemail at work, so I can know what to expect when I get to the office. And then there's those occasions when I listen to a novel. Lately I've been wishing they would put some black erotica on audio cassette. But then I've dismissed that thought 'cause I don't want to be going into the office dripping wet and wondering why folks are really looking at me. When I'm horny, I always get the feeling that it's way too obvious. I guess it all boils down to me just being too busy for any kind of serious relationship. I'm also very demanding, and maybe that prevents men from thinking long term when they see me. Maybe I'm just gonna have to grab some man and mold his ass into what I want him to be.

Speaking of molding, it seems that Nakia is back with Orlando now. I guess I shouldn't be so surprised by that. Even though he and I had our little moment, I know it only happened because his feelings got hurt that day, and he was vulnerable. Humph, a man was feeling vulnerable? That's something to ponder, but let me stop being negative. I guess Orlando humbled himself and is now trying to make up for revealing his weakness. No, Nakia hasn't found out about what happened between me and Orlando, but he ain't exactly the poster boy for monogamy either.

His looks and that sexy-ass voice allow him to get away with a lot. It appears that he's right back where he wants to be. I'd seen him three days ago, slipping into the office, trying not to be seen or heard. His attempt failed. I detected his *hope-I-don't-run-into-Ina* behavior. His ass couldn't fool me. Then, I could see that *shit-I'm-caught* look on his face when I cleared my throat and got his attention. He definitely was caught, and I loved every second of it. At that moment, I realized that I had the upper hand on this man that everyone including myself thought was "the shit." He ain't nothing but a dog. He's a successful dog. A handsome, fine-as-hell, *make-you-wanna-run-off-to-a-hotel-and-get-busy-with-again* dog. But no matter how much he tries to charm his way back into Nakia's life or lie about how good it was to see me, he's still a first class dog, let me tell it.

Well, that had been three days prior to what I originally thought was gonna be a fabulous day to start my week off. Actually, the day ended up being very eventful and not the least bit dull or boring. I'd never imagined that Orlando's visit would touch off some office rumbling, but that's exactly what it did. The aftershocks alone went completely off the Richter scale. In the break room, ladies were talking about the gorgeous flowers inside Nakia's office. In the hallways, they whispered and giggled after greeting me with pretentious hellos and phony *how-was-your-weekend* remarks. A couple of ladies that I'd never spoken to before wanted me to stop and chat with them. I didn't realize that this had anything to do with Orlando until Delores came strutting into the office, talking about "Girl, everybody saw how Nakia's man was looking at you! What's up with that?" As she stood with her arms folded, she was all but certain that I would tell her something delicious. She was tripping, standing there like that, but I didn't say a word—yet. I couldn't recall Orlando doing anything except try to avoid seeing me. Even as he spoke, he acted like everything he said was "Top Secret." He even made his hello seem so discreet, like he didn't want anyone to hear.

At that point, I'd become curious as to what kind of impression Orlando's afternoon visit left behind. If I wanted to know anything, then I needed to entertain sister-friend Delores and see why she was smiling with such delight. I was tempted to ask her if she needed to take notes, but I didn't want to offend Miss Wanna-Know-Everything. She couldn't fool me. I could clearly see that she was chief editor of the office rumor mill. I wondered to myself if I should tell her that I fucked Orlando's brains out a few months ago, or just play dumb and act like I barely know his ass. I decided that my second choice would be my safest decision. If I shared any kind of secret with her, she'd probably run out of here like the place was on fire. Yeah, I decided to play it cool. I wanted to see where she was coming from.

"So, Delores, you had something to say about Mr. Duncan?" I asked in a very professional manner. I pointed to the chair, gesturing to her that it was okay to sit down. She chose to remain standing. I sat down behind my desk and listened to her go on and on.

"Girl," she started, "after the two of you were talking, Orlando kept looking at you like he was remembering some good times! We all got the impression that maybe you two know each other better than you'll both admit."

"Oh, well, maybe he was just daydreaming and not really focusing on me, at that time. He could've just been looking in my direction."

"Uh-huh, I don't think so, Ina. Men are way too easy to read, and I could tell he was looking at you with something on his mind."

"Well, Delores, I'm not gonna spend no amount of time trying to figure out what another woman's man is thinking."

"Uh-huh, okay, Ina."

Delores gave up on her fishing for gossip, and I just smiled as she exited my office. She was up to no good, and it probably didn't matter what I'd tell her because she would surely exaggerate everything. At that moment I began to think that I'd better get to Nakia before the thunderstorm of gossip reached her unexpectedly.

After making a few phone calls and touching base with my boss, I decided to walk through the gauntlet of gossip and snickering so that I could find Nakia. On the way, I ran into a very anxious Avonté.

"What's wrong with you?" I asked him.

"Nothing, just trying to locate Nakia. Maybe see if she wants to have lunch or something."

"Oh, okay. Well, I was looking for her myself."

Avonté didn't respond. His eyes continued to roam around the office in search of Nakia. He also kept looking at Delores as though he wanted to say something to her. I got the impression that his thoughts were pretty serious. I wasn't sure he'd heard a word I was saying to him. Delores was acting like the whole exchange was no big deal. Maybe they got issues with each other.

"You okay?" I asked, interrupting the staring match.

"Huh? Oh, yeah, I'm fine."

"You sure?"

"Yeah. If you see Nakia, tell her I need to talk with her."

"I'll do that, Avonté."

Avonté's behavior was strange to me, but when have I ever been able to figure him out? Right now, I'm just getting used to being able to tolerate looking at his ass again.

Well, I searched high and low for Nakia, not realizing that I should've looked in the obvious place. I knocked on the door to her office and instantly heard her voice, telling me to come in.

"Have you been here all this time, Girlfriend?" I asked.

Nakia had a strange look on her face. She was quiet, like she'd just had a serious conversation with someone. Maybe she's going through some more drama with Orlando. She didn't respond to my first question, so I made another attempt.

"Are you okay, Nakia?"

She nodded "yes."

"Did you talk with Avonté? He was looking for you."

"No," she replied softly.

"Why are you so quiet?

"I just had a conversation with Terence."

"Your ex?"

"Yes."

"Well, you two have a daughter together, so I imagine you have to keep in touch, right?"

"Actually, I spent the night with him."

"You what?"

"I spent the night with him…," she repeated.

"Okay, well, it's not like you're serious with Orlando, right?"

Nakia shrugged her shoulders. She struggled to make sense of her thoughts and wasn't sure what to say.

"You wanna talk about it?" I asked.

She sighed. "It's crazy, Ina. I've got two men trying to get back with me right now. I've never been in this kind of situation before."

"Other women would kill to be in your situation, Nakia."

"It's really not what it's cracked up to be, Ina."

"Why not? How do you really feel?"

"I thought that Orlando was the perfect man. He came close, but he's really not. I'm not even sure if he's the perfect man for me."

"I can't really say anything about that, Nakia. I do remember the effect that he had on you before, but I'm not so sure I see that now."

"No, I've changed. I'm tired of having my heart broken or feeling so disappointed."

"What's going on with Terence?"

"He's so different now…"

"Different how?"

"It's almost like I left him to get my life together, but the opposite happened."

"I don't understand…"

"Terence got his life together and even though I've got a good job and all, my personal life feels so confused right now. Then last night, while having dinner with him, I felt something really crazy…"

"What, Girlfriend?"

"I didn't want to leave him. I didn't want the night to be over. I was so lost in our conversation that I kept ordering stuff like dessert and coffee just so that our dinner date wouldn't be over."

"But you said you spent the night with him, right?"

"Yeah, he always was good at reading my thoughts. He told me that I could spend the night with him, if I wanted to."

"Well, I guess he knew what he wanted, huh?"

"No, Ina, that's the thing..."

"What do you mean?"

"Terence was able to pick up on what I really wanted."

"Oh, I see."

"Yep, and now I'm sitting here with the door closed, trying to fight off the truth and if I tell you, Ina, I'll lose the battle..."

Nakia opened her desk drawer and pulled out a piece of paper. Then she turned on the computer and waited for the system to come up.

"What's that?" I asked, pointing to the piece of paper.

"My password. I can never remember it."

"After all this time?"

"Nope."

"Use something familiar!"

"What good would that do?"

"It would help you remember!"

"Oh, that's okay."

I just looked at Nakia and smiled as she typed in her password and stared at the monitor. I wondered what her thoughts were and marveled at her young features. She didn't appear as though she'd suffered any amount of stress, though I knew she had. I tried to distract her while she was checking her email.

"So, when you gonna ask me about the men in my life, Girlfriend?" I joked.

Nakia looked at me with a smirk on her face. "What men?" she asked.

"Okay, so I don't have a man, rub it in..."

"I'm not trying to rub it in, Ina. I just kind of figured you haven't been seeing anybody—lately."

"I'm not but let me tell you something, Nakia. The only thing a man seems to do well for me these days is get me in trouble and lick my coochie."

Nakia put her hand over her mouth and started laughing.

"I'm gonna pretend you didn't say that, Ina."

"Why?" I asked while joining her in the laughter.

"You need to stop hanging out with me 'cause you the one sounding so ghetto now..."

"I'm just teasing you."

"I'm not so sure you are, Ina."

"Well, I am, but it's all good..."

"See, there you go. I don't remember you using so much slang before."

"Well, I've learned a few things from you, true. But, I just attribute it all to growth and just getting out more to experience my surroundings. You know how I was before, Girl. I'd just go from work to home and back again. Then when it was time to get out and travel, I'd go to the Cayman Islands, Hawaii or someplace else that's tropical and wonderful. I used to find nothing appealing about hanging out here in L.A."

"Yes, I remember hearing stories about all your travels. I'd like to experience some of that myself. You may be loving L.A. right now, but I'm ready to do some traveling and get away for a while."

"Maybe you should, Nakia. I was gonna suggest you go with Orlando but I guess at this point, that might be the wrong thing to say."

Nakia didn't respond to my comment but instead glared at the computer. I guess an email caught her attention, and she didn't hear what I'd said.

"So, how about it, Nakia?"

She looked at me with no expression. I felt strange for a second but I brushed it off.

"How about what?" she replied though I could barely hear her.

"Maybe we could go away for a weekend. Shoot, even if we just go over to Catalina; that would be better than sticking around here when the weather is so nice outside. We could have some fun...Let's go!"

Nakia forced a smile that may have lasted perhaps a tenth of a second. Whatever was bothering her, it took away any desire to think about doing anything that resembled a good time.

I pleaded, "Nakia, what's wrong?"

"I got this email here that…"

"An email, and? Is it something dealing with work?"

Nakia shook her head no.

"Who's it from?"

"It's anonymous…" she replied in a half whisper.

"You're scaring me. Is it bad news or what?"

"Maybe you should read it, Ina."

"Okay, if you want me to."

Nakia nodded her head.

"Okay, I'll come around and read it…"

"No, I'll print it out for you," she said, just before I could get out of my chair. "It's coming out of the printer right now."

"Where?"

"Over there." She pointed.

As I walked toward the printer sitting to the right side of her office door, I could feel some strange tension in the room. I got a feeling this email was not filled with very positive thoughts or comments. It completely changed Nakia's mood, so I wasn't really looking forward to reading it. I bent over slightly and picked up the paper. Instantly, I saw the title in the subject area. It was in bold letters and read, "Anonymously Yours."

As I read the first sentence, I thought this might be a letter asking for Nakia's resignation.

"As a concerned co-worker, I regret to inform you of a situation that may not be in your best interest," the letter began.

I looked over at Nakia, wondering if perhaps she'd been laid off or demoted. "What's this all about?" I asked her.

"Keep reading," she responded.

The look on her face had me worried, so I returned my attention back to the email. I was certain that by reading it, I'd find out the reason behind the tension that hit the room like a tear-gas bomb. I continued to read.

"Sometimes things aren't as they seem, and it should be considered a blessing when someone comes forth to enlighten us, especially when we've been wronged. Well, Nakia, I will get to the point of this letter. Your friend Ina shares something in common with you. On the day that your boyfriend Orlando came to visit with you here at work and left under not-so-positive circumstances, he ended his day by becoming intimately involved with Ms. Ina Sinclair. I felt it was my duty to come forth with this information to prevent you from hearing about it through office gossip. I apologize for not coming forth sooner, but at least you know, now…"

I raised my head slowly while trying to camouflage my anger with innocence and confusion.

"I don't understand what this is about, Nakia," I said to her calmly.

"You mean, you never slept with Orlando?"

I didn't know if I should answer her question. Nakia had me feeling on the defensive right away, and that was only because I couldn't come up with a good convincing lie to tell her.

"You're not saying anything, Ina, so I guess that means you did," she said, while leaning back in her leather chair.

"Nakia, it just kind of happened…"

"So you slept with him, even though you knew how I felt about him?"

"I don't know what else I can say. I mean, when I saw him outside, one thing led to another. We talked. We kind of vibed with one another. He told me that things weren't good between the two of you. He wasn't sure you'd forgive him for not keeping in touch when he went to Miami…"

"So all those things give you the green light to fuck your friend's man? Is that what you're telling me, Ina? You couldn't like, wait until he and I had officially called it quits? Is everybody in this company all about getting theirs when they want it?"

"Nakia, it's not like that at all, and you know it!"

"I know you fucked a man that I was seeing and had strong feelings for. I know you've kept this secret hidden all the while pretending to be a good friend to me. I know this whole company is filled with people gossiping and backstabbing each other. I thought you were different. I've always looked up to you as my mentor, but I'll be damned if I become anything like you."

I just stood there and absorbed all of Nakia's harsh words. I really didn't know what to say except to apologize, but I didn't think that would work at this point. The anger in her eyes convinced me that anything I'd have to say would fall on deaf ears and probably make matters worse. She appeared so disgusted with everything and everyone at the company, especially me.

"Nakia, I wish there was something I could say."

"You should've tried saying something a long time ago, Ina."

"Like what?" I mumbled while not really meaning to ask that question.

"I shouldn't have to find out something like this by reading an email at my job. I don't know who this is from, but if they know, then everybody and they Mama knows, too!"

"Maybe that's why Avonté was looking for you."

"Avonté?"

"Yeah."

"I don't want to hear shit from Avonté. Listen, Ina, you should just leave me alone, okay?"

I just nodded my head and stood in shock for a moment before exiting her office. We'd had some little episodes between us before but nothing like this one. Seconds after I walked out, leaving the door open behind me, I heard a loud bang. I turned around only to find that Nakia had slammed her office door closed. After that, I was the center of attention for the rest of the workday. Everybody could tell that the shit hit the fan between Nakia and me, and I wouldn't be surprised if they already had the details about what happened. This office is really good at spreading gossip. I wish they had the same talent to sell some advertising. Assholes...

After the door slammed shut most likely on my friendship with Nakia, I wasn't the only one in the office who became the center of attention.

As I continued walking away from the scene of my own drama, I overheard an argument going on between Avonté and Delores. They were exchanging some very heated words. They didn't seem to be too concerned that others were staring at them and watching the whole thing unfold like some best of Jerry Springer episode—but with a better set design. I stopped and watched myself because in the midst of their exchange, a confession had been made and all mouths dropped open with that familiar *know-she-didn't* look.

Avonté raised his voice. "Why did you have to say anything? What the hell did you have to send an email for?" Avonté was really animated as he questioned Delores.

Delores just held her hand up as if to warn Avonté of coming closer. She looked pretty serious, but Avonté wasn't finished.

"That's some stupid shit!"

Delores fired right back at him.

"Avonté, you the one that's stupid. You shouldn't be going around telling your best friend's business just so you can get at my coochie! Who do you think you are? You just use people anyway, so you can move up in your career. You don't care about Nakia. You just trying to keep from getting caught. You the one that does some Stu-pid-shit!"

Delores showed her boldness and was all up in Avonté's face. That bit of drama was ten times better than television but only for those who weren't immediately affected. The not-so-cool part about that moment was the fact that Nakia could also hear what was going on. When I looked in the direction of her office, there she stood inside her doorway, watching with no expression on her face. I could only imagine what was beneath the surface of her cold stare. She now knew who sent the email to her while at the same time had discovered that Avonté was the reason that the gossip spread in the first place. He lit the flame and Delores ran with the torch. I know. I'm no angel and I'm the one who gave this whole nightmare the fuel to burn so brightly. I just wish nothing had been said or done before all of this happened. But, wishing in reverse never comes true. I'm just gonna have to accept the fact that my actions took away a wonderful friendship and move on, hoping that I've learned something. I wish Nakia the best, even though she could give a damn what I think.

It's hard to believe that this office was actually gearing up for a big Christmas party this year. I don't see any blinking lights around here. Only thing you'll find is some serious attitudes and drama. I doubt if Santa Claus would want to come into this hostile environment. Even I don't want to be here, at least not today. For now I'll just go inside my office, close the door and get back to being the workaholic that I once was. Friendships in the workplace have never been my cup of tea. I'm done with it, for now.

LIFE AFTER MONTAQUA

EPILOGUE

And so it seems...Montaqua had become a time in my life that opened me up and gave me experience, allowed me to grow and develop my skills in the workplace. I feel like a professional person, a career woman now, but it also reminded me of what's truly important in my life. I mean, I'd been so worried about struggling to provide for my daughter when my relationship with Terence came to an end. I feel so proud that I was able to prove to myself that I could take care of her—and me. Now with that company in my past and a good addition to my resume, I can look ahead and feel confident in myself, knowing that I will reach my dreams and goals.

I'm enjoying a fresh new start at another advertising agency called Farwell Communications, and my personal life is on the upswing, though I've had moments of trying to deny it. You know how when love feels right, sometimes you want to run from it simply because you don't believe it's real? Well, it's definitely on the horizon right now, and I get all giggly inside just thinking about it, about him. New love? In a way it is...Real? Hell, yes!

One day I came home to a letter with a rose attached. It sat on the kitchen table where my mother religiously dumps all of my mail and small items. Even though I hesitated about opening the letter at first, now that I look back in hindsight, that was the moment I'd begun feeling like I was on cloud nine. Reading it was an experience within itself. I began devouring the words as though I were eating pork chops smothered in gravy. The more I read, the more it was on! I was so tickled by what I was seeing. It had been a while since I had blushed or gotten excited about something a man had done for me. Each sentence, each word was like Cupid's arrows except this was on a whole 'nother level. These arrows were directed at my soul. I had to clutch my heart I was so full. My breathing was short and rapid. It felt really tight between my breasts. My eyes went from right to left in amazement as to what I was seeing. Perhaps I was finally witnessing what I'd always dreamed of seeing from a man. And I'd been waiting all along for this one to shed his skin and allow me to see the deepest part of his soul.

I could tell there was no struggle to communicate what he felt. His only flaw might've been that his pen couldn't keep up with his thoughts. He touched me with his sense of awakening, self-awareness and acceptance. I never knew that there was such disbelief in his heart—before.

"Without that anchor of acceptance, I was unable to focus my energy toward commitment," he wrote.

That moved me to silence as I continued to watch his words drip off the pages and into my heart. His honesty blocked any desire for me to question why he couldn't speak this way before. I couldn't disrespect what he was finally trying to say with such an opened, exposed and enlightened heart.

As I continued to read the reflections of his soul written between the lines on each page, I grabbed my coat. I had to go to him. I wanted to be able to lift my head, open my eyes and answer "yes" to his unspoken question of forever. Terence had grown so much, and there was nothing complex behind the meaning of his letter. It was as though he turned everything up a notch or two and was ready to truly commit to being together. I couldn't sense any issues creeping around and no hidden agendas that served as ways to please himself. If I held his letter up to the flicker of flames, only to discover some sort of invisible writing, it would surely say. "Nakia, I love you...," and I'd have to answer by giving my heart to him—completely.

Well, love had surely captured my spirit and given me reason to move on in a positive direction. Speaking of moving on...Those fools and so-called friends back at Montaqua? Well, Ina is doing her thang. She's in management and making big money just like she always wanted to. Her back-stabbing ass ain't happy though. She couldn't buy a man if she wanted to. Still, I hear she walks around looking like she ain't got a care in the world, so I guess I don't need to waste my time trying to hate on her. Plus, I need to focus on being happy with my man, spoiling my daughter and for once, having a career instead of just a...job.

Oh, but hold up! I can't let things go by without talking about Mr. Orlando Duncan and how easily he seems to have moved on from whatever you wanna call what he and I had. I feel like I was just a detour for him anyway. He hadn't been with someone who seemed like they needed him before. All his ladies in the past had been his intellectual equals. They experienced pretty much the same luxuries and travels so he couldn't play too suave and window dress his weaknesses around them 'cause they'd seen it all.

He was so different to me, and I ate it up. He taught me a lot in such a short time, so in one way, I'm grateful to him. I know my fascination with him was like a Fatburger for his ego. He got full off of all that hero-worshipping I was doing. I know I'm acting like I don't care what he's doing now, but quite honestly, I do. I'll never forget when I first met him that night at the club. He gave me the kind of attention that I'd been missing so much. Now I just hope he learned the importance of honesty in not only a developing relationship, but a relationship, period. Now, if he didn't learn anything, then he can go to hell and take Avonté with him.

I try not to think about Avonté Douglas. I felt so hurt and betrayed by what he did. For a while I really stressed over it before realizing that I shouldn't allow him to have any sort of effect on me. My sweetheart told me to let it go 'cause it was getting in the way of my new direction in life. Terence has learned a lot since we've been apart. I listened to him, but I can't help but feel some sort of satisfaction behind my moment of revenge that I had with Avonté. I had his ass thinking that I was gonna forgive him on my last day at Montaqua. I let him help me to my car with all my belongings. He was smiling and thinking that everything was cool between us again. He was so wrong, but I wasn't gonna tell him. I guess that made him "doubly" wrong, if that's a word.

Anyway, on that day, he walked with me to my car. I was carrying a bunch of paperwork and a couple of picture frames. He carried my laptop computer and a box of junk that I had inside my desk. He kept talking all kinds of stuff like he was so happy that we were friends again. "We gotta celebrate your new job, Nakia!"

"Celebrate?"

"Yeah! Let me take you out to lunch or something..."

I started smiling 'cause his invitation was too good to be true. Not that I wanted to go, but it was the perfect opportunity to do my little dirt that I had planned.

"Listen, I have a better idea...," I told him.

"You do?"

He was so anxious to hear what I had to say that he stopped walking. It was like he couldn't wait to hear what I was gonna say 'cause he just knew it had to include the two of us getting together, and he could be rid of the guilt he'd been feeling for doing me wrong.

"Come on," I told him, so that he could keep walking. I didn't want to stick around after I did what I wanted to do.

So, Avonté walked slightly behind me like some anxious little boy, trying to keep up with his mother. Once we made it to my car, I had him place my things in the back seat, and I started my engine.

"So, what's the idea? You got me in suspense!" Avonté said, after rubbing his hands together and smiling with anticipation.

I played it off and acted like I wasn't doing such a big thing. I handed to him slowly, a small invitation card.

"What's this?" he asked.

"It's an invitation. I'm inviting you somewhere as an appreciation for all that you've done and for the really cool friendship that we've had."

"Damn, that's cool...," he said, just before beginning to open the envelope.

I stopped him. "Wait. Open it as I'm driving off."

"Say what?"

"Well, just wait a little bit before you open it..."

"Oh, okay."

I walked around to the driver side of my car, still keeping my eyes on Avonté. I had his ass completely fooled and looking like I gave him a coupon to get some free pussy. Once I got in my car and began backing out of the parking stall, I could see Avonte opening the envelope frantically. He wasn't about to wait for me to drive away before he read what was inside. I tried to keep my eyes on him in my rear-view mirror as I pulled slowly behind the line of cars waiting to exit the parking structure. Avonté's smile fell completely off his face, and his eyes frowned up like his bank account had a zero balance. I'd given him an invite but it wasn't what he'd expected or hoped for.

Dear Avonté,

Thanks for everything. The lesson that your friendship provided is something that I'll carry with me for a long time to come. Now that we won't see each other every day, I wanted to leave you with this very special invitation to go fuck yourself! Friends don't spread rumors about their friends, jerk!

Always grateful,

Nakia

"Good luck to you!" the parking attendant told me just before I drove out of the lot.

"Thank you. Take care, okay...," I responded with a devious smile 'cause I knew that Avonté wasn't feeling too good and at that point, I didn't give a damn. Actually, I still don't, but I'm trying to let all of that negative thinking go. I don't want any more issues in my life. I don't even want to wish that on anybody 'cause it might just come back to me. I can only hope that I've seen all I'm gonna see, but I know I'm just fooling myself if I think it's possible to actually avoid drama for the rest of my life. Oh, well...

Holding on to the past and using
it as a means to sustain your future.
You've got to take responsibility for
your emotional hardships and
blindness to others that wish to grow
and move on with their lives...
You know, everybody got issues but I'm about
to leave mine behind...

Nakia Davidson

ABOUT THE AUTHOR

V. Anthony Rivers has been featured on R.A.W. Sistaz, Sisterdivas.com, and Netnoir. His work is seen monthly on the e-zine, Nubian Chronicles (www.nubianchronicles.net).

V. Anthony Rivers is the author of *Daughter By Spirit* and *Everybody Got Issues*. Both are published by Strebor Books International. He's also featured in the Strebor anthology, *Sistergirls.com*, with a very funny yet sarcastic look at online dating. His short story contribution to the anthology is entitled "Somewhere Between Love & Sarcasm."

He is steadily writing and has short stories and other novels in the works. He hopes to write more novels in the future that bring to light the rich history of our ancestry as well as the stories that feature today's contemporary lifestyles. He's currently working on a novel that combines both those aspects, entitled *Until Again*. In essence, it's a story about love picking up where it once left off, generations ago.

Also in the works is a story about friendship, love and the consequences of hero worship called "Romeo Revelations (Love seems to get in the way)," a very special anthology book called

A Rivers Touch, inspired by and dedicated to his family. And also, a very touching story about a boy with a special gift of sight called "Timothy Beekerwood."

V. Anthony Rivers was born in Los Angeles, California but stays very connected to his East Texas roots where both sides of his family originate. He currently resides in Van Nuys, California.

Printed in the United States
By Bookmasters